SYDNEY STRIKES BACK

He smiled and stopped. "Good old Crystal. You know, I don't think I ever saw her sober. Why are you so loyal to such a drunk, Sydney?"

"You haven't answered my question, Mickey. Did you use Gloria's combination to get in here? Did you brag about it to Crystal?"

"Do you think that's worth killing her for?" He took a step closer.

"Did you have that van with you that night?"

He even laughed. "I drive a Mercedes, babe. You ought to know that."

A siren blared. Then another.

He shook his head back and forth, then his forefinger in the same motion. "Now, why'd you want to go and call the police, Sydney? I'm going to have to leave you now. Nobody's going to believe you, you know." He ran to the front door. The sirens were on our block now. As he leaned over to insert the key back into the supralock housing, I stuck him in the rear with the hypodermic. He screamed, then straightened up, hands on fanny.

That's when I screamed "Take this, babe" and knocked him in the head with my low heel.

MULTIPLE
LISTING

ANNE UNDERWOOD GRANT

A DELL BOOK

Published by
Dell Publishing
a division of
Bantam Doubleday Dell Publishing Group, Inc.
1540 Broadway
New York, New York 10036

ISBN: 0-440-22551-5

Printed in the United States of America

Published simultaneously in Canada

February 1998

10 9 8 7 6 5 4 3 2 1
OPM

For Ruth Pollock Underwood
My mother, My friend

ACKNOWLEDGMENTS

The author would like to thank the following people for the roles they played in the creation of this novel: Lynne Pou for urging me to write mysteries; Elizabeth Grant and Leighton Grant for believing in this dream; and all those real estate agents in Charlotte who couldn't sell my house and unwittingly spawned this story.

Great home. Corner lot.
Ideal for Entertaining. Must See. ML

I feel so alive: Every muscle knows its role without direction; blood seeks its own route, giving pulse to uncharted parts of me; each cell screams in the power of its life. This feeling's stronger than the words I know. Love? Hate? Maybe both, maybe neither. It is a riptide, pushing and pulling me with such power that I cannot stop to name it. For surely then, it will take me under.

All I know is I am doing what I'm here for.

So is she, I suspect.

I press myself hard against her and back her up down the hall. My knee against her thigh, my cock against her stomach. A tango. She tries to move in my rhythm, to dance. She leans back, thinking I will catch her, thinking we will sway into the lighted bedroom, thinking our needs are the same.

I let her fall at the door, and I go down with her, onto her, my cock striking her plate with a force that shoots currents to every part of me. She grimaces, then tries to smile again. Her drunkenness may spoil it all. I will have to work harder.

She hears noise in the living room, looks lopsided at me in concern. I stand and close us off inside the bedroom. She backs to the bed in either invitation or dizziness, I cannot tell.

All she says is "Why are you here?"

1

CRYSTAL BALL WAS A FRIEND OF MINE. IN FACT, she was more than a friend: I felt responsible for her. That happens with your old drinking buddies when you quit drinking and they don't, or they can't, and you have to watch them continuing to mess up their lives; it happens particularly when you're the person responsible for turning your friend's very name into a joke, as I had done with Crystal when I introduced her to Fred Ball.

I was thinking about Crystal as I watched my client Jean Miller thread her way across the huge convention hall with drinks in both hands. I was wondering if Jean had made any progress selling Crystal's house. Of course, I'd introduced Crystal to Jean, too. Like I said, I have this habit of taking responsibility for things, and it was going to get a whole lot worse, only I didn't know that quite yet.

At the time, Jean and I were inside the Charlotte Civic Center at the annual Board of Realtors Roundup. Us and several thousand other overly animated, ambitious women. I felt like one of many cattle at auction.

The place was hot in spite of its lofty ceilings. The stench of battling perfumes mingled with workaday sweat; the boisterous hawk of vendors clashed with high-pitched anxiety. I retreated under a massive set of steps leading to the mezzanine.

I don't sell real estate. My thing's advertising. More precisely, marketing communications since it takes more than mere advertising to sell most things. I own a little agency called Allen Teague, Allen for my birth name and Teague for the man I was married to and divorced from ten years ago. Real estate, both commercial and residential, is a big part of our client mix since Charlotte, North Carolina, has lots of services but very few tangible products. The town is long on pretense, however. Like a newly rich southern woman eager to buy her way into social prominence. Charlotte is a New South city, full of herself with polite aggression, portending to the crown of shifting economic futures, hoping Atlanta will slip, pretending she has no past. An easy place to sell a service like mine if you talk nothing but vision.

"Oooh, Sydney, I'm sooo sorry. Here, I was bringing it to you. You looked as if you could use one." Jean Miller, my client, sloshed Scotch on my linen-clad shoulder and began wiping my shoulder pad with a Hardee's napkin.

"Don't worry about it, Jean," I said. The foam rubber had deflected the amber liquid down my arm. I slid the flax jacket off the shoulder, took her napkin and dragged it up my triceps.

This was the most excitement I had felt in the forty-five minutes I had been here. The Roundup may not be my idea of a fun afternoon, but it's a vendor's dream.

Three thousand consumers, ninety-five percent women, packed into two large rooms for four hours of eating, drinking, and buying from the hundred or so booths set up around the space. Mostly ad specialty guys, I noticed. Those guys who put anything and everything on a key chain or a refrigerator magnet.

"Ran into your favorite competitor at the bar." Jean's voice was light but taunting. Her eyes twinkled. I was being baited.

"Okay, let's see. Who is my favorite competitor?"

Jean laughed. "Mickey Sutton."

I couldn't suppress a groan. I disliked Mickey enough that even the mention of his name could sour my mood. Almost.

Her grin could not have been wider or more self-satisfied. "I thought that'd get a rise out of you."

I had lots of reasons for hating Mickey Sutton, not the least of which was, again, my good friend Crystal. I'd introduced Mickey to Crystal a long time ago. Before I knew either one of them very well. Before he'd screwed me in business and a legion of other women any way he could get to them. Before I'd learned how addictive he'd be to someone with an addictive personality like Crystal's. Of course, I hadn't known what a jerk Fred Ball would turn out to be either at the time I introduced him to Crystal. My own ignorance about the two guys didn't make me feel any better about my part in the mess that her life had become. In fact, I felt like the evil queen presenting Snow White with an entire basket of poisoned apples.

"Whatever his faults, he's the best-looking guy I've seen in a long time."

I looked at her as I imagine a doctor would who's

warning a patient about the recreational use of arsenic. "Look, but don't touch, smell, feel, or talk to him. He's lethal."

As I was folding my jacket over my arm, Gus Georges of Put It On! hit me on the shoulder and knocked what remained of the Scotch on my skirt.

"Hey there, Sydney! Oh, hon, sorry. Didn't see the drink in your hand. Here, let me get it for you." He pulled out a large, rumpled handkerchief and was dabbing between my thighs before I could stop him. "Here"— he gestured from below my waist—"take mine. Looks like I just about finished yours off." He thrust into my one empty hand something darker than the Scotch Jean had brought me. His angle was such that one small wave of the dark stuff rolled out onto my skirt. Smelled like Bourbon. Now I was doused in blend.

Here I stood, Bourbon in one hand, Scotch in the other, my formerly crisp linen suit soggy with liquor in two shades of beige. In the old days that would have meant the evening was off to a good start, but I don't drink at all anymore. Not even a beer with pizza. Not even champagne at toasts. Not even wine at communion, for Christ's sake! Some people don't see the harm in a sip of communion wine, but as far as I'm concerned, it's not the intent of the sip that leads you back to a life of debauchery. It's the alcohol itself. My friend Crystal knew that too, although she kept on drinking, proof that knowledge and action have little in common. I slipped in the early years because I failed to cook the wine out of a stir-fry dish. That was more than ten years ago. I keep turning it over one day at a time, and, through the grace of my higher power—certainly not my fellow man—have not had a drink inside my body since.

"Got a hot new coffee cup, Sydney. Know how ya love that coffee. The expensive kind, right? Foreign brand, right?" Gus was doing what the best of these guys do: letting his target know that she's a person worth listening to; that he, good ol' Gus Georges, is more than a pitchman to her. In this impersonal, rough 'n' tumble world, he's her friend. "From France, right?"

I nodded as I played right into his pitch. "French roast," I said. Jean was softly chuckling beside me, although I noticed she was surveying the room rather than giving Gus her attention.

He patted me on the back while removing his glass of bourbon from my hand. "Ah ha," he guffawed. Every ad specialty guy I've ever met guffaws, a professional trait I find mildly interesting. Gus could see that he had sparked something in me, so he continued. "These are French cups, Sydney gal." He held his hand to his mouth in the mock stifling of a giggle, with his cheeks all puffed out like a stuffed rodent and his head lurching forward down in his neck like an attacking goose. He shifted the drink to his other hand and slapped Jean on the shoulder just as he'd slapped me on the back. She posed obligingly, eyebrows raised in feigned interest. "Not the French cups us men like so much." He giggled outright. "Little muglike cups with saucers." He was rummaging through his bag o' wares when he put down his drink and pulled out a demitasse cup and saucer.

"Demitasse," I said.

"Yeah. French, like I told ya." He turned toward Jean. "It's hard to find something real classy like this in adware." He thrust his hand out. "I'm Gus Georges. President of Put It On! Ad Specialties."

"I'm sorry, Gus. This is Jean Miller of Miller and Associates."

Gus's eyes took on a shine the way only salesmen's eyes can shine when they find themselves in the presence of great opportunity. "You're new," he said with true delight.

"Not really, Gus," I jumped in. "Jean's been one of Charlotte's top producers, both listings and sales, for more than ten years. Used to be with Bishop Cates. Miller and Associates is new."

"Well, well, well," Gus said. "Bishop Cates, huh? You work with Barbara Cates or her old man before he died?"

Jean glared at poor Gus as if he'd asked her if she'd slept with the devil. "Both," she finally said. "But the wrong one died if you ask me."

Gus shuffled his feet, feigned a cough, then hung his head as if he'd dropped something at this feet. What else could he do with a comment like that?

The moment Jean saw my shocked expression she slapped her hip and winced. "Damn, I didn't mean that." She looked at me with an awkward combination of supplication and defiance. "You know I didn't, Sydney. If I hadn't had three drinks, I never would have said that."

Jean was still smarting from the less than amicable parting between herself and Bishop Cates. She had been their top producer for years. Calvin Bishop had promised her a vice-presidency and an override on commissions. When he had died last year, ownership went to his daughter Barbara, who swore on a stack of Bibles that her father had never mentioned such a vice-presidency. The firm had been the undisputed leader in Charlotte until Bishop died. It seemed that old Calvin must have done a lot of promising because, of the two hundred–plus realtors who worked at the firm, all but thirty left within nine months of his death. Alzheimer's, Barbara had said. Nobody believed her, not even I, who'd known her over thirty years. Her dad's brain had been as finely tuned as the mint Packard he drove until the day he turned it into the path of the Carolina Special, Amtrak's latest foray into town. I had heard he had cancer, and rumor had it that he was simply rushing to meet the inevitable. Promises are easier to make when you know you're not going to have to be the one to keep them. Barbara had inherited a mess.

"I thought they were going out of business," Gus said.

"Rumor. Don't you listen to it," I said. Over my shoulder I saw Barbara Cates heading for the bar on the mezzanine.

"Well, I wasn't going to call on her anymore because of what I'd heard. Don't want to get stuck with a bankruptcy, y' know."

I needed to extricate Jean from Gus. I'd seen him work before. Despite her cool, he'd get her. Now he stood with the little demitasse cradled in crossed palms like those of communicants awaiting the body of Christ. Only he looked like the Mad Hatter at tea, somehow devilish and too large for the cup and saucer in his hands.

"Bishop Cates is still much bigger than little Miller and Associates here, Gus," I said. "Barbara just went to the bar. I'd go get her now if I were you."

Gus's rush to the bar was so hasty, he failed to say good-bye. I turned to Jean. "If you're ever tempted to feel special as a small-business owner, remember how quickly Gus just ran to greener pastures." I needed to leave this place; the roundup theme was affecting even my choice of words.

"You've been a good friend to come to this damn thing with me, Sydney. And for sending Crystal to me too."

"Any bites on her house?" I was grateful Jean had brought up the house so I wouldn't have to. Sometimes I felt like Crystal's agent in the world.

"I held an open house last weekend and got a few who're still interested. She's a lot of fun, great sense of humor. With a name like Crystal Ball, I guess she has to."

I laughed. "Crystal's got the best sense of humor of anyone I know. Too bad she's been married for three years to a guy who has none. You met Fred, I guess."

"No, she got his signature on the contract. You sound like you know him though."

"Unfortunately, yes. He's Sally's brother."

"Your secretary Sally? Oh my God, Sydney, the divorce puts you in an awkward situation, doesn't it?"

"A bit." I am fond of understatement.

"Sometimes I think my husband and I are the last happily married couple in Charlotte." She hesitated, looked at me. "You know I didn't mean anything by that."

"Doesn't bother me. Not anymore anyway. I think about marriage the way I do singing. I would give anything if I could carry a tune, but I can't. I messed up a bunch of glee clubs in school proving it to myself. Now I know everybody's better off if I just sit in the audience and keep my mouth shut."

Jean laughed. "I can't believe that. You just haven't found the right guy."

"Right. And anybody can sing if they concentrate hard enough. Fred is Crystal's third attempt at a duet."

"How do you and Crystal know each other?"

"I feel like I've known her forever, but I guess it was when George and I moved to Kingston Avenue. She lived next door with husband number one. I went through that disintegration as well. I should have never introduced her to Fred."

"You introduced the divorcing couple?" Jean shook her head.

Mickey Sutton walked over to a booth no more than ten feet in front of us. His entourage of female account executives surrounded him, reminding me of rock-star groupies. Jean stabbed me with her elbow in case I had not noticed.

"I introduced her to Sutton as well," I said.

Jean said, "God, some friend you are." She could not have known how guilty I already felt.

I wedged the Scotch glass into the midst of some stiff bromeliad leaves that seemed to grow out of the top of a lone laminated pedestal. All of a sudden I was overcome with a clear understanding of the shallowness of this gathering, and I wanted to go home.

"No divorce is pleasant, Sydney."

"Please," I said. "Look who you're talking to. I could teach Divorce 101 at the community college."

She laughed. "They'll certainly need it more than algebra. Figuring out the value of x hasn't helped me one bit."

I looked at my watch. Five-fifteen.

Jean noticed and stooped to put her drink on the floor next to the pedestal. "You need to get home to your kids. Sorry this hasn't been more productive. Should I have bought something, counselor?"

"Not out here in the pasture. Wait till they come to your barn."

"Huh?"

I sighed. "Let's go. I'm not making any sense."

"It may take us an hour just to get to the parking deck."

It didn't take an hour, but it did take a good twenty minutes with one particularly long holdup at four gossiping women who would not budge. As we approached the exit, I was calculating that we had moved about two and a half feet per minute getting out of here. Not aerobic pace, but the sweating was bound to be good for us.

As Jean reached for the door, it flew open in our direction, pushing us back at least five feet into the mayhem. My secretary, Sally, poured into the room like a wave at high tide. Her skin was ashen, her normally well-coiffed hair wet from perspiration and dangling into her eyes. Her eyes were odd. Glazed yet purposeful, afraid. My mother instincts steeled themselves. I searched her eyes for an answer without words.

"What's wrong?" Jean asked when I didn't.

Tears suddenly welled, then flowed over Sally's cheeks that turned from white to red. As she attempted to speak, her jaw lost its mooring and her lower lip crumpled into quivering, staccato lines. The sounds she made verged on incomprehensible.

"Something . . . something horrible."

2

As selfish as it may sound, I now sensed with relief that whatever crisis had brought Sally in search of me was her personal crisis—not mine or that of my kids.

Jean reopened the exit door and I led Sally outside onto the parking deck, where it took her another minute or two to gain control. Jean and I glanced at each other and waited quietly.

"Freddie," she finally gasped. "Freddie's at the police station. They . . . they made him come down there. I think—" She stopped and looked at me. "They think he killed Crystal."

"Killed Crystal?" I must have screamed it because Sally held her palms to her ears, and Jean's look of concern shifted from Sally's face to mine.

I pulled Sally's hands off her ears and stooped so that I could look up into her downcast eyes. She seemed on the verge of fainting; I felt my own stomach drop as well. I had seen Crystal yesterday. She couldn't be dead.

Jean held Sally by the elbow as her knees began to buckle.

"Do you have your car here, Sally? You need to sit down," I said.

She shook her head back and forth, then nodded over her shoulder south down Third Street. I followed her nod to the roof of the Law Enforcement Center, where its massive fan straddled the flat surface like a mismatched toy block.

"I walked," she said in a breathless voice, sounding more like she had just run a 10K.

Jean had already begun a quick clip into the maze of cars. "I'll get mine," she said.

"Oh, God, Sydney," Sally cried. "Murdered. Murdered. Crystal's been murdered. Not Freddie. Freddie could never . . ."

She pulled at her hoop earring as if to fortify her resolve. Too much. The tiny dagger ripped through her lobe, drawing blood, then falling to the floor.

"Shit," she said, leaving the earring on the floor.

Crystal had told me that Fred could be one self-centered son of a bitch. But murder? She had never said anything to me about a temper. In fact, she had complained to me about his lack of passion.

I picked up the hoop, took Sally's limp hand and put the earring in it. I don't think she even noticed.

Sally inhaled deeply and let it out slowly, shuddering in the process. Something tickled the edge of my mouth. I scratched at a thin stream of tears. I hadn't known I was crying.

I hugged her in silence, although I wanted to yell "When?" and "How?" instead. Surely something would tumble out if I could help calm her. By the time Jean pulled her Mercedes alongside the curb and safely beyond the exit door, the story was coming in fits and starts. I opened the back door and instructed Sally to sit while I deposited my body onto the curb.

The "when" was sometime early this morning. Fred had stopped by the house on his way to work.

"Why?" I asked.

"Why not?" In spite of her confusion, Sally was automatically defending Fred.

"I mean why wouldn't he just call her on the phone. Why go by there when he'd already moved out?"

Sally's flaccid jaw turned rigid as she turned to me. "She couldn't answer the phone, now could she, Sydney?"

I turned away from her glare.

Jean tried to break the tension. "I'm sure they still had a lot of details to work out, Sydney." Then she said to Sally: "Come on, Sally, you know that Sydney didn't mean anything. She's upset too. Crystal was a good friend."

Jean opened her door and put a Hardee's napkin into my hand. I tasted the salt from my tears, blinked to hold them back, and instead released a flood upon my face. Even unfolded, the napkin wasn't big enough.

Sally slid out of the car and engulfed me in her arms. "I'm so sorry, Sydney. You loved Crystal. She was your friend. I know you didn't mean anything."

"No, Sally, I was wrong," I said through my tears. "I have no business second-guessing Fred. I'm sure he's as devastated as we are." I fumbled in my pocketbook for a tissue, blew my nose and smiled weakly at Sally, who was likewise doing her best imitation of composure.

She ran both hands through her hair, then pressed her palms above each ear and pushed up her sagging hairdo. One side obeyed and the other didn't. With her red nose, white face, and lopsided hair, Sally looked like a clown, and I immediately felt hot with the shame of noticing.

"Why don't we all sit in the car," Jean said efficiently. "The air-conditioning will feel good."

The car was already cool, quickly turning my sweat and tears into sticky, salty film, like beach residue. The smell of the spilt liquor blasted up my nostrils, and for a second or two I was afraid I was going to be sick.

I sat in the back beside Sally. Jean draped her right arm over the seat so that she could face us.

"Okay, Sally," Jean said. "Fred went by the house this morning on his way to work . . ."

Sally continued carefully, hesitantly, looking over at me for emotional corroboration. "Yes, yes, he did. When Crystal didn't come to the door, he let himself in with his key. He found her in the bedroom." Her voice broke; she cleared her throat. "Freddie told me her neck looked funny. There were marks on it," she said quickly. "And her head was turned weird. He said it just wasn't natural. He could tell right off she was dead."

I automatically stroked my neck as Sally talked. Crystal had been wearing only a short nightgown. The bed was disheveled, the scene of either violent sex or violent struggle. Probably both.

"He called the police himself," Sally said. "Why have they got him down there now when he's the one who called them in the first place? Why? None of this makes any sense to me."

"They probably thought of some more questions to ask him is all," Jean offered before I could. "This is just awful," she added, as if reality was just now pushing itself on her.

"He told them everything he could think of this morning. They kept him there at the house for three hours. I mean, my God, what else could they want from him? Then he came by the office to tell me." Her mouth began to quiver again. "The poor guy didn't know where else to go. I was just coming back from lunch. You'd left to see that client, then come over here. I'm just glad I got to you before you left."

"But what can I do, Sally? Her parents. Has anyone told her parents? She has a brother, doesn't she? What's his name? Lord, somebody's got to tell them."

"Freddie did that. He called them from the office. I thought maybe you could get your brother Bill to run over to the police station and help Fred. I don't think he should be over there without a lawyer, do you?"

"Bill's a corporate lawyer. I'm not sure he could do anything for Fred right now."

"It's the one thing he asked for. I guess I was his one phone call. Is it true about only one phone call? Is that all he gets, just the one? Anyway, what he said was 'Get me a lawyer.'"

"I don't think Fred has a thing to worry about," I said. "How long's he been down there?"

She looked at her watch. "He came by the office at about two and called Crystal's parents and brother from there. I guess that took about an hour." Her voice was steady now and confident, the question of time carrying no emotional triggers. "And it couldn't have been an hour after that when he called to tell me he'd been asked to come downtown. I called your brother myself, but he was with a client, and he hasn't called me back. Hart and the salesman had both gone home, and I couldn't stand waiting anymore. I went down to the police station myself to see if there was anything I could do. I saw Freddie just a few minutes ago to tell him I was coming to get you. Honestly, Sydney, he was white as a sheet. He looked so scared."

It was almost six o'clock, so he had already been at the police station two hours. I wondered myself what they could be asking him that they couldn't have thought to ask this morning.

"Jean," I said, "could you drop us off at the Center? I'll find my brother somewhere, I'm sure. We'll get him to talk with the police and straighten this whole thing out. Don't worry, Sally," I said cautiously as I impulsively patted down the awkwardly high side of her hairdo. "They just don't know who else to talk to about Crystal. Fred will be out in no time."

Sally and Fred sat huddled at the far end of a long metal conference table. They looked like both sides of a bipolar personality, she depressed and he manic.

Fred's voice was strained, a loud, raspy whisper. "I will not stay here any longer. How dare they suggest that I might—"

Our eyes locked. "Hey," I said.

Sally jumped up, grabbed my hands, and led me to the table. "Where'd you go? I thought you were right behind me."

She had bolted from Jean's car and run into the building. It had been the last I'd seen of her until finding her now. "Sally, nobody could've kept up with you."

Fred ran a hand through his collar-length black hair as he stood up. He pushed a stray corner of his wrinkled white shirt back into his pants and extended his hand. "Good to see you again, Sydney. Sorry about the circumstances." He raised an eyebrow toward Sally and added, "I told her not to go after you. No offense, but the last thing I need right now is advertising." The laugh he forced was hollow and had the kind of self-generated energy born of nerves.

Sally said, "Shut up, Freddie. Sydney's getting her brother, aren't you, Sydney?"

"I'll try. I haven't yet."

"I don't need her brother either, not with the prices I'm sure he charges." He turned toward Sally. "I didn't do anything. I don't need anybody, least of all a corporate lawyer." He paced around the conference table, flailing his arms as if a swarm of yellow jackets had been released from the vinyl floor. "Sally, you can be so damn dumb."

I was tempted to respond to Fred in kind. He was the last person in the world I wanted to see at this moment, much less try to help. I felt disloyal to Crystal just being here.

Sally held her head; she looked close to collapse.

I stepped between the two of them hoping to deflect some of the barrage Sally had been getting. "Hold it, Fred," I said. "I'm here because Sally asked me. She's trying to help you, so why don't you stop attacking her, okay?"

His chin and shoulders dropped as air rushed out of his chest, a thick, wet piece of hair falling across his forehead in the process. He slumped into a chair, and I pulled one up between his and Sally's.

"When did Crystal die?" I asked, although the words themselves did not seem real. A slight whimper came from Sally, and I patted her knee as I looked at Fred.

"Sometime during the night," he said. "I don't know if they have ways of getting at exactly when." His quick laugh spit sarcasm. "I was the last one to talk with her last night, and then, of course, I . . ." He hesitated slightly, the first emotion I'd seen other than rage. "I found her this morning. Early. About seven-thirty on my way to work."

"You didn't sleep there last night?"

"Lord, no. Our divorce was due to come through this month. We'd both moved on, you know."

Sally mumbled, "I think you could have worked things out." It set Fred off again, shooting him from his chair like a lit bottle rocket. While he paced and cursed his sister, I suggested she get us all some coffee.

When she had gone, I turned quickly to Fred. "I wouldn't alienate her if I were you. You need all the support you can get right now."

His glare told me that he thought as little of me as I did of him.

"Do you think they suspect you?"

His expression was an ad for disbelief. "No, Sydney, I think they brought me down here to give me a citizenship award." He shook his head, jerked it as if his neck needed oiling.

"Why?"

He laughed. "Oh, I don't know. Is it so surprising that I could get a citizenship award?"

"Why do they suspect you?" He was moving with such deliberate speed around the stark room that he seemed to have a destination. My neck was sore following him.

"How the hell should I know? If I did, I'd straighten them out. As it is, this Thurgood guy is playing cat and mouse. He talks with me for fifteen minutes, then leaves for thirty, then comes back for fifteen, then leaves again. I don't know why in hell they're holding me."

"You don't really think you're being held, now do you, Mr. Ball?" The voice at the door jolted me out of the chair, not so much because it frightened me but because it was so familiar.

I'd rarely seen Tom Thurgood in anything except tennis shorts, sometimes even less, but that had been eight or nine years ago when we were steady tennis partners. I did a double-take, seeing his lanky frame in a sport coat and khaki pants.

His raised eyebrows belied his shock of recognition as well, but the grin that spread across his face was genuine.

"Hello, Sydney. I'm surprised to see you here."

His easy manner relaxed me, and despite my currently grim surroundings, I allowed myself to remember how attracted I'd been to this man at one time. I glanced at Fred, who had frozen midstep with mouth open at our exchange, then back to Tom Thurgood.

"Fred's sister works for me," I said. "And Crystal was a good friend." In spite of much effort, my voice cracked on these last two words.

Tom quickly squeezed and released my shoulder while seeking my eyes. "Sorry about your friend."

"And her brother's a lawyer," Fred said.

"Isn't everybody's?" Thurgood asked.

"Excuse me," I said.

"Isn't everybody's brother a lawyer? Some days it seems as if everybody's a lawyer." He turned a chair around backward and eased himself onto it. "I don't think Mr. Ball needs a lawyer. He's not being held for anything. We just needed to ask him some questions since he found the body." He shifted his gaze to Fred. "You don't think you need a lawyer, do you, Mr. Ball?"

Fred looked uneasy, in a quieter way than before.

"Why do you keep asking me questions and then disappearing for thirty minutes at a time?"

"Just checking with the rest of the team." He dipped the back of his chair against the table, then pushed off, landing upright. "I don't do the typing." He held up a sheaf of papers toward Fred. "If you'll just sign your statement here, you can leave."

When Fred didn't show any inclination toward taking the papers, I did. I took them right over to the table in front of the chair where Fred had sat earlier, pulled out the chair, and motioned Fred to sit.

Thurgood smiled and said softly, "Rush that net, Sydney."

3

"WHAT IS THIS?" FRED ASKED AS HE SAT DOWN and stared at the paperwork before him. His lips began to move silently as he read.

"I taped it," Thurgood said as he reached for the doorknob, "so, if there's a problem, it's with the typist. I'll be just down the hall. Step outside if you need me." He closed the door as he left.

I sat beside Fred.

"What should I do?" he asked. "Should I sign this without a lawyer?" The sarcasm was gone.

"I don't know. If you've incriminated yourself, you've already done it when you were taped. Did you know he was taping you?"

"He mentioned it so I guess I did."

Fred began to read, his lips again forming each word like a nervous actor waiting in the wings for his cue. When he finished the first page, he laid it upright between us. I slid it over just enough to read it myself, and, when finished, turned it facedown in the middle of the table.

There were over thirty pages in all, and it read like a script. But not one with a very happy ending. Neither Fred nor I said much during the forty-five minutes that we read. Not even when Sally returned with the coffee and placed it before us. She sat and began to read from the accumulating facedown stack of papers in the middle of the table.

Much of the interview had to do with Fred and Crystal's divorce. Was it hostile? Did they ever fight physically? Fred said no to both questions. Crystal had told me he didn't care enough to fight. What was the settlement? Were they both satisfied? Fred's responses all read as if he had been captain of the Good Ship Lollipop and Crystal had been a bad little girl. I felt an immediate rush of anger and suppressed the urge to defend my dead friend. What did I expect from Fred under these circumstances? Self-preservation was literally all he cared about right now, and it was true Crystal drank too much at times, and she did continue to find men attractive both during and after her marriages, Fred being number three. Still, it was hard for me to read this stuff. Crystal's drinking had escalated during her marriage to Fred. She told me she could and would get her life together after the divorce, and I believed she would have. I am living proof that the facts of a person's life say very little about the spirit of that life. I had known Crystal's soul, and knew she was a good and kind person. I didn't recognize her in Fred's words.

The middle pages of the transcript dealt with Fred finding her. I couldn't bring myself to read his description of her body, but I read everything before and after that part. He said he stopped by the house to discuss the disposition of furniture and appliances, items that had not been divided as part of the divorce. When Thurgood asked Fred what time he arrived at the house, Fred's response was "just before nine," not the seven-thirty he'd told me and Sally.

I pushed the page in front of Fred and said, "Look here. This nine o'clock's a mistake. You told us seven-thirty."

"Shhh," Fred said as he hit my knuckles and glanced quickly at the closed door. "I couldn't tell them I was there for over an hour before calling them."

Sally nodded as if she understood.

I just sat there waiting for some kind of explanation.

"What did you do for over an hour?" I finally asked.

"Everything was gone. All three TVs, the stereo, the video camera, the computers, the PC as well as the laptop . . ." He turned to Sally. "You remember my laptop." Then back to me. "I brought that laptop into the marriage. I looked everywhere. It was gone just like everything else that had any value."

I couldn't believe this. "You mean you spent close to an hour and a half rummaging through the house while Crystal lay dead in the bedroom?" My disbelief was as strong as my anger. The combination cut my air supply, and I had to stop talking. How could anybody be capable of this level of materialism? Crystal had been right: Fred was one self-centered son of a bitch.

I had a hard time reading the rest of it, but I did. Fred reported that everything had looked normal at the house except for the missing items, the messy master bedroom, and his dead ex-wife. That is the order in which he said it too. He saw no signs anybody had tried to break in before he arrived. Dishes were in the kitchen sink, a paper had been read and left in sections on the kitchen table. I wondered briefly if the paper's date had been this morning's or yesterday's. A bottle of vodka and a pitcher of warm orange juice were together on the coffee table in the living room. Most of the lights were on throughout the house, including the ceiling light in the master bedroom. Fred had called her last night to say he'd like to stop by the house this morning. Although he hadn't looked at a clock, he guessed he'd made the call around eight o'clock. No, he'd said, he didn't hear anything unusual in her voice and, no, he didn't get the feeling that anybody was with Crystal at the time of their phone conversation. Thurgood had ended the interview by asking Fred if he was seeing anyone special now that his divorce was almost final. Fred said he'd dated, at the most, three or four times since his separation, but that Crystal regularly saw an army of men. His exact words. He also said, and the bitterness showed up on the page, she had begun recruiting long before their separation. When I finished reading the last page, I saw Fred's signature and date, September eighteenth, at the bottom of the page.

Before I could look up, Fred had stood up, opened the door, and was in the hall looking for Thurgood. I took the last sheet of paper from Sally to stack for Thurgood, and I noticed my hands shaking. I looked into Sally's eyes, and the horror I saw there I felt in my soul. Crystal's murder had been acknowledged by my head but was now washing deeper, flooding me with feelings that my head couldn't touch. Sally's eyes told me she was drowning as well, but I suspected that although the intensity of our feelings was similar, the feelings themselves were most likely different. Strange how the deepest of sorrows and the deepest of fears showed up the same.

* * *

In the parking lot I hugged Sally and told her not to worry about coming in tomorrow. I didn't want to, but I hugged Fred as well. If he had shown any remorse for Crystal's death, I would have had some feelings for the guy. As it was, I sensed, in some egocentric way he felt she'd deserved what she got.

The instant they disappeared in Fred's car, I realized I'd left the Trooper at the Mint Museum, where Jean had picked me up. The Mint was at least five miles from here, so walking was out. I went back inside to search for a phone and ran into Tom. He was about to leave, he said, and offered to drive me.

We had known each other much better than either of us had let on in front of Sally and Fred. We had been a couple for a few months in the late eighties when the kids and the divorce were still young, as was my sobriety. I'd fought the desire to let him move in when he asked. Too much for me at the time. I just couldn't open the door that far. Vulnerability was an option I no longer allowed myself. Besides, what he had really wanted was a wife.

I couldn't resist asking him if he'd found the woman he was looking for.

"Sure did," he said without taking his eyes off the road.

"Any children?"

"No." He hesitated, then added, "We never had any."

I laughed. "Uh oh, that's past tense, Tom. I never thought you'd be among the divorced."

"I'm not," Tom said, and looked away. "Carol died. Lymphoma took her out of my life as quickly as she had come in. Five years now."

"Oh my God, Tom, forgive me. I'm so sorry. It was stupid of me to assume . . ."

He turned onto Museum Drive, and the streetlight caught the wetness in his eyes. "It's okay," he said. "Five years can be an eternity. My memories are good."

He drove in silence the remaining three blocks.

When he pulled in next to my Trooper, he turned off the ignition and maneuvered to face me. "Why do I get the feeling you've never remarried?"

"Strong vibes, huh?"

"The strongest." He grinned.

"I've been busy. I had to earn a living," I explained. "And the kids still aren't grown. Sometimes I wonder if they ever will be."

He put a forefinger to his temple and closed his eyes for a second. "Joanie and little George, right?" he said as he pointed the same forefinger at me.

"Right!" I was pleased. "Only little George is twelve now so he's George junior and sometimes he fights even the junior so he's just George."

"Tennis sometime?"

"Maybe." I opened the car door.

He held my wrist to stop me. "Sydney, how close are you to this Ball fellow?"

I hoped I hadn't given the wrong impression. "I'm not. Not at all." I looked into his eyes and saw relief.

"Good. You don't want to get in the middle of this."

"What do you mean by 'get in the middle'? Crystal was a really great friend of mine for close to twenty years. What do you want me to do, pretend she died in a car wreck?"

"All I meant is domestic disputes are the ugliest cases we handle, especially when they end with murder."

I stared at his shadow behind the steering wheel for a full thirty seconds before answering him. "If you're convinced Fred killed her, why didn't you arrest him tonight?" I wondered why I was defending Fred as I heard my voice rise an octave.

He turned his profile to me. In the dark of the car, I watched his chest swell and quickly fall in sync with a sound that was somewhere between anger and exhaustion. When he turned to face me again, his words came out sharp and distinct. "I haven't said I'm convinced of anything, and I'm not going to say anything else I might regret."

He suddenly opened his door, came around to my side, and escorted me to the Trooper without a word. I knew I had crossed a line. Well, so had he.

I am a closet smoker, so of course the first thing I did after I revved my big engine at Thurgood, was to light a Vantage. It took a mere three drags to calm down, the miracle drug being what it is. A cigarette does for me what Scotch used to, although not as well. Automatic mood-switching devices. Up, down, in, or out. Wherever I wanted or needed to go, alcohol took me there until it put me down for the count. I breathed deeply and hoped that my lungs were holding out better than my nerves had.

My house is a 1920s rip-off Tudor on a deep narrow lot in an old section of Charlotte. Because of the skinny land allotment, each of its three floors had three rooms lined up one behind the other with steep stairs at the back of long connecting halls. I drove into the drive that barely fits between the house and the lot line and watched the

lights fall like dominoes as the kids turned off the basement TV room light, and then the first-floor bathroom
light, and then the kitchen light. As I was locking the
kitchen door behind me, my daughter Joan called down
from her bedroom.

"How was your real estate thing, Mom?"

"I'm glad to be home," I yelled back, and thought
about small dishonesties. What good would it do to confront them about their homework? What good would it
do for me to tell them about Crystal tonight?

Instead, I fixed us grilled cheese sandwiches topped off
with bowls of ice cream. Normally we eat van-cho-straw,
but not tonight. I needed comfort anyplace I could find
it. Tonight I pulled out the "company" ice cream, Pierre's
toffee crunch made from bits of real Heath bars.

"Any messages?" I asked, nodding toward the answering machine on the kitchen counter.

"A couple," Joan said, "but I think they came in last
night after we went to bed. Don't worry," she quickly
added when she saw my concern, "they're not business.
Just friends. I punched Save."

More and more lately I was cutting the phones' sound
off at night and letting the answering machine get it. The
practice had begun as a way of keeping homework time
uninterrupted. I liked the quiet so much that I'd sometimes conveniently forget to turn the phones back on.

"George junior, score any goals in soccer practice
today?"

He beamed. "Two."

"Wow," I said. "No problem getting home?"

"Naw, rode my bike."

Joan had been gradually inching her nose toward my

upper arm and finally said, "Mom, you smell awful. What have you been doing?"

My perennial defender, little Georgie, said, "I think Mom smells good."

I laughed. "No, I don't, honey. I've been dodging slippery liquor at the Civic Center all afternoon." I stood up and took my jacket off. "Who knows what's on this jacket at this point. Is everyone ready for bed?"

Sixteen-year-old Joan looked shocked at the suggestion. "Mom," she said in that exasperated tone only teenagers have, "it's only nine o'clock."

I put my bowl in the sink and started toward the stairs. "Well, then, come do your homework, and don't tell me it's done because I saw the big rush when I was coming down the driveway."

No protests this time as they moved single file past me and up the stairs.

That night I both showered and bathed. The steamy spikes of the shower couldn't dissipate the grief that had sunk to my gut nor penetrate the shell hardening around it. Crystal's face came at me in the pulsating waves of the shower head, and her laugh echoed off the slick tile walls. My tears mixed with the clear water and bathed me in remorse.

I felt as though the alcohol had seeped through my suit and invaded my pores, leaving me nauseous and headachy. Like old times, I thought. Lying in the full tub, I eased my eyes down to bubble level. I lingered for a good thirty minutes, feeling my muscles finally begin to unravel, letting some water out twice to replenish with hot. My pores opened and the poison flowed out. I dragged deeply on my Vantage and blew large, thick rings of smoke, better than the best I'd produced as a teenager. Blowing smoke rings was quite private now. I could count on one hand the people I knew who still appreciated such a skill, and one of them was Crystal. If she had been here now, she would have told me what I already knew: that these smoke rings were pretty damn near perfect.

Not surprisingly I couldn't sleep. The more I willed my mind to wipe out all thoughts, the more alert I became. Then, in the midst of the effort, I'd remember that Crystal was dead. Like a stream at the base of a broken dam, my mind would flood with sadness. Worse than sadness. Sadness tinged with anger.

At midnight I gave up and went to the kitchen in search of milk to go with my aspirin. After I poured the milk and put the carton back into the refrigerator, I noticed the red blinking of the answering machine. If I didn't clear it now, it would just have more messages tomorrow. There were two, the first of which was my cousin announcing the marriage of her son last weekend down in South Carolina. I wondered what I was supposed to do with that information. What was the postmodern protocol? Send a gift? Call her back? Call her back with the gift of my voice?

This multiple choice was dancing around in my head when the second message began: "Sydney, this is Crystal. You in bed already?" She laughed as I gasped.

I slammed my hand atop the machine, one finger pushing the Save button, another finger the Stop button. All the blood in my body rushed through my head at once. Its roar was all I could hear. I held on to the edge of the counter with one hand and pushed the other hand against the rapids inside my head. I held on like this for at least a minute while I forced slow breathing and thought about the voice on the machine. Slowly I realized the message had come in last night after I'd turned off the phone ringers. Even with that understanding, hitting the Play button was one of the hardest things I have ever done.

It began where I had stopped it, in the middle of her laugh. Throaty, loose, fluid. Crystal had been drinking last night. When she wasn't, her laugh was more girlish, a nervous giggle.

"Oh, Sydney, we are going in different directions with our lives, aren't we? Two extremes, I'd say." A shorter laugh. "But listen, friend, I need to talk. I've got to tell you something our Mickey is planning. Lunch tomorrow? Please try. You don't want to miss hearing what I have to tell you. Anyway, call my machine in the morning and let me know when and where and I'll be there." A five-second pause. "You were right about him, you know. Mickey is a genuine sleaze." The computerized voice had recorded the message at seven a.m., Friday, September nineteenth. What? It was midnight now. The nineteenth was just beginning. This time was seven hours into the future. Then it dawned on me: I had failed to reset the machine's clock after one of this summer's thunderstorms. Had the answering machine jumped forward in time during the blackout? I had grown accustomed to my machine's quirks, but now under these circumstances, it was more than I could bear. I vowed to unravel this problem later.

My hands were still shaking as I washed down the two aspirin.

Mickey Sutton. The damn bastard. What was she going to tell me about him? Was it bad enough for him to try to stop her?

He was coming to my office tomorrow. Even if I had to confront him, I'd find out.

Crystal used to say God intended us to go through life a little high. "Fuzzy," she called it. No hard edges. Reality was the devil's venue. To Crystal, sober people were oftentimes brittle, unhappy and disappointed. A little booze in the system at all times, she preached, guaranteed seamless experiences, unexpected humor, and a good night's sleep. Part of me thought she was right.

Without opening my eyes, I felt for the blaring alarm and turned it off. I pulled the second pillow to my chest and hugged it, letting its soft fibers caress my body. The mornings are so much better sober, I'd told her: no daggers in the head, no stomachs in the throat. She had laughed and said she didn't need convincing. Fuzzy was gone, long ago replaced with drunk. I could still hear her the last time we'd discussed her stopping. "I know, I know. I can't maintain the buzz anymore, Sydney, but I would if I could. I still feel it's the ideal way to be."

In quick succession, Joan's, then George's alarms went off. I let the pillow go and rolled over and up, feeling my feet hit the wool Berber throw rug. The hard edge of today's particular reality shot through me as if the Berber were an ungrounded wire. I froze at the side of my bed. An image of Crystal dead overtook me. Brown laughing eyes turned lifeless. A doll's glass eyes. Rich olive skin a mask of dingy Naugahyde. I shook my head to rid it of this horror and took the deepest breath I could. If God is merciful, then surely He let Crystal be drunk when she died.

* * *

Telling the kids about her death was harder than I'd expected. Crystal had been a fixture in their lives, part of their earliest memories. I should have been more sensitive to their relationships with her when I'd only been thinking of my own. I blurted it out over toast and bacon, even the fact that she had been murdered.

Joanie burst into tears. "She was my friend too, Mom." And she had been. All of a sudden, I could see through Joanie's eyes. "I could talk to Crystal. She taught me to dance, she showed me how to put on makeup . . . she was funny." Her face broke into a hundred tiny pieces of grief. I cried too, perhaps more honestly than at any time last night. Being with someone else who loved her helped my tears cleanse me, somehow reaffirming life in the grieving of her death.

George junior's reaction was more troubling. He wanted details. How did she die? Was she asleep when it happened? Did someone break into her house? Could her murderer be someone we knew? There was fear in his eyes, fear for himself, fear for me. He hugged me longer and tighter than he had in many years.

I was late getting to the office. Sally had come in even though I'd told her she didn't need to. She said Fred convinced her there was nothing to worry about. After listening to Thurgood last night, I had my doubts. And watching Sally polish the same spot on her desk for five minutes, I thought she might be worried as well.

"Where are Hart and the salesman?" I asked. "We need a staff meeting." I hoped to convert Sally's busywork into real work. Today was Friday, and what had slid all week must hop out of here now.

"Hart's upstairs. Who knows where the salesman is." She was separating paper clips as she spoke.

Neither Hart, Sally, nor I called the salesman by his given name anymore. Unless, of course, he was around, which he rarely was and shouldn't have been. Not if he was going to sell our services. We had contracted six different commissioned salesmen this past year and learned after the first two, to whom we'd become attached, that account executives didn't stay anywhere very long. They either produced quickly and built a base or they moved on. I couldn't afford to get too attached to people I fired regularly.

Hart was crouched over his drawing board in what probably had been the master bedroom of this monstrous old house that was home to Allen Teague. After two winters of electric bills, I had put the house back on the market with Miller and Associates. All we needed were three or four good-sized rooms in an energy-efficient office building. In this house, as much as I loved its comfort and charm, I could have put an entire village of Haitian refugees. Last winter, each time I passed a group of ragged men huddled outside St. Peter's soup kitchen, I felt guilty that I'd used this space so wantonly.

"You shouldn't be so winded climbing those stairs now that you've stopped smoking." Hart was watching me pause at the top of the banister. It had been immensely important to Hart that I stop smoking, so I never lit up around him anymore. I've never actually told him I've stopped, so we've been in what I like to think of as an extended misunderstanding.

"Whew! We'd do better to rent this place out as an exercise studio," I said.

Hart put down his X-Acto and swiveled his chair toward me. "The high ceilings," he said. "Makes the stairs steeper. Want some coffee?" The morning sun brushed across his forehead, and I could see a network of blue veins just beneath his porcelain skin.

I sat on the old leather love seat across from his board. "Got a cup downstairs. I think we probably need to meet for about fifteen minutes 'cause I don't know what's due out today. Have you got a pretty good handle on it?"

"I know what you're given me. Sally hasn't brought me anything," he said.

"You know about Sally's brother?" I asked.

Hart nodded and widened his eyes, the blue paler than his veins. "What a mess. She said he'd been released."

"For now, but I think she has reason to be worried. Do you know Fred?"

Hart shook his head. "Never met him."

"Consider yourself lucky," I said. "Not a very ingratiating guy. Hard to believe he's Sally's brother. He's more concerned about some missing electronics than he is about Crystal's murder."

"I'm sorry, Sydney. I know you and Crystal were close. Are you okay?"

Hart is generally so unemotional, any gesture like this on his part surprises me. I looked into his almost transparent eyes to let him know how much his asking meant to me. "Yes, we were. Thanks."

A slight crease appeared on his forehead, a harbinger of wrinkles twenty years down the road. "Do you think he killed her?"

"No, no, I don't."

"Why not, if he's such a jerk?"

I thought about his question for a second before answering. "Because he is a jerk. Something about the way Crystal seemed less than the objects in his life. He wouldn't be so upset about a stupid missing television. Somebody's bound to have taken that stuff and killed her in the process."

Hart smiled that wry smile of his. "Too self-absorbed to murder, huh?" He shook his thin head. "That's a defense I've never heard before."

"Well, think about it. It makes sense in this case if you knew them both. I'm just not sure the police think about things like that. And I'm not so sure Sally believes he didn't kill her."

He wrinkled his forehead again. "But he's her brother. Surely she can't believe he'd do something so barbaric."

I raised my eyebrows. "I know it sounds stupid, Hart, but Sally thinks Fred has normal emotions. If she saw him the way I do . . ." I stopped when I saw the confused expression on his face. "Oh, well, it's moot, isn't it? He's been released."

I got up and walked over to his board, where the Miller and Associates logo was pinned. "Looks good. Jean'll be here after lunch to go over signage and billboards. I think we'd better meet downstairs in fifteen minutes. If for no other reason, Sally and I both need a focus today."

Hart Johnson had been my art director for seven years. I'd been in business less than two years when I plucked him from the graduating class at UNC-Charlotte. The man is still under thirty. Yet he is older than I in so many ways. He never lets people get to him; I am entangled at every turn. He is not influenced by trends: political, social, or fashion. Not even advertising trends. He listens to and watches only public broadcasting. His reading range is broad as long as the material was written before the twentieth century. His sexual inclinations, I admit, remain a mystery to me and to others of both sexes. But he does have a great love of the human race precisely because, I believe, he has graciously and determinedly kept us all at arm's length.

Around eleven o'clock I heard my brother, Bill, talking with Sally in the reception room. I'd been yelling at the software consultant on the other end of my phone line, so I'd missed Bill's entrance. I hadn't wanted the fancy software, just a simple system to coordinate all our jobs. There certainly were plenty such programs on the market. But I guess I'm still insecure in the computer realm and was ripe pickings for the "consultant." This guy had us so screwed up that we were writing checks to clients and billing our vendors. When I told him I wanted my money back and the program removed from the computer, he told me he couldn't.

"Custom work," he said blandly.

"Then fix it by next week or I'll hire someone who can take it off, and I'll see you in court." I said the part about court loud enough for Bill to hear. I had yet to reap the rewards of having a brother in the legal profession.

By the time I had slammed the phone onto the hook, Bill and Sally were standing in my doorway.

"We're having a little software problem," I said by way of explanation.

Bill grinned. "I haven't heard you yell that loudly since I beat you at marbles thirty years ago." He sauntered in and sat on one of my straightbacks.

Sally lingered at the door.

"I thought I'd return your call in person," he said.

I pushed my chair back and looked at my watch. "Fifteen hours late, Bill."

"Sally says the emergency is over," he said, making light of it. How did he know one of my children had not been hit by a car? "She told me about her brother, that he's been released."

Sally was nodding in rhythm to Bill's words, so eager she was to believe Fred's close call was over.

Bill's boyish face makes him look younger than me by as much as ten years, but, in fact, he is two years my senior. I inherited the angular bone structure of the Allens; he has our mother's softness.

"I'm really sorry about Crystal. I know you two go way back." His round cheeks dropped into the hint of future jowls as he stared at me in concern.

"Yeah," I said. "Way back."

I looked up at Sally. "I don't think it would hurt for Bill to call Fred, do you? Refer him to a good defense lawyer, just in case?"

Sally's eyes got that hunted animal look I'd seen in them last night.

"Just in case," I said again.

I motioned toward Bill. "He's here. He may as well talk with Fred."

"Do they have any other suspects that you know of?" Bill asked me.

I shook my head and noticed that Sally was shaking her head as well.

"Maybe you should call Freddie," she said softly.

"It wouldn't hurt for you to call Tom Thurgood either," I said. "See if you can get any information out of him."

Bill's eyes twinkled. With his rosy, round cheeks, he could have been a cherub. "The Tom Thurgood you used to see?"

I don't know why I was embarrassed all of a sudden, but I was. "He's the detective handling this case," I said as quickly as I could.

"I've heard he's the best homicide has, Sydney." Bill looked at me as if I should have known that fact. "You bet he's handling it. Upscale neighborhood, break-in in the middle of the night, attractive woman, raped, strangled . . ." He stopped abruptly when he saw my lower lip quivering.

"God, I'm sorry. I forgot for a moment . . ."

"How do you know she was raped?" I asked.

He looked at Sally, then back at me. "It was in the paper this morning. On television too. I thought you knew everything."

"Not that." Perspiration began to form beads on my upper lip. I picked up an oversize *Ad Age* magazine and began to fan myself. "Check the thermostat, please, Sally. I'll bet Hart is sweltering upstairs."

When she was gone, I leaned over my desk to whisper to Bill. "I don't think they're through with Fred. Get him some help." I pointed where Sally had stood a moment earlier. "She's not facing the reality of this situation."

4

"TO TELL YOU THE TRUTH," JEAN SAID TO ME, "I think I had a little too much to drink at the Roundup. The last thing I felt like doing this morning was reading the paper even though I knew it would have more details on poor Crystal." We were back in my office after meeting with Sally and Hart. She nodded in the direction of my closed door. "How's Sally holding up? I know you were close to Crystal, but what about Sally? Were she and Crystal close?"

I lowered my voice. These old walls didn't provide much of a sound barrier. "She'd like to think they were close now that Crystal's dead. It's easier that way. Something like this isn't supposed to happen while you are actively hating someone. However she's feeling, you can bet it's driven by guilt."

"Mixed up with loyalty to her brother probably too."

"Speaking of the brother," I said, "I don't see any of that wonderful guilt in him. He hasn't even said he's sorry she's dead. What a jerk."

"I'm beginning to be glad I never met hm." She smoothed back her dark hair and pressed her skirt down with perfectly manicured fingers.

"Oh, the showing's at six. Will y'all be out of here by then?"

The house had been listed for only three days, so this would have been good news if anybody other than Mickey Sutton were looking at it. Even if Crystal had never left me the message about him, I would not consider letting Mickey into my office without being present.

"We can be, but I'm staying."

Jean smiled. She knew how I felt about Mickey. The creep calls his agency Mickey Sutton Esquire Inc. How's that for subtlety? A walking ego full of outrageous ideas and applications. His personal style borrows from side-show barkers at country carnivals. Some people, however, are actually smitten with Mickey and think his approach makes good advertising.

"I wish now it weren't in Multiple Listing. I'd have more control over who sees it."

"His money's as good as anybody's, Sydney. You don't want to run off a perfectly good buyer just because you don't like him."

"I don't? It seems to me the best reason to run someone off. Besides, I think he's just playing games coming here. He'll go through our files and go after our clients."

"Barbara Cates will not let him get into your stuff." She got up, walked over to my desk and patted my hand. "Come on," she said. "Show me how you want me to attach the supralock. We can put it on the doorknob or the porch railing."

The supralock, it turned out, was a metal box like a large, old-fashioned bicycle lock. Its face had a vertical, three-number combination instead of one circular set like regular combination locks.

"How's this going to let realtors in?" I asked. "It doesn't even lock anything."

"Your house key's inside. You use your personal combination plus your supralock key to get inside and get the house key. Did you make me a copy?" She was stooped by the railing where she'd hooked the key housing around a skinny spoke. Immediately it slid to the brick landing and played hide-and-seek among the sweet autumn clematis. "This would be a lot easier to get to if we put it on the doorknob, Sydney."

She held on to the rail and pulled herself up. Perspiration had formed on her forehead. She removed a handkerchief from her pocketbook and dabbed at her face, then smoothed her Liz Claiborne gabardine suit.

"Naw," I said. "I don't want to fight my way through that thing to get to the doorknob every morning. I like it being inconspicuous."

She exhaled as she put her handkerchief away. "God, it's hot," she said. "When's it going to cool off?"

"Last year even October wasn't even any better, remember? I think I wore summer clothes until Thanksgiving week. The leaves never got their full color; they just shriveled, turned brown, and fell off."

We moved back into my reception room, the old parlor, where Sally was putting her phone on the hook. She appeared almost as distraught as she had been yesterday. "It's the detective, Sydney. From last night."

"Thurgood?" I asked. I looked at her blinking phone line. "Is he still on the phone?"

"Yeah." Her voice had that quiver to it again.

"What did he say to upset you?"

Her eyes met mine as if she had just caught me in the middle of cheating on finals. "He asked if he could speak with you, that's what. Why? What could you tell him that I couldn't?"

Sally said quickly as she was about to pick up the phone again, "Don't talk to him, Sydney. I'll tell him you've left for the day."

I put my hand on top of hers. "This is crazy. Of course I'll talk to him. I'm sure it has nothing to do with Fred, Sally."

Jean stayed in the reception room with Sally while I returned to my office to take the call. I couldn't have been more surprised at what Tom Thurgood wanted. I shouldn't have been, though. Tennis had been important to him eight years ago. Why should it not be now?

"Well, will you play with me? An hour? Thirty minutes if that's too long."

I held the phone as if it was a conduit to some remote memory. A time machine when I had expected immediacy.

The topic was immediate to Tom. His speech sounded almost rehearsed. "You need to be honest with me, Sydney. If you don't want to hit with me, you need to tell me. As I recall, you had a hard time telling me that eight years ago."

His memory was accurate. Golfers have handicaps; tennis players have the alphabet. The closer you are to its beginning, the better you are. Eight years ago I was a solid A player, Tom a mere C. By the time we stopped seeing each other, he had progressed to a C+ and I was barely hanging on to an A−.

"I've improved," he continued. It didn't seem to matter that I had not said a word the entire time we had been on the phone.

I finally laughed. "Tom, you're probably better than I am. I've played maybe five times in eight years. You'll be sorry you asked me."

We settled on five o'clock tomorrow afternoon at Freedom Park.

"Look," he began haltingly as we started to hang up, "I'm sorry about our misunderstanding last night."

Finally the topic I had expected. "What misunderstanding?"

"Fred Ball."

Here we go, I thought. "What about Fred Ball, Tom?"

"Dammit, Sydney. You know you misunderstood what I was saying. You misunderstood my warning about getting mixed up with Fred Ball."

"We didn't have a misunderstanding. I thought we were both perfectly clear."

In the silence that followed, I could hear the intercom at his office. I had memories of this kind of silence between us from years before.

"Your brother called down here a few minutes ago." He'd decided to act as if we had not just disagreed again.

"Good for Bill," I said. I hoped he had been able to find out what this guy was thinking.

"Remember the fun we used to have playing doubles with him and . . . what was his wife's name?"

"Karen. And she wasn't his wife. She is now though."

He couldn't hide his surprise. "I don't think I knew that. I just assumed, I guess."

I said "Don't worry about it. He plays with somebody named Terry now. Karen sits at home just as the first wife did." I knew I was sounding harsh.

"Well . . ." He hesitated as if weighing the merits of

continuing this conversation. "It was good talking with him again. He's a nice guy, Sydney."

I really didn't want to agree with Thurgood on anything. "Sometimes he's nice. Everybody's nice sometime. See you tomorrow, Tom."

When I opened my office door, both Sally and Jean were shuffling aimlessly right on the other side. In unison, they said, "Well?"

"It had absolutely nothing to do with anything of concern to anybody. Except him. He wants me to play tennis."

Sally still looked worried.

Jean hung around upstairs with Hart until four-thirty. They were going over myriad logo applications. I had not particularly liked the plain MA for Miller and Associates but Jean did, especially since she could say "Call MA" and "MA Knows Best" on her billboards and in her radio spots. There was so much clutter and clamor in real estate advertising these days that the simple MA probably would help. Perhaps twenty new firms had sprung up since the exodus from Bishop Cates, but I hoped Jean would fare better than the others with this campaign, too cute though it was. We'd tackle dignity and integrity later—after some of those twenty dropped out of the market.

I stayed in my office and returned some phone calls that had been on my desk since yesterday while I was at the Civic Center. Sally was on the trail of the salesman, but it was pretty stale. The list he had left us of people he was seeing today proved a day old. My guess was he'd gone to the mountains or the beach to escape this heat. It was okay by me; he didn't sell, he didn't get paid. We were busy enough without him right now anyway. I sometimes worried that I was becoming callous.

After Hart left at five-thirty and Sally was packing up, I settled in to wait for Mickey and Barbara. I was going to find out if he'd been at Crystal's the night she was killed. Besides, no matter how good a real estate agent Barbara Cates was, I couldn't imagine her convincing Mickey Sutton to move to quaint Dilworth. Mickey loved Charlotte's glass towers downtown or "uptown" as city PR was dictating we call it these days. That's where he was now and I didn't see him moving his firm here—ever. He was definitely up to something.

For me Dilworth is the only part of Charlotte that doesn't seem to have been created during the eighties. I have a friend who thinks the massive growth in Charlotte is a direct result of the state-sponsored highway seeding program, a wildflower beautification thing. Only difference, she says, is Jesse Helms and Ronald Reagan seeded the Charlotte area direct themselves and up sprang all these glass towers and manicured neighborhoods. And banks. Everywhere banks. The same friend points out that a large portion of Charlotte's workforce has never made anything but money. Banking deregulation doesn't make very interesting cities.

I both live and work in the Dilworth neighborhood, the former on a shady sidestreet called Kingston and the latter on the main thoroughfare, East Boulevard. The neighborhood was first laid out in the second half of the nineteenth century and bustling by the 1890s. It experienced most of its growth then, making it a wonderful example of Southern Victorian America. The houses are substantial, not necessarily in size but in construction quality. Styles are hodgepodge from Tudor, to Queen Anne, to early Craftsman. Sidewalks are abundant and wide, except on its major business corridor, East Boulevard, where my office is. Every yard has at least one hundred-year-old tree, usually an oak. The neighborhood was hit hard in 1989 when Hurricane Hugo came up Interstate 77 from Charleston and smashed into Charlotte. A lot of those oaks ended up in people's beds.

The best part of the neighborhood to me has always been the roofline. All the roofs are steep-pitched, multi-angled and multigabled—no matter what the style. The rest of Charlotte is uniformly Georgian, especially the newer streets. If I were a bird and looking for an interesting place to roost in Charlotte, North Carolina, I'd make a beeline straight for the roofs of Dilworth.

I was finishing a cigarette when Sally stuck her head into my office before leaving. She knew I still smoked but said she was proud that I'd cut back. Even so, she hated it, even coughed if she got into my line of fire. Consequently, I always exhaled into my wastebasket whenever she was present. Thus I experienced firsthand and second-hand smoke simultaneously.

"I didn't know you played tennis anymore," she said. "When's the last time you played?"

I was stubbing out my Vantage as I answered. "Oh, I don't know. I played in that Holiday Classic thing in Raleigh last year. With those casket manufacturers, remember? My partner and I won the mixed doubles. I can still hold my own."

I saw the concern on her face and was touched by it. "Don't worry about me, Sally. Just because I'm five years older than you doesn't mean I'm over the hill."

"That's not what I'm worried about," she said. "I'm

afraid you'll beat him, and that's the last thing we need. Promise me you won't beat him, Sydney. For Fred's sake. For mine?"

After Sally was gone, I walked around the rooms putting work-in-progress out of sight. Paperwork went in drawers and art too big went into the closets where I covered them with tablecloths and winter coats arranged haphazardly on the floors. Mickey wouldn't dare pick them up, I thought. Not with me and Barbara at his sides.

Mickey Sutton has the kind of features that invite good vibes from strangers. His eyes are wide and sparkle as if he were a true innocent. His mouth is full as if he were generous and his jaw is strong as if he had character. Other people trust him because of his looks. I know first-hand that he is a snake.

When they did arrive, Barbara and Mickey were both surprised to see me still there. I greeted them at the front door as if I were hosting a cocktail party and they were my first arrivals.

"Isn't that smell heady?" I said to the two of them. Barbara was crouched in the sweet autumn clematis attempting to combine her numbers. From the spread of her hips, she had not been doing her deep knee-bends. "Get up from there and you two come in the house!"

As I expected, Mickey immediately suggested to Barbara that they leave and come some other time. Barbara seemed pleased to see me and amused at the situation, as if it were only now dawning on her what Mickey was up to.

"No, no, no," I chimed. "Don't you dare think of leaving now. We're through for the day. Everybody's gone home for the weekend. When I heard the showing was for you, Mickey, I knew I wanted to show you around myself. In fact I said to myself this morning, 'Sydney Teague, you should be flattered Mickey Sutton thinks so much of you that he wants to see your little office.' " I was raised in a southern home where my parents instilled in me the fine art of repeating to others conversations I've had with myself. I hate to admit this sort of behavior comes naturally when I need it.

Mickey smiled politely, but his cold eyes revealed his disappointment in the situation. As he turned to survey my office space, and no doubt noticed the cleared desks and absence of materials waiting for his perusal, he sighed heavily. "You must have better lighting than this," he said, "to do top-rate advertising."

I played along and answered, "We prefer more subtlety in our approach."

"I was talking about the light, not the work itself," he snapped.

"Of course, my mistake."

The showing, such as it was, was over in fifteen minutes, with Mickey looking at his watch for the final five. He was pacing the front yard as Barbara and I closed up.

"Sorry," I said to her, "but he was up to no good. I had to be here to protect my turf."

Barbara looked worn. We were the same age, had gone through junior high and high school together. She had lost her softness; wiry gray cut through her brown hair randomly and her features were sharp. Her eyes lacked all definable color, and her back curved a bit like early osteoporosis. She was either sick, not aging well, or going through a difficult time emotionally. Knowing what

I knew about her decaying company, I assumed it was the last.

"I should have known. I don't know where my mind is these days, Sydney," she said. "I sometimes feel that I'm losing my grip." Her eyes turned liquid, she blinked and smiled. "Ugh. These ragweeds. They'll be the death of me."

"Allergies are tough," I said softly.

She blew her nose. "I've been wanting to talk to you. You slipped out of the Civic Center before I could get to you yesterday." Then she straightened her shoulders in some kind of physical resolve, and her body jerked itself once as if halting in the midst of a minor convulsion. Her tone perked up. "How about dinner. I'd love to talk. It's been ages."

A horn blew. I automatically waved. It was a friend of Joan's in an old VW convertible. "Tonight? I can't tonight. Joan has volleyball."

"What about Monday?" came her quick reply.

Gee, what a mood swing, I thought. "Well, okay," I answered. "I can get dinner Monday. I'll stop by your office at six. We'll go to SouthPark."

Between Barbara's keys and mine, it seemed to take us forever to get out the front door. A sullen Mickey stood silently in the front yard, hands in the pockets of his European pants.

Now was the time. I took a deep breath, strode purposefully toward Mickey, and stopped no more than two feet in front of him. Startled, he stepped back.

"Mickey," I said with no hesitation, "why haven't you told anybody that you were at Crystal's house the night she died?"

I had never seen a fearful snake until this moment. His

eyes shrank to slits and darted everywhere but at mine, which held him fixed like a target locked on radar.

"So what if I was? It's nobody's business."

Bingo. Dammit. It had been a bluff, but what was I supposed to do now?

Barbara stood at her car and looked from me to Mickey, then sighed.

Mickey turned and walked to her car.

They were out of my sight before I could close my mouth.

5

I WISH I WEREN'T SO COMPETITIVE. THE QUALI-
ty makes me do things against my better judgment. Like letting Joan come home "sick" after her
American lit test so that she could rest for her volleyball game.

You have to understand that Charlotte is serious about
its sports, and volleyball, even at the high school level, is
no exception. Joan plays for the Charlotte Bees, a junior
olympic team composed of the best of the sixteen-year-
olds in the city. The deeper the girls go into the season,
the more obnoxious we parents become. Today's game
against Raleigh was only their fourth this year, so my behavior was still contained. Some parents are much worse
than I am. Too involved in both the team and their
daughter's position on it. When Joan sprained her ankle
going into the play-offs last year, I could swear I saw
Melissa Downey's mother smile. Melissa had been Joan's
sub and, with Joan on the bench, got her chance to start.

Tonight we were tied with Raleigh two games apiece when the mandatory fifteen-minute break was called. Frank and Cynthia Hyatt came down from the top bleachers, each taking a side of me. George junior moved even farther away than he'd already been; the only thing worse than being with your mother, I assumed, was having to watch her socialize.

"Want a Coke, Sydney?" Frank asked. "I'm going to get Cynthia and myself one."

As soon as Frank had disappeared on the crowded gym floor, Cynthia jumped right in. "We heard about Crystal. God, it's getting dangerous to go for a divorce in this city. Can you believe it?"

"What?" was the only response that seemed to make any sense. "Cynthia, what are you talking about?" Gossip traveled quicker on these bleachers than any other place I knew.

She looked taken aback for a second as if she was shocked, but she didn't stop. "I don't know how I first heard about it. Somebody said something yesterday in the grocery store, I think. This morning I read the newspaper like everybody else. It said that Crystal Ball was found dead by her ex-husband yesterday morning. That she'd been strangled, probably raped, and that the husband was being questioned. True?"

Frank returned with our Cokes. Again I sat wedged between them. "I was there for his questioning, Cynthia. They had no reason to suspect him so they let him go. It's as simple as that."

Frank sipped his Coke and looked at his wife. "I agree with Sydney, Cynthia. You and all your friends are going to convict the poor man just because he was getting a divorce. Just like you did the other guy."

"You've got to admit it's quite a coincidence," she said.

Some important part of the conversation had passed me by. "Hold it a minute. What other guy?"

Cynthia wasted no time in telling me. "Same thing happened last week. Couple separated. He'd moved out. She's there in the house alone with their kid, right?" She sipped her Coke so eagerly that it dribbled down both sides of her mouth as she talked. "Kid walked in to wake her mother and finds her dead. Just like the Ball situation. The kid never heard anything. No sign anybody'd broken in. Doors locked. If you ask me, the only person it can be is the husband."

"Ex-husband," said Frank.

Her eyes locked with his. "Not quite," she said. "I'll bet they each had nice big insurance policies."

Cynthia's imagination had always been vivid, but this was too much even for her. One more bit of evidence to add to my list of the negative effects of too much television. I would tell Joan and George junior about it when we got home if I remembered.

"Whew! Cynthia," I said, "I'd think the husband would be the last person you'd suspect. His own child in the house? Think about it."

"I have thought about it. You need to look up 'male' in the dictionary, Sydney. They're not like us. They're capable of rage bigger than fatherhood."

Frank made a small noise in defense of his gender.

Cynthia stroked the sides of her mouth with her middle finger annd sighed. "I guess someone else could have had a key."

The girls returned to the court.

"When a woman divorces her husband, she meets all kinds of characters," I said. "Some not so nice."

"Is that the voice of experience, Sydney?" Her laugh was almost a schoolgirl giggle, but it carried too much cynicism.

Frank said, "Cool it, Cynthia. Fact is Charlotte's crime is skyrocketing. I hate it, but it's true."

"Well, I'll never give you a divorce so don't even think about it, Frank Hyatt."

As the first serve of the deciding game scorched its way across the net, Cynthia and Frank took their Cokes and moved away. That wasn't too obvious, I said to myself; they certainly weren't interested in watching the game with me. I flexed my larynx to yell for Charlotte.

"Side out!" the umpire screamed as the ball, dodged by our girls, sailed out-of-bounds. Cindi Hyatt stepped up to serve and put a floater just over the heads of Raleigh's front line. It was the kind of move that demoralizes the opponent, making them scramble, run into each other, and end up on the floor in a heap. Cindi served seven in a row after that, working off the single psychological victory from her floater. Finally, someone woke up on Raleigh's team and spiked a ball at the net into Joan's chest. She herself had been lulled into the rhythms of Cindi's winning serves and had not even brought her hands up to basic ready position during the serve. She turned a medium shade of red and covered her faced with her hands, concerning the umpire enough to stop the game and ask her if she was okay. I knew it was embarrassment, not air loss, when she sought my eyes in the stands. Hers read humiliation, not hurt.

I gave her a thumbs-up and considered to myself that, if her chest were larger, she might be able to return a spike like that with the force of her own body. I really needed to do something else with this competitive streak of mine.

Eventually Charlotte pulled it out, winning 15 to 13, thanks to some pro-level spikes by Joan and incredibly deep digs by Cindi. I watched the girls milling around on the floor, shaking hands with the Raleigh girls, high-fiving each other, and getting pats on the back and sometimes hugs from other teenagers. Barbara and Oscar Cates's son, Buddy, ambled up to Joan and gave her a particularly long and hard squeeze. Joan sought my eyes, and I registered my disapproval at its length. She squeezed him back, of course, in defiance of me.

It wasn't that I thought Buddy a bad kid. I'd known him all his life. Barbara's only child, extremely intelligent in a brooding kind of way. Totally devoted to his mother. He'd been held back a year because of a long adolescent depression, making him a nineteen-year-old senior, three years older than Joan. When he came back to school after that illness, he started hanging out with a rougher crowd and getting into minor scrapes, the worst of which was taking one of his grandfather's vintage cars last year and selling it for parts in South Carolina. Barbara and Oscar had shielded him from any repercussions and sent him off to military school, from which he'd been expelled over the summer. His head still had one of those military buzzes.

Also, Buddy had a strange assortment of friends, including a scraggly fellow who seemed to be casing the gym while Buddy hugged my daughter. I didn't recognize him from the high school, which didn't surprise me since he looked as though he was in his early twenties. He had below-the-ears hair a rat would have been at home in and eyes that told me he was up to no good. After eleven years of hanging around AA, I knew the eyes of someone using, especially if the drug of choice puts the user above reality or considerably below it. As I watched his eyes dart around the crowded gym, I bet myself he was on crack, cocaine, or amphetamines. It was clear to me that Buddy was on the wrong track with this guy, and I wondered if Barbara knew he was hanging out with somebody like this.

I chose not to bring up Buddy myself, but Joan was icy to me on the ride home. She wouldn't even participate in my postgame analysis. Finally she spoke. "Buddy doesn't need condemnation from you, Mom. Everybody else's parents are down on him, but I'm surprised at you. You've always taught us not to judge."

I thought about her remarks for a minute and decided two things. First, I was proud of her use of the word "condemnation"; she could have said merely "put down." Secondly, she was probably right.

"I am sorry," I said. "You are right about that. It probably won't help for me to say it's his friend who worries me, not Buddy."

"Yuk. Jake. I can't stand him. He's so dumb; he dropped out of school when he was in junior high somewhere. He's been doing construction ever since. He can't talk to you about anything. Believe me, I've tried. But he's Buddy's friend and always hanging around it seems . . ."

Her response was a relief. "So where does he come from? He seems too old to be interested in the high school crowd. And Buddy's so smart. I wouldn't think they'd have anything in common." I didn't want to come right out and say what I was thinking about the drugs, but I hoped that Joan would put together her own questions.

"Buddy says he works for Mr. Cates. Does handyman stuff with their rentals. I don't like Jake at all, but please don't judge Buddy because of him. At least Buddy's not depressed anymore."

"Mom wouldn't judge anybody," George junior piped from the backseat. Sounds good, I thought, but not true.

The three of us had Sealtest van-choc-straw when we got home. As always, I was left primarily straw. The inequality had become tradition in our home.

I was exhausted but stayed up for the eleven o'clock news out of habit. I was staring at the screen, not really listening when the lead segment began. Close-up of Fred's confused face; then the angle widening to show the deputies on either side of him. Alongside them walked Tom Thurgood, or who I assumed to be Thurgood since the camera took him in from the jawline down. The voice-over was saying that Fred Ball had been arrested to-night for the murder of his wife. A hearing was scheduled for Monday morning. Good God! "Wake up," I said out loud.

I called Sally. How could this have happened? Why now? When we all left the police station last night, I was convinced that Thurgood was letting Fred go for good. Unless, of course, they were to come up with some new evidence. Now all of a sudden . . . What could they have found out?

Sally had been crying, but she was coherent this time. She had tried to reach me, she said, but when she couldn't, she called Bill directly. Bill sent over Craig Diehl. Well, good for Bill; at last he'd done something. So now what? What could I do to help?

"It seems the police have talked to his old neighbors," she said. "They told them Fred arrived at the house a lot earlier than he said he did. They also told the police that Fred had been at the house the night before and there was a loud argument. This has all got to be a big misunderstanding, don't you think?" She hesitated, and when I didn't answer, she added, "I don't think Fred's neighbors like him."

"Like him? What does popularity have to do with this?"

"Well . . . why would his neighbors make up stuff about him if they liked him?" A tinge of defensiveness in her tone, sounding as if she had been defending him all her life. She probably had.

I took a deep breath.

"Sally, how much earlier did the neighbors say he showed up yesterday?"

"They say seven-thirty."

"We knew that already." I was almost shouting. "He told us. Don't you remember? He didn't want the police to know how callous he'd been."

"Callous?" The word jumped off her tongue.

"Sally, he'd been inventorying his electronic losses instead of calling for help." I couldn't control the sarcasm. "Callous is a mild word for that behavior, don't you think?"

"I don't know what I'm supposed to think. What about the night before? Why would the neighbors say he'd been there the night before?" I no longer heard any defensiveness. Sally was groping for lost faith.

"Because he was, I guess. There'd be no reason for them to lie."

Silence.

"Sally, why would the neighbors lie?"

She tried to muffle her sobs, but she couldn't. Not completely. "Freddie couldn't . . ." She choked; the rest of her words never came out.

"Sally . . . Sally, stop. I don't think Fred did anything except love his toys more than the woman he was divorcing."

"You? You don't think Freddie killed Crystal?"

"No, I don't."

"Sydney, I've been thinking you hated Freddie."

I was relieved this wasn't a question.

"I don't think he's capable, Sally."

A quiet little sniff came through the phone. "You've made me feel so much better." She hesitated again. "I thought maybe he was guilty and I've been feeling so guilty for thinking that, Sydney."

I had suspected as much but saw no reason to comment on it. "Look. Fred has a lawyer now, and he's going to be fine. I just wish we could get the police to look for the real killer."

Sleep didn't come any easier tonight than it had last night. I took two disk-shaped pastel Tums and chased their chalky residue with a glass of water, then returned to bed. My pillow had developed a terminal lump. No matter how much I fluffed it, the little mountain rose again. I took the pillow case off and put it on the throw pillow that normally sat on a chair in my bedroom.

Whoever decided to call guilt an emotion? It felt more like a sawing blade, a physical assault begging for a bandage. I couldn't turn my head off after the conversation with Sally. I kept hearing Crystal complaining about Fred. Over and over again, she had said, "Fred doesn't have an ounce of passion. How in hell did I marry a guy with no passion?" I couldn't get it out of my head. But I felt so damn guilty for defending him to anyone. Even to his own sister.

Poor Sally. Her guilt was in thinking he might be guilty while my guilt was in thinking he wasn't.

I awakened to one of the most beautiful sounds a single mother can hear: a lawnmower busy peeling the foot or so of weeds that had adapted themselves so well to my backyard. As I brushed my teeth, I peeped through the blinds at George junior sweating his way through our deep lot. We didn't use to have all that grass. Not until two or so years after Hurricane Hugo took all the trees, and with them, the shade. My second-story bed had been one of those with an oak tree in it. Come November, it might be a good idea to plant a few trees. Or at least kill off a big section of grass so that George junior wouldn't have to mow a pasture anymore.

I looked at myself in the mirror, and all of a sudden I knew I had to do something about Fred. No, it wasn't really Fred. Maybe that's what made the decision so easy. It was really about Crystal. About finding some integrity for her in all this. Integrity lies nowhere if not in truth, and the truth was, her killer was still out there. In my gut I knew that Mickey Sutton was more likely her killer than Fred. Mickey acted on his emotions, and some of his emotions seemed pretty base. Fred didn't seem to have any at all.

The phone rang and was answered after the first ring. This efficiency meant Joan was up and attending to her social life. When she screamed that it was for me, the sound of disappointment in her voice was obvious.

Crystal's mother sounded so much like her that my first reaction was shock. I had met Ruth Simmons many times, even had her and Hal and Crystal's brother Curt to dinner when they were in town visiting Crystal. Familiarity didn't make talking to her any easier today. They were all three staying downtown at the Radisson because they didn't know if the police would allow them to stay at Crystal's.

"I couldn't anyway," she said, her voice breaking. "Not tonight. Maybe tomorrow."

"I couldn't either if I were you," I said.

"Hal has gone to the police station to find out when we can get her body released. We'll have the funeral as soon as we can. We thought about burying her back in Pennsylvania, but Hal said no, she'd lived here all her adult life and is bound to have made more friends in Charlotte than are still back home. Do you think that's the right thing to do, dear? Do you?"

I told her I did. Crystal's friends, however, consisted of me, a few women she hung out with in bars, and many men, most of whom—like Mickey Sutton—could not attend her funeral because their wives might then suspect the truth.

"We can't find Fred though. He's not at his apartment or at Crystal's. You don't suppose he's made arrangements without us, do you? He wouldn't do that, would he?"

Oh my God. They didn't know anything about Fred's involvement. He was the only person they had talked with since Crystal's death, and now he was sitting in jail accused of committing it himself.

"I don't think he's made any arrangements, Mrs. Simmons," I said. "Is Curt there with you?"

"Yes, Curt's right here with me."

"Can I speak to him for just a second, please?" I thought the news about her son-in-law would sound better coming from her son.

Curt Simmons had the same reaction I would have had. "Goddamn self-centered bastard. I told her not to marry the slime."

I didn't talk to Ruth Simmons again that day because Curt was so angry, he wouldn't give the phone back to her. I don't even think he heard me when I told him I thought Fred was innocent.

In spite of the phone call, my stomach, and my pillow problems, I felt rested. Like I could take on the whole world. Well, except maybe Joan.

She was on the phone in the kitchen when I padded in to get my juice and make the coffee. Her voice immediately dropped, she put her hand over the receiver and pleaded a two-syllable "Mom. Can't you go in another room? I'm on the phone."

I filled the coffeepot anyway, trying to remain as cheerful as I'd felt three minutes earlier. "Good morning to you too. I can't get breakfast in the living room, Joan. Otherwise, I'd be glad to accommodate you."

A long, windy "God" came out of the child as she returned to whispering low tones into the phone.

I plugged in the coffee and poured my juice. "I'm leaving," I rasped in my best imitation of her camouflaged voice. "Call me when my coffee's ready."

I put on a Paul Simon tape and curled up on my living room sofa, appreciating the coolness of its old leather beneath my thighs. My living room is my favorite place. Its hodgepodge of mismatched pieces comforts me. I can't recall a time when being in this room didn't make me feel better. Even when I was feeling good already. Like I was today. Even though my parents' living room had been the only really large room in their home, it was off-limits to us kids. It was where they took company. I never could figure out why it was called the living room. Everything had matched and been so symmetrical. Two identical end tables with two identical gold columnar lamps with their plastic shades still on. I thought that was how things were supposed to be. George senior had to tell me to take the plastic off our lamps after we were married. Once I did that, the whole spell of my parents' living room had been broken. In their house, everything about the living room was gold. Maybe that's why I stayed away from it. Mine was rich in deep reds and blues. Black accents rather than gold. Three of my four walls had built-in bookshelves all the way to the twelve-foot ceilings. The fourth had a massive stone fireplace that I made a habit of using most winter nights. I pulled friends and family into this room every chance I got.

The lawnmower had puttered down the side of the house and was making its way in front of my picture window when I returned with my coffee. Joan had sequestered herself inside her bedroom with some music that even Paul Simon could not harmonize with. I picked up the paper off the front porch and read the article on Fred's arrest.

No neighbor's name was used. No mention of why he'd been arrested except for one quote from Thurgood about inconsistencies in his story. I knew what the inconsistencies were, but, dammit, I needed some neighbors' names.

I read my comics and checked the commercial real estate section to see if Jean had advertised the office today. She hadn't. Weekends were for houses, not offices. I didn't have time for the rest of the paper, so I folded it over and put it in the recycling bin.

My tennis shoes seemed snug. I wondered if my feet were still growing, but I dismissed the thought and decided that the heat had swelled them. Or maybe these new socks were too thick. All this fretting was the result of dread. I hadn't played tennis in longer than I was willing to admit, and the prospect of making a fool of myself in front of Tom Thurgood seemed highly likely. As George junior had come in from his mowing drenched from the deadly combination of heat and humidity, I reconsidered my wardrobe and changed from a lightweight tennis sweater to a T-shirt. As I watched him down his fourth glass of water, I hoped it would cool off by five. I didn't want to faint in front of the man.

Grocery store, cleaners, George junior's soccer practice, tennis. My list of Saturday chores was longer than usual, and I had to create an hour or two to talk to Crystal's neighbors. From a distance, Mickey and Fred looked alike to me. I was hoping they would to the neighbors as well.

While George junior showered, I ran to the grocery store and picked up beans, hot dogs, chips, and Cokes. That would hold everybody until tomorrow when I'd have time to plan the week. And when Cindi Hyatt came by to pick up Joan, I bribed them to pick up my cleaning by offering to stake them both to a movie.

Now I was set. While George junior was scrimmaging, I would take a walk in Crystal's neighborhood. I hoped that the heat wouldn't keep all her neighbors inside.

6

I DRIVE A BIG BLACK TROOPER WITH A V-6 AND four gigantic all-terrain tires that cost me a hundred dollars each. Just in case. At least once a year Charlotte gets some snow. That's when I make my impact. Allen Teague has never missed a deadline. Never. One of the reasons is that I pick up Sally, Hart, and the salesman on snow days. I've even taken the salesman to his appointments only to find that the appointees haven't shown up themselves.

So this is a great car, an easy one to find in mall parking lots, a memorable car. But it's not the best vehicle to look inconspicuous in. For that reason, I parked on Blue Sky Lane, one street over from Crystal's house on Sunshine Place, and I set out on foot. At the last minute, I decided to carry a can of tennis balls and my racquet. It was important to look as if I lived in the neighborhood.

The Happy Valley subdivision is about thirty minutes south of Dilworth, in the general direction Charlotte has spread. With street names like Blue Sky and Sunshine, I wondered if I would find perky people, friendly dogs, and grinning cats outside today. Living within the boundaries of that nomenclature was bound to affect its inhabitants somehow.

The two blocks I walked on Blue Sky Lane before turning onto Sunshine Place yielded nothing more than two seven-year-old girls running through a front yard sprinkler. Perspiration had worked its way through my thick mane of streaked hair and was threatening to break through its surface. The racquet slipped once from my hand; I would have to remember to put on a wristband before meeting Thurgood at Freedom Park.

As I hit Sunshine, I checked my watch. I would have to hurry in order to pick up George junior at four as his practice ended. I wished I'd asked another parent to give him a ride.

Fred and Crystal's house was 806. As many times as I'd driven this neighborhood, I'd never noticed the houses. They were typical of the ones in the hundred or so subdivisions that seemed to grow on Charlotte like a twenty-year-old epidemic of measles. I guess you would have called these updated ranches. Each of the houses had some feature, like a cathedral pitch on a great room or a jutting entrance, to keep it from being a true ranch. Why didn't developers ever angle homes on their lots? Why did they square them all up with straight-away drives dividing each little postage-stamp lot from its neighbor? Advertising had progressed from the T-square approach, so why hadn't land planning?

The first thing I noticed about the Ball house was the FOR SALE sign in the yard. My reaction was revulsion at the generic typography, a reaction that quickly turned to revulsion at myself for noticing it. As if this stroll were a sales junket rather than a desperate attempt to garner justice for Crystal. My second thought was to take the damn sign down completely. Jean didn't need her phone number advertising a murder scene.

The house was on the corner, its side yard flanking the major subdivision thoroughfare of Rainbow Road. As many times as I'd been here, I had somehow forgotten that. Maybe because the driveway ran off Sunshine.

I was in luck. Directly across Sunshine an elderly man was running what looked like a weed-whacker in his side yard, the one that ran beside Rainbow. I approached him as casually as I knew how, a curious new neighbor out for a stroll.

"Hi," I said, "I'm Happy Smith. My husband and I just moved in over on Blue Sky." Dammit! This is the sort of stupidity that comes out of a mouth when nothing is planned. I should have planned a name as well as a story. It was too late to take it back.

He turned off his machine, probably the quietest weed-whacker I'd ever heard. "Well, you've certainly moved into the right neighborhood, Happy. Isn't that something? What'd y' say your last name is?"

"Smith. And you're?"

"Collins. Dave Collins. Welcome to Happy Valley, Happy. What's your husband's name? Doc? Sneezy?" His accompanying laugh was long, rattling and grating. I could tell that Mr. Collins would have fun with my pseudonym for weeks to come.

"No sir, it's Jim. Being new here, we were a bit worried when we read about the murder at the Ball house. Quite frankly, it just scared me to death." I was hoping he would tell me the kinds of things I wanted to know without my having to ask him directly.

"You shouldn't worry. Who would want to kill a pretty young thing named Happy?" He laughed some more. "I don't know a thing myself 'cept what's been on the TV. It's a strange world, Happy. Nothing people do surprises me anymore."

Mr. Collins was obviously not one of the neighbors Thurgood had interviewed. He started his weed-whacker again, but it didn't have any wire to cut through the weeds. I asked him how it worked without the wire.

"This isn't a weed-whacker, it's a detector, Happy. I'm gonna find me some dropped coins or maybe even some buried treasure." He turned it off again and pointed across Rainbow to the house whose front yard faced the Balls' side yard. "The Kirbys over there are the ones done talked to the police if you want to hear firsthand about the murder." Then he picked up his metal detector, turned it on and thrust it at my pocketbook, which I'd thrown over my shoulder. When it buzzed loudly, he said, "Now ain't that the prettiest sound you ever heard, Happy?"

I smiled broadly as I backed away, leaving the man to his treasure hunt. At the curb I turned around and walked across the street to the Kirby house. It would have been easier if a Kirby had been in the yard, but I guess that would have been asking too much. This time I chose a name as I approached the door. If Mr. Collins were later to mention the Happy woman to the Kirbys, the Kirbys might think him short an oar. I had a strong hunch some neighbors saw him as rowing disabled already.

* * *

"Debbie Smith, did you say? Come in, Debbie. I'm Ken Kirby and my wife here is Anne. Welcome to Happy Valley."

I joined the Kirbys in their living room with its bay window perfectly framing Crystal's side yard. We chit-chatted for several minutes about my fictional husband Jim's equally fictional management position with Sears, then I came to the point. Again I expressed my concern and my need to understand what really happened in the house across the street from them.

Anne did most of the talking. "Of course you're afraid, dear. But don't you worry. It was a clear case of her husband killing her out of passion and greed."

I was willing to bet that Anne Kirby watched soaps regularly. "What makes you think it was that simple, Mrs. Kirby?"

"Call me Anne, Debbie. And what makes you think passion and greed are simple?" Her question sounded rhetorical, so I shrugged. Anne Kirby had a point.

"Like I told that detective," she said, "Crystal Ball had many male admirers after she and her husband separated last year. He didn't like that. He didn't want to sell the house." She looked over at her husband. "Right, Ken? Didn't he tell you he was going to try to get the house back?"

Ken hesitated, not so free with his words as Anne. "I don't think it was the house so much as all the things in the house. He told me one time he didn't like the idea of other men in his bed, watching his television, eating at his dining table. You know what I mean. He wanted what he thought was his, I guess."

"How do you know that? Did you hear them fighting?" I asked.

Anne gave me a strange look, not quite suspicion, but if I wasn't more careful with my questions, it would be.

"Now, honey," she began, "how could knowing that make you any less scared?"

I looked to the floor and fumbled with my racquet strings. If she had caught my eyes at this moment, she would have known I was a lying impostor.

"It's, well . . . it's like I told Jim. If I can convince myself that what happened over there was really just between those two people, then maybe we'll be able to stay in the neighborhood. If I can't convince myself"—I paused here for effect—"I've already told Jim we'll have to move."

"You don't need to move," Ken said. "That's ridiculous. The husband killed her. We know what we saw." He looked at his wife. "Anne, tell Debbie what we saw so she'll stop worrying."

At least momentarily. Anne accepted that my need was genuine. "We told the police what we heard," she said. "We also told them what we saw. Fred, he's the husband, showed up over there the other night when Crystal already had company. She had company quite a bit. Certainly more than the average." Anne stood up, walked to the bay window, and began gesturing toward the Ball house as a lecturer might point toward an overhead.

"We heard him before we saw his car and van," she continued. "His car was in the drive that goes up to the front of the house; he'd left the van right out there on Rainbow. Since the nights have started cooling off a bit, Crystal left her windows open. Their fight was impossible not to hear."

I wanted to ask about the car. And what was this business

about a van? Instead, I asked Anne what I sensed she wanted to tell me.

"Did you hear any of what the fight was about?"

Ken looked embarrassed. "We couldn't help," he said. "Our windows were open too."

Anne said, "Fred called her a slut at least three times. The fellow who was visiting her ran out the door and drove off after the first slut was yelled. Can't you see, honey, this doesn't affect you and Jim at all?" She looked over at her husband with a dutiful expression. "Ken says it's none of our business, but it is our business when somebody dies."

"The whole neighborhood's business really . . . when somebody in it is killed," I said hopefully.

Anne nodded in what I prayed was agreement.

"Anything else?" I asked.

"He was screaming about the furniture and the house. He kept yelling 'Mine! Mine!' and threatened to prove her unfit in court." She raised her eyebrows and said, "Can you imagine? You would've thought they were fighting over a kid. The Balls didn't even have a dog, much less a child. It sounded like a custody fight, but it was all over their things."

"And then what happened?" I asked.

"You mean did I hear him hit her or anything? No. No, I didn't. But, like I told Ken, you don't hear someone get strangled, do you? No, I saw him run out the front door, mad as all get-out." She looked at Ken again. "Then we got our ice cream, didn't we, Ken?"

This was beginning to sound like a Movie of the Week for the Kirbys. "What about the van?" I finally asked. "You say he had a car and a van?"

"When we came back in here from the kitchen," Ken said, "Fred's BMW was gone."

Fred would have a BMW, of course; Crystal had driven a Honda hatchback.

She continued. "He was loading some things into the van by then. He'd moved it to the driveway with its side doors pushed back."

My confusion must have shown. Anne asked, "What's bothering you now, Debbie?"

"How could he have two vehicles with him?"

"We didn't think that was strange. Fred's had a van over there three or four times since they separated. He brought friends to help him every time. Somebody was in it that night too while Fred was yelling at Crystal."

I decided to push my luck and hope that Anne Kirby was caught up in telling her story enough to not notice my pushiness.

"What kind of van was it?" I held my breath.

"One of those old Ford Econolines or something like it. You know the kind. No windows, strictly utility. I think it was light blue, don't you think, Ken? Or maybe it was light green. That street light out there isn't too good."

"Did Fred's friend drive his BMW off?"

"Who else?" Anne looked very self-satisfied.

"How long were you in the kitchen?" I asked Ken.

The couple looked at each other and answered together, "No more than a long TV commercial." It really had been like a show for them.

"So you actually saw the husband loading things?"

Anne and Ken locked eyes and nodded.

"We saw him with the big TV, the one they kept in the den," Ken said. "Can't miss him with all that hair hanging down to his collar. I've never understood why young people think more hair makes 'em look better."

I looked at my watch and saw that I had twenty minutes to drive the thirty-minute distance to George junior's soccer practice. "Oh, I hate to run, but I have to pick up my son, and I'm going to be late."

At their front door, Anne said, "Where are you playing tennis, Debbie?"

I was thrown by that and stammered before I could get a sentence out. "Oh, at the neighborhood courts."

Ken said, "Happy Valley doesn't have any courts, Debbie." His shoulders drooped as if he knew this revelation would be more than I could take.

"Oh no!" I tried to sound exasperated.

Anne patted my arm. "Oh, dear," she said. "Oh, dear, Debbie. You mustn't let these unexpected things upset you so. It's really a very happy neighborhood."

The sprint to my car did not leave a lot of reflection time for the happiness of Happy Valley except for the sure knowledge that Crystal and Fred had both been exceptions. I would take Dilworth any day of the week and be depressed whenever I felt like it.

My poor son was standing alone on the edge of the soccer field. George junior was as upset with me as he can get. It translates as disappointment and tugs at my heart. Since his father and I separated when he was only two, and his father chose to keep his distance, George junior endows me with qualities I oftentimes cannot embody. I wish I were as good a parent as he believes I am.

That I was going to dump him back at home for the rest of the day and most of the evening did nothing to allay the guilt I now felt. I have never believed in quality time. There is no substitute for hanging out for long stretches. Boredom, getting in each other's way, bad moods, long talks, observing one another: aren't these experiences better preparation for life than two hours at the zoo?

"I'm going to have to drop you and run, kiddo," I said. "Got tennis, then my meeting. Why don't you have someone over? There're hot dogs and Cokes you can have."

He smiled, unable to hold a pout for long. "Cindi Hyatt's staying over with Joan. Can I ask Jimmy?"

I told him okay as long as the Hyatts didn't mind both their children staying here when I wouldn't be in until ten. Cynthia and Frank could have themselves a good time if they took advantage of this unexpected empty nest.

7

FREEDOM PARK LIES ON THE EASTERN EDGE OF Dilworth, part of its acreage distinctly Dilworth and part of it flowing into the more upscale streets of the Myers Park neighborhood. The tennis courts are just off East Boulevard, four blocks from my house, so I was ten minutes early. I sopped my forehead with the wristband before pulling it over my hand. The car radio said it was eighty-two degrees outside, down from a high of ninety. I would have bet the humidity was up.

I turned off the car, opened the door and just sat there, trying to sort through what the Kirbys had told me. Why hadn't Fred told me he was at Crystal's the night before? Had he lied or had he just failed to mention it? He had said they'd talked on the phone but nothing about going over there. Could it have been Mickey with the TV? Why would Mickey take the TV? And, if it was Mickey with the TV, who ran out the door when Fred arrived? If it was Fred with the TV, whose van did he have at the house, and who helped him? And, dammit, Fred would never let anybody drive his BMW. If it had been his BMW. Crystal's house, the night she died, was beginning to resemble Grand Central Station at rush hour.

"You're an easy mark" a voice behind me said.

My breath caught on an exhale, and my body prepared itself for flight. Since I had jumped off the seat already, I thought I would look more in control if I continued my motion out the door. I grabbed the balls, the racquet, and my keys before closing the car door and answering him.

"You wouldn't say that to a man," I said with only a slight quiver.

His laugh was wry and light. "Oh yes, I would. And I have. This park's where the closet gays vent their frustration after dark. It's also where a couple of teen gangs roam in hopes of some quick hit-and-runs."

"Why don't I remember this cop mentality you've got? Why did I think you were in insurance?"

He laughed. "I was with the Fraud Unit."

He tested my door handle and, when it opened, punched the electronic lock so that all doors would be secured. "Funny, I didn't really know what you did either. I tried to find you once a year or so ago and called every television station in town. Could've sworn you were in television."

"Why didn't you call my home number?"

"I did. A couple of times." He placed his racquet and can of balls on the hood of the Trooper and tucked his shirttail into his shorts. "Got your machine once, your daughter another time."

"Did you tell her who you were?"

"She wouldn't have remembered me. You were out of town on business. She wanted to know if I wanted to speak to the sitter. I told her I'd call back."

"But you didn't."

He placed his right hand at the small of my back and led me toward the tennis courts. His touch was so gentle, yet firm, that I felt I was being led onto a dance floor.

I couldn't help but like the man. There was this old-shoe quality to him that I found very appealing. He was at ease with himself; I'd remembered that because, at the time, I'd been the opposite. Somewhere around six and a half feet tall, I figured, but he stooped a bit so as not to tower. I guess that's why I had thought he was shorter. At almost five-nine, I always notice a man's height. His auburn hair was close-cropped on the sides and back, just as it had been eight years ago, but a couple of long pieces spilled over his eyebrows in front. His eyes crinkled to slits when he smiled, and I couldn't tell, or remember, what color they were. I could tell, though, that he still laughed a lot from the deep creases that were etched beside his temples.

Tom Thurgood was a little better than eight years ago, but I was pretty rusty. His height and upper body strength gave him a natural advantage at the net. In fact, given the time to get himself situated up there, he didn't let anything go by. I had to quicken the pace by taking the ball on the rise in order to pass him. Or, and I hated this tactic, I had to lob over him. No easy task since the man is six and a half feet tall. He also had a powerful serve when it went in, which was maybe a third of the time. Not enough. His second serve was a powder puff, and I jumped on it every time. By six-thirty I had beaten him 6–4 and 6–3. The heat and humidity had beaten us both.

"I owe you a lemonade at Wad's," he said. "It's the least I can offer. Or dinner, if you don't have plans." He raised his eyebrows as if the idea had just entered his mind, and I thought it probably had. With Thurgood, I was beginning to remember, there was no pretense.

I wanted to politely pump him for information about his arrest of Fred Ball so the lemonade offer would give me a chance. Saturday nights had meant an AA meeting for me for the past eleven years, however, and it would have taken more than a dinner invitation to shift that priority. "Can't do dinner," I said. "Lemonade sounds great."

He accepted my rejection as graciously as he had accepted defeat on the tennis court.

Wad's Sundries has been a Charlotte landmark since the early sixties. It is, I suppose, a drugstore, but its reputation hinges on its hot dogs and freshly squeezed lemonade they still serve at the counter. The lemonade that day tasted better than I'd ever remembered.

"You were great out there. Are you sure you haven't been practicing?"

I shook my head as I continued to sip lemonade through my straw.

"You said you were going to when your children got older." He waited, then said, "They have, so why haven't you?"

"Why haven't I what?" The straw was still in my mouth.

"Tennis. You should be playing regularly."

I looked up at him. "It's habit," I said. "Like everything else. It used to be habit to play. Now it's habit not to play."

"I still say we'd make a solid doubles team," he said. Aha, so this is where those compliments were leading.

"Maybe," I said, without looking at him.

"We're balanced," he continued as if I'd agreed. "You

just don't miss from the baseline, and your serve's stronger than any woman's I've seen."

I wondered briefly which other woman's serve he might have seen recently before I responded. "Yeah. I live in Charlotte under a pseudonym. My real name is Steffi Graf." I did not want to discuss tennis but didn't know how to redirect our conversation.

"Don't answer now, but I'd like you to be my partner. I don't feel I have to compensate with you on the same side of the net. We could start with the city tournament. Will you promise me you'll just consider it?"

He looked at me with a strange pleading, as if he'd proposed an offer of marriage. The words were the same as a marriage proposal; for some people this was probably the more important of the two questions. As I remembered it, Tom had not sounded this sincere when he had asked to move into my home.

I smiled at the thought of it. "We do complement, don't we? I'll think about it. We ought to try it on the same side of the net before we make a commitment."

He drained his lemonade. "Your brother was right about your forehand. It's still a killer."

It was a small opening, not "killer" but "brother." I jumped in. "Has my brother called you since you arrested Fred? He's the one who sent Diehl to the rescue, you know." For the first time, I could see into his eyes. They were green. Why hadn't I remembered them? They were so clear.

His relaxed manner remained. Maybe getting him to open up about the case would be easier than I had thought. "I was off today, but I spoke with both Diehl and Bill last night. Ball gets a probable cause and bond hearing Monday morning. Your brother Bill's done right by sending in Diehl."

I decided to ask directly. "Why did you arrest him?"

"Come on, Sydney, I don't think we should talk about this. Not now."

"Why not? You talked to the newspaper. You talked to the TV news crew."

He kept staring into his empty cup.

"Look," I continued, "I know he was there at seven-thirty instead of nine like he told you. All he was trying to hide was his character." Although I was concentrating my stare directly at his face, he never looked at me.

"He lied to us." He folded the already tiny paper napkin and wiped the sweat from his glass off the old Formica counter. "He told us he wasn't at the house when he actually was. It's real simple. You can't do that when there's been a murder."

I followed his lead and began to mop the liquid residue off the counter in front of me. "Have you asked him about the van?"

He straightened his stooped shoulders. This was the first nonathletic adrenaline I had seen in him. "He says he knows nothing about a van. How did you hear about the van?"

I stood up and pulled my salt-laden shorts off my thighs. "I was in Happy Valley earlier today," I said.

"And?" He stood up as well.

"And what?" I asked. "They don't have any tennis courts out there. They don't have little happy families playing outside. They don't have very good streetlights either. Did the Kirbys tell you that too? I'll bet it wasn't Fred loading the TV in the van."

We were walking back toward our cars. He stopped

and scratched the inside of his calf with his racquet. I waited. He took his time.

"Why's that?" he finally asked. Was he playing along or was he willing to listen?

I took a chance he was willing. "Anne Kirby said herself the streetlight was poor. It was a utility van with no windows in the back. If it was parked in the drive with the sliding door nearest the Ball house open, how could the Kirbys tell it was Fred?"

"He walked from the front door to the van," he explained.

"Yes," I said, "but that's ten feet. With a van between their view and him the whole way. And he had a thirty-inch TV in front of his face. They just assumed it was Fred since they'd seen him earlier."

We were standing at the Trooper. I added, "And where was the BMW after the van pulled into the driveway?"

I climbed into the driver's seat, and he shut the door.

He looked thoughtful. "I don't know the answer to the BMW. Maybe whoever was with him drove it off." He was literally crouched to keep eye contact with me inside the Trooper. "Who said the TV was a thirty-inch?" he asked.

"Nobody," I said a bit defensively. "But you're getting to know Fred. He has a BMW, doesn't he? You've heard him go on about his wonderful electronics, haven't you? I figured a thirty-inch was as small as he'd consider owning."

Thurgood smiled broadly and his eyes disappeared into the folds above his cheeks. "You have a law degree, Sydney?"

"No. I can't stand the profession," I answered.

I had put my elbow on the window ledge. He put his

hand on my upper arm and let it slide down to my forearm where he held it. "I wouldn't want to answer your questions in court."

I held his gaze. "Somebody has to answer those questions," I said.

He moved his large hand to the back of my neck and squeezed it for a brief second, then tousled my hair. "There's a process, Sydney. Let it work."

Then he stood up and backed up at least five feet so he could look me directly in the eyes. "No ma'am. I wouldn't want to be on opposite sides of any court from you." His smile was contagious.

I smiled too; I couldn't help it. Tom Thurgood had a presence that made smiling quite easy.

I have been sober eleven years now. These past few years the compulsion to drink has lifted since the habit of sobriety is eventually as strong as the habit of oblivion.

Like most others, my home group meets in the basement of a church. I've always taken comfort in being beneath a church, as if we're trying but we can't quite get up there. That's important because the second an alcoholic thinks she's arrived at wherever it is she thinks she's going, she's bound to be headed for disaster. "Cunning, baffling, powerful," our literature tells us. Our foe is forever in us waiting to fuel the fire that is never completely out. So the habit of sobriety I am leery of as well, and I need reminders of who and what I really am.

When it was my turn to share, I told them all about Crystal's death. She had been with me to the group twice, kept saying she'd come back when she was ready to quit. They grieved with me and let me talk. It was all about letting go, but I found I couldn't. I had thought that going to her neighborhood today would help me answer the questions that had been nagging me so. Instead, the experience had introduced new ones. Like scratching the itch that spreads the poison ivy. You can't take back what you have done so you treat new eruptions like the original, trying your best not to scratch them as well.

I went home frustrated and depressed.

As I entered my kitchen from the driveway, I was greeted by the sound of hard rock from the basement and a cold hot dog on a hard bun that someone must have abandoned earlier in the evening. I screamed hello into the deep stairwell leading to the den and assumed I was heard from the chorus of hellos echoing back up the stairs.

I suddenly realized that with the exception of juice this morning, lemonade after tennis, and tons of bad coffee at the meeting, I had not eaten today. After a moment's hesitation, I picked up the hot dog, musing that I was so hungry, I could have eaten cardboard, which was, not surprisingly, what the hot dog tasted like.

It was not enough. I rummaged through the pantry and found a box of angel hair pasta. A can of condensed tomato soup was the only "sauce" I could find. Why not? Funny the difference between appetite and real hunger. As I waited for the water for the pasta to boil, I tore apart the one remaining hot dog bun, smothered it in butter and sprinkled garlic salt on it, then thrust it under the broiler for my own version of garlic bread. The pleasant aroma was filling the kitchen as George junior and Jimmy Hyatt came bounding in.

"What happened to Buddy's hot dog?" George junior said. "He sent me for it."

"Buddy Cates is here?" I asked, removing the bread from the oven, my mouth watering ever so slightly. "I didn't see an extra car."

"He got dropped off," George junior said. He grabbed a bag of chips off the counter and opened the refrigerator. "Did you see the hot dog, Mom?"

I made a show of looking around the kitchen. "No hot dog here," I said, feeling a slight twinge of guilt over the lie I couldn't help telling. "Hi, Jimmy. Is your sister here?"

"Hello, Mrs. Teague. Yes, ma'am, she and Joan and Buddy are in the den." Jimmy had always been so polite to me. Was he like this at home with Cynthia and Frank? I would feel uncomfortable with such a formal kid.

I stood to take my plate over to the sink and felt the muscles in the back of my legs resist. Tennis every six months had not kept my hamstrings well strung. While I was at the sink waiting for the water to heat up, I held on to the counter and did three deep knee-bends. Maybe I could get myself back in shape after all. Being part of a doubles team again might jump-start my body. I needed someplace to put my competitiveness anyway, someplace other than my kids' lives.

The last time I'd seriously played mixed doubles was with George senior. I'd often thought that was why he'd married me, the winning team we'd become. I'd made him look good on the tennis court. Surely I could perform the same service for him in marriage. After marriage, his sense of competition had veered in a direction I couldn't follow. More and more I caught a glimpse of it. I ceased being a person apart and became, instead, an extension of some need in him. Not only how I looked, but what I said, how I carried myself, what I did with the children—babies at the time. I stopped playing tennis and drank. It made our lives so much easier. For both of us. As long as I did it well (without passing out), it was okay by George. The sloppy times, the sick times, did not bother him anywhere near as much as my sober time. Sobriety killed what was left between us. It happens to a lot of alcoholics when we finally take a look at what we've become.

I followed the boys into the den, where Buddy Cates sat on the sofa between Joan and Cindi, an arm around each. He stood to shake my hand, and I thought that the military school, no matter how brief, had probably been good for him in the long run. I decided to come clean.

"I ate your hot dog, Buddy," I said. "I hope it was just a snack and that you'd gotten your supper earlier."

"Yes ma'am," he answered without hesitation. "I ate at home before coming over."

"I didn't see your car."

He eyed Joan before answering. "A friend dropped me off. He'll be back any minute."

Joan pulled her legs up under her body. "Buddy's lost his license for a little while, Mom. His friend Jake gave him a ride." Her eyes said shut up, Mom, and stop asking so many questions.

I sought a safer subject. "I'm seeing your mother for dinner Monday night. How've she and your dad been doing?"

Buddy hesitated. "Mom's been under a lot of pressure since Gramps died. Business hasn't been so good. That's why I came home from school."

I had heard he'd been expelled, but I didn't pursue the

discrepancy—not with the female Gestapo at his side. Instead I said, "The economy's been hard on everyone, Buddy. Your mother's a smart woman. She'll get the company back on track. How's your dad?"

Buddy went rigid. "You mean Oscar? He's not my dad. My dad died when I was a baby. Oscar's my stepfather."

"Oh, I didn't know that." And I really didn't. Before I'd married George senior, I'd been in graduate school in Chapel Hill. By the time we were settled here and I was pregnant with Joan, Oscar and Barbara were married and had Buddy. So I'd just assumed that Buddy was Oscar's child as well as Barbara's.

"I should have," I continued, "since I've known your mom my entire life. One little gap of time when I wasn't here and up you sprout." I grinned, but only Cindi joined me. "Was your dad a Charlottean?"

"No." He remained rigid.

I wanted to relax the boy, so I smiled and winked at him. "Come to think of it, I've always seen you and your mom as a twosome. Oscar hasn't been too involved, has he?"

Buddy looked me in the eyes, and, for a brief second, I saw years of resentment.

"No," he said, "and now's not the time to start."

Joan got off the sofa and turned on the tape player, sending blasts of Pink Floyd into my shoulder muscles.

I could tell that I'd been asked to leave, but I wasn't going until I got a smile out of Buddy Cates. "I like your haircut," I screamed, running a flat palm across the top of my head.

Joan stood between us. "You're being sarcastic, Mom."

Cindi stifled a giggle.

I leaned to the left to see Buddy on the other side of my daughter. "No, I'm not. I really like it." I touched my cheek. "Makes you look very mature. Very masculine." I smiled the biggest smile I could muster.

Finally Buddy smiled back as he ran his own hand over his stubby head. "Thank you, Ms. Teague. Mom likes it too."

Joan turned the music even louder.

I ran the water in the tub as hot as I thought I could stand it, then eased my decrepit parts in one limb at a time until I was as numb as a boiling lobster. I wiggled my toes, then bent my knees some more. They had turned red.

I decided I'd call Tom Thurgood tomorrow for mixed doubles. First I'd see if Bill and Karen would take us on. Then maybe we'd all cook out over here. Like we used to. Bill and wife number one had often been the opposing team for George senior and me. It had been a fun time in the beginning. For all of us.

No matter how hard I tried, I couldn't blow a seamless ring tonight. I stubbed the butt out, half unsmoked. Cigarettes, after all, weren't good for the athlete. After the water had drained, I lay in the tub and raised my arms over my head five times to the count of twenty. As I toweled myself off, I heard a horn honk and an engine roar. The front door slammed and Pink Floyd stopped singing in the middle of a word.

Owner Must sell. A lot of house for the money. Bring all offers. ML

They had a lake. I spent a lot of time there. Mostly staring. Reflections: trees, clouds, myself and sometimes her.

In the spring the ducks would fuck. The male, he'd climb onto the female's back and grab her by the neck, plunging her head into the water. She'd struggle, break away, feathers flying, scream or squawk or whatever it is ducks do to get attention.

Oh let's save her, she'd said to me. So we waded into the frigid lake. It was March. My balls froze to ice cubes against my thighs.

The female duck, she pecked at us, like saying: Go away, you Assholes. You're not ducks. You just don't know.

From the shore again we watched the female go under, protesting still, tailfeathers up in welcome to the male.

She was shivering. I pulled her back against my chest and tried to warm her in my own wet body. That's when it began. First a tingle, my thawing parts awakening, demanding. I pressed into her back to soothe the odd sensation.

I felt the rhythm for the first time: thrusting, plowing, drilling. Separate from me, leading me. I was alive, truly alive for the first time.

She didn't understand, and I didn't care. No one understood. The moment had changed me, freed me. I was not who I had been. You just don't know.

8

"Eight p.m., Monday, September twenty-second." The computerized voice on the answering machine sounded like a talent we had used for a bug-spray spot last year.

"What difference does it make?" Joan asked, a bit winded from having run back from our neighbor's house after using their phone and leaving a message on ours.

I was literally scratching the back of my head, hoping to dislodge the logic of word problems from the seventh grade. "It should tell us when Crystal really left that message."

"I know that, Mom. What I mean is why does it matter when she called us?" She was perched on the kitchen counter, her long, smooth legs crossed at the ankles. Although the kids knew Fred Ball was suspected of Crystal's murder, they did not know anything else. Not my suspicion of Mickey Sutton nor my charade in Happy

Valley yesterday. What purpose would involving them serve?

"This information will help the police," I said. "It'll at least tell them she was alive at a certain time." I sat at the table, solar calculator, Bic pen, and steno pad in front of me. I wrote *Eight p.m., Monday, September 22.*

"Okay," I said, "I played Crystal's message at twelve a.m., Friday, September nineteenth. The machine said it was seven a.m., Friday, September nineteenth." I swear it hurt just to say all these numbers in the same breath. Math is not my strong suit.

"The difference between twelve a.m. and seven a.m. is seven hours." I wrote "seven" on my pad. "It's eleven a.m. on the twenty-first right now, but the machine says it's eight p.m. on the twenty-second." I realized that the calculator didn't serve much purpose with this kind of situation, so I looked up at Joan instead.

She was grinning at me. "Mom, forget when we listened to her message. Take what we learned just now and apply it to the night Crystal called."

I must have looked as helpless as I felt, for she hopped off the counter and was looming over my shoulders. "Get rid of the seven, Mom. It doesn't mean anything." She pointed at the paper.

I crossed through the seven.

"We know that the difference today between when I placed the call and when it says I placed the call is . . . what?" She paused dramatically. "It's eleven a.m. now, right? The machine says tomorrow at eight p.m."

Joan continued to wait.

"Good Lord, Joan. Don't play teacher with me. What are we looking for? The value of x?"

She patted my shoulder. "Sort of."

I would have to tell Jean there was value in algebra after all.

"Look, Mom," Joan continued. "The difference today is thirty-three hours, so apply that information to the other night."

I closed my mouth, thought for a minute, then opened it again. "You mean I count back thirty-three hours from seven a.m. to get the time that she really called?"

"Right. Ten p.m. on Wednesday night." Joan spoke quickly, her teacher instincts waning. "Crystal left her message at ten p.m. Wednesday. Will that help the police?"

I realized I hadn't asked the Kirbys about specific times. I knew the sequence of events, just not the exact time that it all happened. If I could get Fred to be honest with me about being there, maybe I could get the time out of him.

I looked at my daughter. "I don't know, honey. Tom Thurgood will be here for supper, so I'll tell him." I punched her elbow with my knuckles. "Where do you get those math skills? I'm jealous."

"Thank goodness for the Teague genes." She smiled and punched me back.

I fought with myself over calling the Kirbys, being Debbie Smith again and asking them for the time specifics. I literally had the phone in front of me, touching it, then removing my hand. Finally I decided simply to give the information to Thurgood tonight.

Then I opened the phone book, found Mickey Sutton's home number, and called him. I held my breath as the rings accumulated. Just as I was taking the receiver away from my ear, Gloria Sutton picked up.

I had been so intent on confronting Mickey that I wasn't prepared for his wife to answer. Gloria was a realtor like most others I'd been talking to these days, so I began the conversation as I always do with these people.

"How's business, Gloria?"

"Okay, I guess. It's hard adjusting to a new firm." Gloria had been with Bishop Cates too.

"If it makes you feel any better," I said, "you have a lot of company. Getting used to their new firms, I mean."

"Barbara did her best to keep me from ever working again. Anywhere." Her voice was tinged with resentment. "When I told her I was leaving, she asked me which firms I was considering going with." She laughed derisively. "I thought she asked so she could help me."

"And did she?" I asked.

"She got on the phone and called every one of the firms. Told them all that I was more trouble than I was worth." She waited to see if I was going to comment. "Can you believe that?"

No, I actually couldn't. Why would Barbara do such a thing?

"I'm sure there was some misunderstanding with that, Gloria. Did Barbara ever admit this to you?"

"Of course not. Barbara never admits to anything."

She waited a few seconds before sighing heavily. "You

ought to be glad you're in advertising. That's what I tell Mickey."

"Speaking of Mickey—"

"You want to speak with him? He's on the rowing machine, but I can get him."

Rowing machine? Mickey sweat? I would love to have seen it.

"No, no, Gloria, not yet. I want to talk to him, but I wanted to asked you something first."

"What is it, Sydney?" I thought I heard a shift in her voice. Heavy and guarded. Was there some question she dreaded my asking?

"It's no big deal, Gloria. You sound like I'm all of a sudden the IRS. I just want to know why Mickey had Barbara Cates show him my office instead of you. I thought it odd since you're in real estate yourself."

She hesitated. "He what?"

Uh oh. Mickey hadn't even told Gloria he was looking at my office.

"He hasn't said a word to me. As badly as I need business these days, you'd think my own husband would . . . and Barbara of all people." Realization and anger joined to halt her words.

"I'm sorry, Gloria." And I was sorry for her, sorry she'd chosen to stay married for so many years to such a lowlife. However, I was delighted to cause trouble for my nemesis any way I could.

"I'll get him," she said abruptly.

I could tell by his cheerful tone that Gloria had neither confronted him nor told him who was waiting on the phone. I ended his facade by merely saying hello.

"Look, Teague, I have nothing to say to you."

"Is Gloria in the room with you, Mickey?"

"No, but what does Gloria have to do with anything?"

"She knows about all your bad habits then?"

The air in his head blew out his nose so quickly that he snorted. Not very attractive.

He said, "Are you threatening me?"

"Threatening? With what? Seems I have a choice. Gloria's actually going to be angrier about your using Barbara as your agent than she'll be about your visits to Crystal's house." I shouldn't have been enjoying this so much.

"You didn't tell her about Crystal, did you?"

"No, but I will," I lied. "I want to know what time you were at Crystal's, and I want to know what you told her that she thought I should know."

I could hear him breathing again, this time through his mouth.

"I'm waiting," I said.

"Okay." He lowered his voice. "I was there most of the night. I left when her crazy husband showed up around eleven, maybe before."

"She called me at ten. Did you know that?"

"No."

"Where were you at ten?"

"Watching the Braves on TV. Crystal and I never sat around talking all night." He said it with such sarcasm that I wanted to spit at the phone.

"What was she trying to tell me about you?"

"How should I know? She was drunk as hell that night."

I sat thinking, not knowing what more to ask him.

"Sydney?" he said.

"Yeah?"

"Your office looks like a place to make cookies, not advertising. I'm surprised you've got any clients."

He was trying to get a rise out of me, so I sat quietly. When neither of us had said anything for fifteen or twenty seconds, I heard the click of his receiver.

9

BROTHER BILL SHOWED UP AT THE TENNIS courts with Terry instead of wife Karen, throwing a wrench into my mood from the outset. It seemed that marriage number three had maybe a year to go at most.

In view of the fact that what Bill and Terry were doing on the court had little to do with tennis, Tom and I beat them easily. I found myself wishing I hadn't extended the dinner invitation. Just because our blood has the same source doesn't mean I have to like everything about my brother.

My feelings have a way of seeping into the atmosphere. The result is less like wearing them on my shirt sleeve, more like coloring everyone's mood. The quality is a part of myself I try to check. When Terry asked to beg off the cookout, I genuinely felt bad. I had not said anything, but what I thought was sitting on my forehead, beaded in perspiration. I really didn't blame her.

The heat would not let up. Even now at seven, the air

was oppressive. The sky had not been blue, it seemed to me, since June. Carolina gray, more like the color of worn cement.

"You shouldn't have been so hard on them," Tom said. We were in his old Honda, having taken separate cars from Bill and Terry to the courts.

"I didn't know it showed so much," I said. "I feel bad about it; I really do. I don't go around trying to make people feel uncomfortable. It just happens." I looked at his profile as I spoke. For some reason, it was important that he believe me.

As he turned into my driveway, he returned my gaze. "No. No you don't. I think I know that about you."

"Bill's on his third marriage, Tom. It doesn't take a psychologist to see it's crumbling too. I just don't like to watch it."

"I have a hard time spotting bad marriages. I guess I'm an optimist. I think all marriages are as healthy as Carol's and mine was."

I took a good look at Tom Thurgood and decided that he was telling the truth about his marriage. "Why didn't you two have children?"

His crinkled smile appeared. "She was a lawyer. I was a cop. Modern career couple we were." His laugh was ironic. "She wanted to wait."

I squeezed his hand and let it go quickly. "Oh God. And I told you how much I despise lawyers."

His laugh had more body now. "No. You said the profession. There's a difference, believe me. A lot of people hate law enforcement, but get confused and hate me instead."

"That would be very hard to do," I said in all seriousness.

*   *   *

George junior had the charcoal started. With just the three of us, it was always my job. I had noticed before tonight that he was more responsible whenever a man came to the house. Even if it was just Hart. It must have been some sort of primitive territorial instinct, to lay claim just in case one of these men thought about taking over. Common, I decided, in female-headed households. I'd seen it with Barbara and Buddy, too, in spite of Oscar's weak presence.

Having driven Terry home, Bill pulled in just as we were getting out of the car. Either he was oblivious to the fact that I had run Terry off or he just did not care. Whichever it was, he showed no irritation with me. In fact, he was in a better mood than I'd seen him in months. George junior had assumed the task of cooking the burgers as well, so I watched as Bill monopolized Thurgood. I could tell that he liked the man. He did a lot of ribbing, always a sure sign from Bill. He teased him about his net play, calling him an illegal octopus.

My own mood, never quite up since arriving at the tennis court, had deteriorated. I found myself forcing the joviality that flowed so naturally from Tom and Bill. I had soaked up more than my share of the humidity. My arms felt like sponges and unseen insects hovered about my neck, occasionally pricking me beneath my hair. When we ate, the potato salad and hamburger tumbled like rocks into my stomach. I drank two Cokes trying to dissolve them. As I stood up from the picnic table, I found my thighs attached to each other like Velcro. Sometimes it's best to end the day early.

"I don't mean to be rude," I said, "but I've had it for today. Tennis two days in a row seems to be more than I can take at this stage in my career."

Joan laughed. "It's great to see you playing again, Mom." She turned to Thurgood. "It's good for her. Keep making her play."

He flushed, then grinned, obviously pleased and embarrassed at the same time. Looking for something to do with himself, he took my paper plate to the garbage can I had pulled out from the carport. When he returned, he stood behind me and massaged my shoulders. "Better?" he asked.

I closed my eyes to his touch as the tension eased out of me. I was left merely exhausted, much preferable to the creeping depression of moments earlier. Without thinking, I said, "What's going to happen to Fred?" I had really not intended to discuss that.

He continued to rub my shoulders. "I told you. A hearing. He'll probably be released on bond before noon tomorrow."

"I mean in the long run," I said.

Bill interjected, "He has a good lawyer. He might even be able to beat the probable cause." Always the lawyer, I thought.

"What about the other guy who strangled his wife last week?" I blurted this out, and added, "Is he still in jail?"

"What are you talking about?" Bill asked. Thurgood had stopped rubbing my shoulders and moved around to the other side of the picnic table.

"I heard it at a volleyball game. That another man had killed his wife. They were almost divorced too, just like Fred and Crystal." I looked across the table at Thurgood.

He answered slowly in the way he might answer a curious child. "Charlotte's murders are over a hundred a year now," he said. "Of those hundred, I'd say thirty or more are domestic. That two men strangled wives in the same month is par for the course."

"Are you sure there are only two?" I asked.

Bill was working up to a lecture, I could tell. "Come on, Sydney. We're a big city now. We've got big-city crime, right, Tom? If it were as easy to get a divorce as it is to get married, people wouldn't resort to violence like they do." The part about the difficulty of divorce was as much for himself as it was for me.

The weariness was overtaking me. If I didn't leave the table now, I feared I might sleep on the bench. As I pushed myself up with both hands, I attempted to smile apologetically at Thurgood.

The smile he returned me was kind and thoughtful. He said, "If it'll make you feel better, I'll check it out."

"Thank you. It would." I began a slow walk toward the house. Just before reaching the door, I remembered the message on the machine. "By the way," I called out, "Crystal left a message on my answering machine at ten p.m. the night she died."

Thurgood looked up from the conversation he had already begun with Bill. He didn't say anything. "Don't you want to know what she said?" I asked, tired of his restraint.

"If it's pertinent," he said evenly.

"Oh, it's pertinent, all right," I said smugly. I really wanted him to ask. Some part of me wanted him to beg.

He sat waiting instead.

I blurted it out: "She said Mickey Sutton was planning something terrible—not her words exactly—but she wanted to see me the next day to talk about it and, of course, by the next day she was dead."

He still sat quietly, almost as if he were watching a movie.

"I confronted Mickey on Friday at my office. He admitted he was at Crystal's house Wednesday night, but he wouldn't say anything more. Don't you think that's pertinent?"

"Who is Mickey Sutton?" he asked.

"The biggest jerk in all of Charlotte, that's who." Now we were getting somewhere.

He stared for a moment more, then said, "Why did you confront this Mickey Sutton?"

"Why? Because he was at my office, and I had a hunch. That's why." I didn't like being questioned as if I had done something illegal. As far as I was concerned, I was the only person trying to get to the bottom of this nightmare.

He didn't praise me. He didn't even thank me. He merely said, "You shouldn't have done that, Sydney."

I left the four of them and retreated to my cool, dry house.

Normally I hate to go to bed dirty. My legs get stuck to the sheets and don't move freely. Tonight it didn't matter because once I lay down, I didn't move again. Not until the phone beside the bed rang.

"Yeah?" I growled.

"Why such a grouch?" came Sally's upbeat voice.

"You woke me. Why're you calling in the middle of the night?"

"It's not even eleven," she said. "I knew you wouldn't be asleep."

I could hear water running in the hall bathroom and knew that Joan was still up. I struggled my poor body into a sitting position. "I was tired and went to bed early. What's going on?" I tried to run fingers through my hair and got caught on a snag immediately. God, I was a mess.

"Just wanted you to know I won't be in until after lunch," she said. "Fred's hearing's in the morning and I want to be there. I might need to help arrange the bond."

I told her not to worry, that Hart and I could answer the phones. Again I assured her that I had faith in Fred's innocence and that she should too.

She sounded stronger, maybe not confident but not on the verge of collapse either.

We hung up, and I showered. As soon as I returned to bed, I threw my legs about with abandon. I pretended I was swimming. First the scissor kick, then the butterfly. On my second lap of the old standby side kick, I could see the finish line and, in gratitude at having made it, fell asleep.

Monday mornings at Allen Teague are like they are at most small businesses. We discuss what's on our plate and then panic, either because it's too much for a firm as small as ours to handle or not enough to keep us going. Today it was the latter so I dispensed the salesman to his rounds with an urgency I find unflattering in myself. I then called a couple of clients who'd been holding back campaigns. Of the two, I snared one. I don't like this part of advertising. After all, we aren't selling bread to the hungry. Not as bad as snake oil, but sometimes I feel close.

Hart said he'd need the rest of the day to get all of Jean Miller's art camera-ready. I called to tell her she could approve the final work tomorrow.

"I hear they arrested the Ball husband over the weekend," she said. "I know Sally must be upset."

"He'll be getting out in the next hour or so," I said as I looked at the school clock I keep on the wall by my conference table.

"I've been wondering what I'm supposed to do about the house. Is he going to move back in?" she asked.

The thought hadn't entered my mind, and I found it abhorrent now as she suggested it. "My God, I hope not. Her parents and brother are probably in there by now. Funeral's tomorrow, and I suspect they'll be there a few days after that."

"Technically, though, Sydney, does the murder take the house off the market?"

"I don't know. I doubt if anybody's given that any thought. Why?"

"Trying to figure out how to market it after this. Anything to make the house appear different from the way it looked at the time of the murder." I heard a sigh on her end. "Oh, well, never mind. I doubt it'll sell now anyway. Once something like that happens, it's doomed." She laughed in resignation. "I bet Lizzie Borden couldn't give her house away."

"Wrong, Jean. About Lizzie Borden anyway. Her place is a bed-and-breakfast now."

She didn't skip a beat. "Oh really? Don't think the zoning allows that usage in Happy Valley."

I was hanging up from talking with Jean when Hart yelled from upstairs that Thurgood was on the other line.

He asked if I'd recovered from my athletic weekend. I told him I had even as I massaged my forearm-serving muscle. There was a consistent sincerity in Tom Thurgood's voice. My experience of people, both men and women, was that sincerity came and went—depending on the mood and circumstances. Not so with this man.

He came to the point quickly. There'd been three strangulations in the last three months. All autopsies showed evidence of recent intercourse. During the same time one other woman had been stabbed to death in her home. She appeared to be a rape victim as well.

He waited for some comment from me. "I know what you said about statistics, Tom, but isn't that a little much?"

He answered slowly, a style I'd come to expect. "Maybe. Maybe not. What is odd is that all four of them were part of robberies—if we count the Ball case as a robbery."

Surely this combination was statistically unusual enough for someone to check further. "Even stranger," he continued, "is that none of these robberies was breaking and entering. Just like the Ball case."

"Even I know that's strange," I said.

He neither agreed nor disagreed. "We could have a very large coincidence. Or someone could be gaining entry through a scam. A few years back we had a guy who had a pet-sitting service. You know one of those businesses where, when you go out of town, someone comes over every day to feed and walk your dog, maybe water your plants."

"Yes?"

"This guy had copies of his clients' keys made, waited six months so the clients wouldn't make the connection, then returned to rob five of them in five consecutive days."

"How'd you catch him?" I asked.

I could hear a weariness tinged with anger in his answer. "Never did. By the time we figured it out, made all the connections, he was long gone. Warrant's still out, but I doubt if anybody'll ever find him unless he pulls the same scam in another state."

"Did he murder his victims?" I asked tentatively.

He hesitated. "No. In fact, he made sure they weren't at home."

"Well, that makes this very different, doesn't it?"

I could almost hear his mind sorting things through, the way you hear the roots of plants taking in water. Finally he said, "I'm going to put someone on this. Look for what else these four cases might have in common. By the way, Ball's being released as we speak. The judge set $75,000. Ball used his house."

I looked at my watch. Almost noon. "Are those four cases in some form you can fax to me? I'd like to take a look at them myself."

"You know I can't send you internal information on cases in progress," he said apologetically.

"What part's public record? Can't you just send me the who, what, where parts? Surely some of it is okay for me to see." I swiveled my chair around to watch the traffic on East Boulevard. The road had those wavy lines on it they get when the heat of the air and the heat of the traffic combine to cook un-air-conditioned drivers. "I guess I could come down there myself and get whatever can be made public. God, it's hot outside."

"Why don't you go to the paper or library and take a look at all of it on microfiche? You'll find every bit of what I'd be allowed to send you."

"Sure I could if I had the afternoon to give to the project. Tom, public record, remember?" Damn he was thickheaded.

Reluctantly, he agreed. Said he'd fax me something by midafternoon.

10

I SPENT LUNCHTIME AS I OFTEN DO ON MON-
days, grocery shopping. The only way to have a
totally free weekend is to spread the household work
throughout the five-day part of the work week. But today
my mind kept wandering back to the conversation I'd
had with Tom, and to the other women in Charlotte
who'd died so recently—and so anonymously. Perhaps
that's why I wound up with such an odd assortment of
groceries. The frozen pizza and head of lettuce would do
for tonight while I had dinner with Barbara, but what
were we going to do with the four different kinds of
cheeses that looked so elegant and the eight-pound bag
of russet potatoes on special? Grocery shopping in a
hurry without a list is not only expensive, it results in
some unbalanced menus.

Before I relocked the house to return to the office, I
studied my key. All my doors had the same dead bolt,
even the ones at the office, so that I wouldn't have to go
through three or four to find the right one. How had

someone found a way to gain entry to four women's houses without having to break a lock? I wondered if the murdered women had dead bolts or if they had those old-fashioned kinds with the locks inside the doorknob itself. Those kinds could be fooled with, I thought, and no one would know that there'd been a break-in. I was sure, though, that everybody had started using dead bolts by now.

Sally had returned from court by the time I got back to the office. She and Hart could have been modeling for some leisure-life publication as they sat sipping coffee on the twin love seats that make up the reception area of Sally's office.

"Hey there," I said. "You look like a star witness." I was going for lightness, hoping that her nerves had calmed and her mood had lifted.

Her smile told me that at least the latter was true. "It really wasn't bad," she said. "Over in a sec. Freddie's gone to my house to shower and sleep."

I poured myself a cup of coffee and wished that I could light myself a cigarette as well. "Don't you keep some flats around here?" The woman had heels on. "You ought to get out of those," I said, pointing at them. "What are they? Two inches?"

"You're bothered by them 'cause they make me as tall as you. You can't tower over me when I wear these things." She rose up and stood head to head with me at five nine. I stood on my toes.

Hart said, "Cut that out or I'll stand up and tower over the both of you."

The three of us laughed, something we had not done together since the middle of last week.

Sally then mentioned that Crystal's mom had called her.

"Why?" I asked bluntly, our momentary lightheartedness gone.

"Why shouldn't she?" she said defensively. "She wants me to have any of our family jewelry that Crystal still had."

"That's kind of her." Why was this bothering me? I don't think I wanted Crystal to give up anything, not even in death.

"Look, Sydney, I just want my mother's engagement ring. It's a two-carat emerald-cut diamond that's been in my family for three generations. That's not a whole lot to ask. Besides, her mom's the one who offered. I didn't call her."

When the phone rang, I was relieved. The whole idea of possessions and what belongs to whom and who deserves this residue or that made my chest heavy. Families were as much keepers of treasured things as they were of treasured people. I was grateful I didn't have much.

The phone call brought more business, a quick public service effort to alert people to the dangers of roadside fires this fall. A full eight years after Hurricane Hugo hit the area in and around Charlotte, the felled trees constituted hundreds of acres of kindling awaiting a match. The guy from Raleigh said that legislators had panicked after a sudden realization that we were in a drought. They had quickly set aside $50,000 for some brochures, billboards, and public service TV spots. The catch, of course, was that the whole campaign had to be up and running in ten days. Could I do it? the Raleigh man asked. I had a distinct feeling that I was not the first agency called to handle this "emergency." Obviously, however, I was the first one to say yes.

The tea party between Sally and Hart was just breaking up as I reentered the reception room. Before I could share our good fortune at going from work famine to work feast in half a day, Sally was out the door to collect the family jewel. Hart acted as if he were about to return upstairs to his lair, when I stopped him.

"Please have another cup with me," I said. "I've not had thirty seconds of a social life today, and I could use a half cup or so of civility." I poured myself another cup and sat on the love seat catty-cornered to him, both of us having crossed our legs, our feet touching. For Hart and me, this was intimate; I felt human for the first time today.

Hart gardens, so I asked him how it was going. "Dregs," he said dolefully. "Drought, heat, bursts of rain that run off and never soak. Annuals are leggy, my perennials spent. Asters and mums not blooming yet." He sighed. "I've come to the conclusion that this is the season of death, not after frost. My garden is a painful scene to watch these days."

"Nothing's doing well?" I asked.

"Not for me. Maybe it's the season to harvest parchment paper."

He'd brought it up, not me, so I thought here was my opening to discuss the drought ads I'd just obligated us to do. Hart cannot stand tight deadlines, while I, to be honest, thrive on them. It's when I do my best work and so does he, although he won't admit it.

So I told him.

He began to show early anxiety signs, the most obvious of which was the involuntary swinging of his foot against my own.

"It won't be so bad," I said. "I'll work on all the concepts while you finish Jean Miller today. By Wednesday, we can both get on it and have the brochures to the printer by Friday. We can use stock video for the PSA and use voice-overs and sound effects. It'll be a cinch, you'll see."

His foot slowed considerably. "Wasn't it just this morning that you said we'd all starve if we didn't get some work in here?"

I nodded in agreement.

He continued. "I thought you already had the Textile Museum coming at three to start their campaign."

I laughed and pushed Hart's foot with my own. "Oh, well, what a lovely feast we'll have. You won't need to worry," I said. "I can't do it tonight, but, if I need to work every other night this week to get these jobs out of here, I will. I live two blocks away, remember?"

Hart sipped the last of his coffee and stood up. "You're going to kill yourself one of these days, Sydney."

I remained seated. "You know I love it" was all I could think to say, and I meant it.

He put his hand on the banister, then turned back toward me. "By the way, did you beat the detective in tennis over the weekend? Sally was afraid to ask you."

"Why would she be afraid to ask me?"

"Because she's afraid you won, and the whole police department will retaliate against her brother." His smile broke into a grin. "You did beat him, didn't you?"

I felt only slightly defensive. "What if I did? Whether I did or not has nothing to do with Fred's case. Actually

Tom Thurgood is probably a very good detective although he doesn't talk about his work much. I assume he'd bend over backwards to be fair to Fred. I'm just not sure he has enough information to put his good detecting to work." Now I smiled too. "He's probably a better detective than he is a tennis player though."

Hart was laughing out loud. "You beat him. I can tell. I know you, Sydney Teague."

Following him to the base of the stairs, I pulled my right arm across my waist and thrust it toward him in a mock backhand. "Beat him in straight sets," I said. "Don't tell Sally."

As Hart reached the top of the stairs, I called out, still playfully, "Do we know anybody with a light blue or green Econoline van?"

"Not right offhand," he said as he continued walking. "Sutton's got a gray one, hasn't he?"

Then he was out of my sight. Into his cocoon. At his board, I assumed. Where everything always squares up.

Working with the Textile Museum curator is a lot like working with my old Sears washing machine. I can't put too much in at one time or the whole thing malfunctions, emitting one of those off-balance buzzes. The Sears man tells me there's crack in the main housing, whatever that is. I don't know what the curator's problem is, but his symptoms are similar.

Today he could not grasp all the elements of his campaign. So I gave him the general goal, which was to entice anyone whose family had never owned a textile mill to enter the museum at all. Since the curator is a third-generation mill-owning family member, the one of the current generation deemed incapable of running the mill, he could not even grasp the need for such a goal.

I was trying to explain the general public's attitude toward the history of textile machinery, when the phone rang. It was Thurgood. A voice so sane and sensible. He said he was getting ready to fax to me. He'd appreciate it, he said, if I'd keep the information in the fax to myself. I didn't remind him about public information again.

"I'll call you tonight," he said as he was about to hang up.

"Whoa," I said quickly. "I'll be out tonight. We'll talk tomorrow."

With that he was gone, and I returned my attention to the curator. As I talked, and talked, and talked and felt I was accomplishing nothing except perhaps cracked housing of my own, I could hear the fax in the reception room churning out page after page.

I was listening to a lecture on the integrity of intimate fiber blending and the revolution it had created, when Hart left for the day. The clock by my conference table had moved to 5:25 before I finally said, "I understand. The goal will be to convey the importance of that revolution."

That satisfied him. I knew it would. I felt dishonest. I'd wanted two things at that point: for him to leave and for me to have work to do that we at least partially agreed on. Now I would create a campaign that I could not execute with passion and that I knew from experience would not bring in visitors. Maybe, just maybe, they didn't want visitors anyway. Maybe we'd been talking about family pride all along, and I just didn't know it.

When he was finally out the door, I had only twenty minutes to drive to the Bishop Cates office near South-Park. I would be pushing it to make that in the middle of rush hour. I grabbed the seven or eight pages of fax that Thurgood had sent and locked up for the day.

SouthPark is more than a mall, although that's how it began a little over twenty years ago. According to the state commerce department, SouthPark is the third largest city in the state, after downtown Charlotte and downtown Raleigh. The parameters of the definition have something to do with working population as opposed to living population, but still the distinction makes SouthPark a phenomenon that has simultaneously spurred Charlotte's growth and added to its lack of soul. No city whose impetus is a mall can expect true distinction any more than Sylvester Stallone can expect knighthood.

The Bishop Cates building was one of the first buildings to go up after the mall was built. Much of the land surrounding the mall had been owned by Calvin Bishop, a fact that played heavily in his firm's dominance for so many years. At least ten distinct neighborhoods surround the central business area, the restaurants, and the mall. Last I heard, Bishop, and now, I assumed, Barbara, owned at least twenty rental houses in those neighborhoods. Her brokerage may have been in trouble, but Barbara herself wasn't.

As I pulled into the Bishop Cates parking lot, I repressed the guilt that I knew made no sense. Jean Miller was my client, and Barbara Cates was not. There's an unwritten rule in advertising that you don't represent two clients in the same industry if they are going head-to-head for the same business.

I reminded myself that I wasn't representing Barbara. My God, I'd known her for thirty years. Ever since she was Barbie Bishop and I was Sydney Allen, awkward thirteen-year-olds who both seemed to have problems fitting in. I was the tomboy who put on nail polish, lipstick, and a bra but still begged the boys to let me play basketball. They didn't know quite how to take me. Barbara, on the other hand, was desperate to fit in with the girls, but she wasn't sure how to do that, and consequently broke some cardinal rules of sisterhood you just don't break. She'd talk behind backs, sabotage other friendships, and lie to make herself look good. I never understood it, so much energy vested in her own destruction.

With boys she was even worse. She'd set her sights on someone else's boyfriend and chip away at his resistance. When she'd won him over, it was as if she owned him, manipulating him to do and say things the boy would never have thought on his own. Even my brother's considerable ego fell prey to Barbara. Bill said he almost swore off girls after the experience. He should have, I told myself as I approached the front door. But through it all I was Barbara's friend and I guessed I always would be.

The Bishop Cates building was long and low, in need of a face-lift to bring it into the nineties. Yellow brick, low-pitched roof, and lots of windows—all with copper-tinted mini-blinds. The reception room was massive, probably thirty by forty, with a large horseshoe-shaped dark wood reception desk smack in the middle.

I was impressed, but not received. The reception area was empty. All its walls were lined with work stations, those modular divisions—these were lined in a beige tweed—that separate people from one another. The ones I could see into were empty. In the middle of each of the walls perpendicular to the front door there were doors leading to the rest of the rooms in the office building.

I didn't want to go wandering down Barbara's halls, so I searched for a bell to ring at the reception desk. No bell, but I did find a phone system with an extension for Barbara. She answered, "Bishop Cates. May I help you?"

"Hey," I echoed in the cavernous room. "It's Sydney here for dinner. I'm at your reception desk. No one's out here so I buzzed your extension."

"Everyone's gone home." She sounded rushed. "Come on down the hall to your right from the front door. I have a couple of things to finish up before we go."

Real offices, the kind with drywalls and doors, lined each side of the long hall, which ended in a fairly large office. Barbara sat at a computer terminal, and Oscar, a cellular phone in his hand, paced back and forth in front of an expansive window.

Oscar waved and put his finger to his lips in one hand movement, letting me know that he acknowledged my presence but certainly didn't want me to speak. Okay by me. I didn't particularly want to speak to Oscar. He was one of those guys who typified what I'd grown to dislike about Charlotte: aggressive, in both business and his social life, he was a people user. I didn't like his looks either. Not because he was ugly because he wasn't. His features fought each other so, when I looked at him, I saw tension. He'd lost his hair in the middle, but what hair remained along the sides was very thick. His eyes were round like giant gray marbles, but his ears were much too small for his globe of a head. He was the only man I'd ever known who had a peaked nose and still looked like a pig. His face was classic Disney pink.

Barbara looked just as drawn as she had on Friday. Living with Oscar would have done that to me, but I knew the business, or lack of it, had pulled her down. It must have been a rotten feeling to inherit a thriving family firm and have it disintegrate before your eyes.

"Just a sec, Sydney," she said as she stared into the green fluorescence of her computer screen. "Gotta clear two listings that expired."

I whispered, "That's okay. I've got some paperwork I can study myself." Of course, all I had with me were Thurgood's fax pages, so I sat in a burgundy leather armchair and took a look. Each of the four murders had at least two pages of computerized information; several had three pages. All of them had space gaps as if Thurgood had removed what I was not allowed to see but did not bother to delete the space after removing the words. Maybe he'd used Liquid Paper.

I started with Crystal's death since it was the only one I knew anything about. Crystal Simmons Ball. 806 Sunshine Place. Strangulation was listed as cause of death, and I'd known that too. Then a paragraph or two on Fred's 911 call, chronology of the investigation that ensued, and a list of the officers working the case, Homicide Detective Tom Thurgood in charge. The general description of the body was deleted except for what she was wearing. I think I already knew everything on Crystal's piece of paper. These were obviously only summary sheets. I don't suppose I should have expected anything more.

I wished I'd asked Cynthia Hyatt the name of the woman in the case she'd thought so similar. That would have seemed the next most logical page to look at. I decided to put them in chronological order since the similar case happened a little under a week before Fred found Crystal. Sara Gurney, age 32, 78 Tamarin Way. Cause of death, strangulation. Was it by hand or a rope or what?

Were the three strangulations all committed by the same means? Didn't say. Body wearing a T-shirt. This was the woman whose poor child had found her.

I was so deeply engrossed in Thurgood's paperwork that I didn't notice Barbara standing by my side looking over my shoulder.

Oscar thrust his hand at me in the robust manner he might display with a long-lost fraternity brother. Somehow I felt violated before he'd even said a word.

"Hi, Oscar," I said as I withdrew my arm. "You seem good and busy these days."

"Creditors as much as anything else, I'm afraid." He glanced at Barbara, who raised an eyebrow in disapproval.

"Barbara," he continued, "doesn't like me to air our professional and personal problems in public. But, hell, Sydney, what's an old friend like you for if not to see her through the hard times, huh? She doesn't sleep; she doesn't eat; she doesn't talk to a soul in the world except the kid." He patted me on the back. "Yes, ma'am, I think it's a good thing you've come over to help her with her marketing. A fresh approach is just what old Bishop Cates needs."

I was speechless. The whole time Oscar had been talking I had been staring at Barbara, who stared at the wall and seemed to be disconnected from us. She had never asked me to help her, of course, but Oscar's remarks didn't spark a protest in her either. I thought I'd better set the record straight.

"Actually, Oscar," I said, "I'd love to help Barbara, but I have a conflict. Jean Miller has already hired me. I can't have two real estate clients at the same time." I looked at Barbara for a reaction. She was still staring at the wall.

Oscar straightened his tie and put his jacket on, chuckling to himself the whole time. "No, you can't have two. Not two that people know about." He winked at me. "That just wouldn't look right, now would it?" He headed toward the door. "You two have a good gossip over dinner," he added as he reached for the doorknob. "I'll feed the kid."

"Buddy," Barbara said without inflection of any kind.

"What?" Oscar said.

She finally looked at him. "The kid's name is Buddy, Oscar. Please call him by his name."

Oscar looked at me, shook his head as if in defiance of an order, and left the room.

Neither Barbara nor I spoke until hearing his car engine start. "Sorry about him," she finally said, and I detected a sadness stronger than anger.

"Barbara, you've never asked me to help you market the company. Did you tell Oscar that I—"

She cut me off with a flip of her wrist. "Of course I didn't tell him such a thing. Oscar has his own agenda and makes way too many assumptions."

I asked her to please set him straight again when she got home tonight. I didn't need Oscar's big mouth spreading those kinds of lies about me.

I shuffled the paperwork in my lap.

"What's that?" Barbara asked.

"Some information about Crystal Ball's death," I said.

"She was your secretary's sister-in-law, wasn't she?"

I nodded. Most people, including Barbara, didn't know that the upstanding ad agency owner and the barfly had been such good friends.

"Forgive me for thinking this way, but that's going to be a hard house to sell."

"I'm afraid there are more houses in Charlotte where the same thing has happened."

Barbara reached for my papers. "You mean murders where the houses are on the market?"

I held on to the papers, remembering Tom's request. "I don't know about being for sale; I just mean women being killed in their houses. Coincidence enough, don't you think?"

She let go of my paperwork and rubbed the back of her neck. "Oscar and I have noticed some kind of trend in robberies of houses on the market."

"How can you do that?"

"Multiple Listing," she said. "We can see robberies from the listings that are removed before their contracts are up."

"What do you mean? Multiple Listing is just a cooperative listing service among all Charlotte's brokerages. It doesn't flag robberies, does it?"

"Multiple Listing doesn't, but I do. Daddy taught me years ago to call either Multiple Listing or the listing agency when a house drops out of the computer. A lot of agents go after homes that drop out."

"Yeah, that's happened to me before. Phone calls and letters too." I was going to add "Like vultures" but checked myself when I realized I was talking to one.

Barbara continued: "But it's sort of stupid to call those homeowners without first finding out elsewhere why they've removed their houses. You can just as easily make an enemy as a friend if you don't check first. So a lot of houses have been removed recently because they've had robberies while on the market It made the owners nervous. Wouldn't it you?"

I was still confused. "You mean homeowners think their houses were robbed because they were on the market?"

Barbara nodded.

"Do you really think there's a connection?"

"Yes I do," she said. "Come over here. I want to show you something." She moved over to her computer and clicked on the screen. "Here. Pull this swivel chair up beside me."

I clutched Thurgood's fax, now wadded like a half-formed ball, and joined Barbara at her computer. The familiar green glare flashed in my face as the box fed itself enough power to communicate with us.

"Okay," she said as her fingers tapped three or four keys in a row. "Everybody gets drop-outs downloaded from Multiple Listing. Like I told you, we prospect from it."

"Do all agents belong to Multiple Listing?" I asked.

"Probably ninety-nine percent of us do. If it weren't for Multiple Listing, Charlotte real estate would come to a halt. The city's just too big and spread out to sell its houses any other way." She shifted in her chair. "I go to the trouble to find out why each homeowner takes his house off the market and record that too along with the addresses that Multiple Listing downloads."

Numbers and words danced across the screen. "Look here," she said. "I created myself a program summarizing the drop-outs by reason, listing agency, neighborhood, time-frame. Anything I want. Everything I need to prospect smarter than my competitors."

The screen held still with the title *Drop-Out Causes/ 6–97 through 9–97.* Literally hundreds of addresses, dates, and abbreviations for codes scrolled themselves up and back into Barbara's hard drive. "Rob stands for robbery," she explained. "Dis stands for dissatisfaction with realtor.

That's the one I'm looking for, the one that makes me pick up the phone. Look at all the robs, Sydney!"

There were indeed quite a few of them. Of the two or three hundred drop-outs, it looked like every sixth or seventh entry listed rob as its reason. "Good God," I said. "There are at least thirty. Is that normal? Are houses on the market targeted by thieves?"

She shrugged. "Not really. Not unless the homeowner has already moved and left all his furniture until the house sells. Sometimes those houses are more vulnerable. But, generally, no."

"I don't suppose your program can tell us if any of these robberies were not forced entry, can it?"

She crinkled her eyebrows. "You mean like if the thief had a key or something?"

Thurgood had said it had to be coincidence or scam. What I was thinking terrified me. "Barbara, isn't every homeowner's house key inside a Multiple Listing supra-lock?"

She dropped her hands from the keyboard. "Oh, God, Sydney. You're not thinking there are real estate agents involved in these robberies, are you?"

I could not tell her my thoughts; they were too embedded in my fears. I took the crushed papers in my hand and began to smooth them out on my skirt. "Barbara, will your program let you key in by address to see if a particular house could be on this list?"

"Yes," she answered nervously. "I can put it in about any way I want to see it." She had not taken her eyes off the screen.

So I gave her the addresses of the murdered women one at a time. In chronological order, the way I'd last arranged them. I held my breath on each one, willing it

not to show up on her screen. When each one did—
except Crystal, who was too new—why wasn't I surprised? I was overwhelmed with what felt like sadness,
but not surprised.

"These women were murdered, Barbara," I whispered, barely able to find the breath for that much.

11

Though neither one of us felt much like eating, we went to Charley's in the mall. We took a comfortable, dark corner booth hoping to escape the claustrophobia that had settled over Barbara's office with our recent discovery.

I had called the Law Enforcement Center before we even left Barbara's office, but Tom Thurgood was gone for the day. There wasn't anybody else I could talk with, since what Thurgood had sent me was in confidence. I left a message for him to call me as soon as he got in the next day.

"What do you think the police will do, Sydney?" Barbara's hand shook as she took a very long drink of Scotch. It would have been my choice too.

"I don't know. I guess the first thing they'll do is match their breaking-and-entering information against the robberies we found in Multiple Listing."

She dabbed at her chin with her napkin, the Scotch

having dribbled its overflow past her lips. "And if they match?" she asked. "What will they do then?"

I sipped my coffee and yearned for a Vantage. "I don't know. Maybe it'll give them a place to start looking." I couldn't stand it any longer. "I've got to smoke, Barbara. I'm sorry, but you'll have to indulge me." I pulled the pack out of my pocketbook without even waiting for her response.

She waved her hand as if to indicate she could stand it under the circumstances, then said: "Of course we know what it means. It means that real eatate agents are involved in this." She licked some Scotch off her lips. "There's some kind of horrible conspiracy among a group of agents in this town." Her eyes were bright in their certainty.

"Conspiracy?" What an odd choice of words. "Conspiracy to do what?"

"What else could it be?" she asked. She set her mouth in a straight line, then spoke through her teeth. "More than one house means almost certainly more than one realtor."

She paused. I waited, not knowing enough to say anything. She seemed angry at my ignorance.

"If so many robberies involve houses in Multiple Listing," she continued, as if talking to a child, "and if there's no sign of breaking and entering, realtors must be involved. How can you dispute that?"

"I don't, Barbara." Gee, was she looking for a fight? "I don't think it necessarily means conspiracy though." I was still not convinced, but what did I know? She was the real estate expert, not I. "Does each realtor have her own separate combination for opening a supralock, one that no one else can know?"

She nodded and, on the uptake, her Scotch followed.

"How about the key they use in conjunction with their combinations?" I asked. "Is that individualized, or does everybody have the same key?"

"Everybody has the same key."

"Is there a way to find out which realtors have been in these houses?" I asked.

"Yes, of course," she said. "There's a roll of paper inside the lock where a mechanical imprint of your numbers is left when you put in your combination. A history of all showings for a particular house appears on the paper. When the house sells—"

"Or is taken off the market like the ones we're talking about. Right?"

She smiled, slightly embarrassed. "Right," she said. "When it goes off market for whatever reason," she continued, "the listing agent takes the lock back to the Multiple Listing office. They put in a fresh roll so they can use the lock for another house."

I dragged deeply. "Then we may never know who got into these houses." I exhaled a mass of smoke so thick that I could not see Barbara. I waved the excess away. "They'd all be cleared by now, don't you think?" It was eight o'clock almost, and my stomach reached through its turmoil to announce itself. "Can we go ahead and order? I'm going to need to get home to my kids."

We both opened our menus. "One last thing though," she said from behind the laminated piece of paper. "The police will have to shut down Multiple Listing until they get to the bottom of this."

"Why?" Maybe I'd missed something.

She shook her head, then tapped her forefinger on her eyebrow. "Sydney, think. Charlotte doesn't need any more of this while its infamously slow police department does its thing."

"That'll make some clients of mine a bit upset."

"More than upset, I'd say." Barbara wiped the perspiration off her Scotch glass with a cocktail napkin. "With no Multiple Listing, new firms won't survive."

I choked on a sip of water.

"I think I'll have the Cobb salad," she said. "What about you?"

"I don't see what I had my heart set on," I answered.

"What's that? Maybe they can make it up for you."

"Two aspirin," I answered.

We laughed, perhaps a bit too loudly, too nervously, the hint of cackle in both of our voices. She hoisted her tapestried suitcase of a pocketbook from the floor and rummaged through it. When at last she produced a bottle of aspirin and lined up her arrows, the top popped off and rolled into the aisle, where our waiter picked it up and hesitantly approached us. We were laughing so hard that, at first, we could not respond to the poor guy's attempt to take our order. The whole scene felt like junior high again to me.

I finally ordered the eggs benedict. Not too heavy, not too light. I hadn't eaten an egg in six months at least. Besides, tomorrow I could tell myself that I'd eaten a good breakfast. I know it makes no sense, but it works psychologically.

Barbara got a second Scotch, and I had a refill of black coffee, which curiously calms me when it should do the opposite. It might just be the ritual memory of putting liquid to mouth that soothes me, but who cares as long as it works. I was beginning to relax. When Barbara said to go ahead and smoke all the cigarettes I wanted, I finally felt the awful knot in my chest dissolve itself. Barbara seemed to be easing out of her anxiety as well.

Changing the subject seemed almost medicinally necessary to me. Neither of us needed to regress. "I saw Buddy Saturday night," I said. "He looks great with that military haircut." I smiled across the booth in the hopes that she'd want to keep the conversation light.

She smiled in return. We were trying

"He is handsome, isn't he? I like his hair short too. I hope he'll keep it that way even though the school didn't work out." She tensed again and fiddled with her spoon, removing it from its place beside the knife and setting it on the starched napkin next to the fork. "Where did you see him?" she asked.

"A friend of his dropped him at the house. He was visiting with Joan and Cindi Hyatt. We didn't talk much. Not that I didn't want to. Joan turned up the music on me. Her idea of climate control. You know kids."

She said, "Sometimes I wish I understood them better."

"We're not meant to understand each other," I said. "That's what I think. They make no effort to understand us, do they?" I halted what was the beginning of one of my philosophical speeches on parenthood when I saw a pained expression on Barbara's face.

"You okay?" I asked. "Did I say something?"

For a long minute she did not say anything at all. Her eyes filled with water the way I'd seen them at my office last week, but she tried to smile. "No, you didn't say anything. Home isn't perfect right now."

"Barbara," I said as softly as I could. "I know Buddy doesn't get along with Oscar. He told me as much. I think I can imagine how hard that is on you." The tears spilled over, and she held my eyes through it all. All of a sudden, I wanted to reach over and protect her from all that had gone wrong in her life. "Buddy told me that Oscar's not his father. I can almost hear the arguments they must have."

"It's awful" was all that she could say before she pulled the napkin out from under the fork and spoon and covered her face. It was my turn to hunt through my pocketbook for a Kleenex. Before I could find one, she excused herself and left the booth.

As I watched her go, I realized that this was not the first time I was grateful that I had not remarried after George left. George junior would have a hard time, too, with anybody who took attention away from him. What could I possibly discuss with Barbara that wasn't a reminder of trauma? Her business was crumbling, so I wanted to stay away from that as well. While I was still thinking, her Cobb salad and my eggs benedict arrived at the table. I had finished my first egg and was about to start on my second before she returned.

The mood shift was as severe as the one I'd seen in my office, and it made me uncomfortable. I prefer a slow rise as well as a slow fall.

"I hope you'll forgive me, Sydney," she said smiling. "I've been so worried about the business the last six months. With Oscar and Buddy at each other's throats, I just had to send Buddy off to Virginia Military Academy." She laughed nervously, and a piece of lettuce fell into her lap without her noticing. "When he was sent back home this summer, the two of them started in on each other again."

"You didn't withdraw him voluntarily? Buddy implied that he left for financial reasons." I was afraid I might trigger something, so I bit my lip to keep from saying more.

"Oh, we've got financial problems, but we're lucky we don't have more. His education is safe. Daddy left an educational trust so we're okay there. Buddy's probably embarrassed." She paused and looked at me as if trying to determine whether I measured up to some unknown standard known only to Barbara. "They shouldn't let girls into military schools. That's the reason we send our sons to them, isn't it? Some boys just can't take the distraction." She had eaten at the most maybe five pieces of lettuce, nothing more.

I laughed and expected Barbara to join me, but she didn't. So I said, "Barbara, no mother can keep her child from knowing there's another sex. The most we can do is play it down, like it's no big thing."

I was grateful George junior was not into girls yet. As a younger sister, I could remember how Bill's personality had shifted during those teenage years. In my home, Joan's reverence for boys imbued our atmosphere with enough hormones for the time being.

Barbara continued, miraculously upbeat: "Buddy's like his father in so many ways. I'm grateful he never knew him though. You never knew him either, Sydney. Count your lucky stars."

"He's not dead?"

"Would be nice, but no. Just gone. Actually, he could be dead, I guess. I never wanted Buddy to know anything about him, but good old take-charge Daddy had to tell him everything. Buddy's father wasn't a very nice person." A glazed film swept across her eyes, cataracts looking for a home.

She drained the watered-down Scotch as her expression shifted yet again. "I'm going to pull the business out, Sydney." A fierce, glistening determination now shone in her eyes. "Daddy damn near ruined me, but I'll show them." She sloppily refolded her napkin and put it on top of her unused knife. "I really am going to survive." She said this as if it were a discovery she herself had just made.

Luckily I had finished the second egg because Barbara decided that dinner was over. My personal feeling was that her business might survive, but she herself might not. Some kind of breakdown seemed inevitable. Her symptoms were alcoholic, but I didn't think she drank enough. Removing the bottle probably wouldn't help. We'd known each other most of our lives; I'd seen her through a lot of scrapes, but I didn't know how to help her now.

12

_____

By THE TIME I GOT HOME, IT WAS AFTER NINE, and nobody had done homework. Pink Floyd had yielded to somebody Joan called Ugly Arms, whom I cut off immediately. The crust of the pizza I'd bought lay on various side tables beside chairs near the TV.

Joan recognized the mood I was in as one she shouldn't fool with. She quickly opened her Hemingway and began to stare into the book. George junior yawned and said he thought he'd go on to bed.

"No, you won't," I said crisply. "Not until you show me your math homework."

"But I'm sleepy," he whined.

"And you'll be sleepier tomorrow 'cause you're staying up until your math homework is done. Understand?"

Now he recognized the mood too and backed into his room. I followed him in and pulled the chair at his desk out for him. Then I opened his bookbag and handed him the algebra book. "Okay?" I asked rhetorically. He cowered.

I stomped from his room to Joan's door, which she had wisely closed. "Joan, I don't want you seeing any more of Buddy Cates. Do you hear me?"

"Why?" came her exasperated reply through the door. "I'm supposed to see him this weekend."

I thought about getting into a shouting match with her, but I decided not to pursue it. To tell the truth, I didn't know why I didn't want them together right now. Gut, I guess. Barbara's mental state scared me, made me uneasy, and now that I knew for sure that Buddy had indeed been kicked out of school, I didn't want my daughter too close to any of that. And what kind of kid sells his dying grandfather's car for parts anyway?

I stepped out of my skirt at my closet door and left it there. My blouse somehow made it to the clothes hamper. The agitation reached to every part of my body, wiring me and shooting me around the house on a crust-hunting expedition and a general cleanup of all that seemed out of place. I needed to control everything I could.

The phone book listed no Tom Thurgood. Information told me his number was unlisted. I was angry at him for guarding his privacy. I'd needed to dump what I had learned in Barbara's office somewhere, and he had denied me that.

The morning seemed a long time from now, a physical presence so far away. Early sobriety had sometimes felt like this. Like the morning would never arrive, and if it did, I would be irreversibly insane and it wouldn't matter anyhow.

Barbara was probably right about Multiple Listing.

They'd have to shut it down until they got to the bottom of these break-ins. Without the Multiple Listing service, real estate would come to a standstill in a place as spread out as Charlotte. Realtors would again have to go to each other's offices to pick up keys for showings. Like thirty years ago. Such a hassle would slow everything down and cut volume in half at least. Jean Miller would probably have to shut down. Hell, as top-heavy as Allen Teague was in real estate, we might go out of business too.

I spent a good hour worrying about Jean Miller and all the new agencies who depended so much on Multiple Listing to build up their businesses. Then I put another hour into berating myself for worrying more about them than about Crystal and the women who had died.

Just before midnight Joan knocked lightly on my bedroom door.

"Come on in," I said. I noticed my voice sounded only tired, not threatening as I'm sure it had sounded to the kids earlier.

"You in a better mood now, Mom?"

"I'm sorry, honey. I've had a hard day, but I shouldn't take it out on you."

"I wanted to tell you, but you didn't give me a chance. Mrs. Simmons called and the funeral is at ten tomorrow morning."

I stared at her.

"Georgie and I want to go. We talked about it. It's like our aunt died or something, like she was your sister, Mom. We decided, if you say no, we'll figure out a way to go anyway so—"

"Joanie, stop."

Her eyes were pleading.

"Of course you'll go. We'll go together. As a family." I felt a solitary tear slide past my cheekbone.

Joan looked as if she were going to cry too. She said, "She was like your sister, wasn't she, Mom?"

I am well practiced at achieving serenity. The key is to act on what you can do something about immediately and to truly accept what you cannot change. Because I couldn't reach Thurgood, I had to take stuff to bed with me that I couldn't let go of. I fell asleep around four.

13

EXHAUSTION ON A HOT, MUGGY DAY IS HARDER to manage than exhaustion on a cool, crisp one. It's as if my skin sinks into itself like red clay in a creek bed. No spring, no resiliency. So everything that comes my way is absorbed rather than repelled. I fill up with inconsequential things that otherwise I wouldn't even notice.

Like the broken light at the intersection of two of the Queens Roads—Charlotte has three. I had overslept anyway, then realized that my only clean suit was at the cleaners, so I needed to drive there, come back, get dressed, and go to my good friend's funeral before I could even start the day.

Portions of the sky were blue this morning, but a lingering haze on the ground and in the trees would rise by noon and paint the afternoon pale gray. It had been the pattern since midsummer. The second broken light at Kings and Queens told me we'd had a thunderstorm sometime after four this morning. The oak limbs and leaves near storm drains indicated it had been pretty severe. I must have slept even deeper than usual not to have heard a thunderstorm as big as this one must have been.

Crystal's body had been released to Harry and Bryant, Charlotte's oldest funeral home. I wished I'd had time to call all the people who owed me something and get them to the funeral home this morning. I wanted Crystal's family to believe in a life Crystal never had. I wanted them to be proud in their sadness, to feel good about her life as they mourned her death.

I pulled into the shopping strip to get our cleaning and took a deep breath before opening the car door. "Sorry, Crystal," I said. "Some PR person I've been for you during all this."

My linen suit looked new beneath its clear plastic. I pulled the see-through up and took a whiff. Not even a hint of Bourbon and Scotch. God, was that only last week? If only I could have been sent to the cleaners and rid myself of the garbage I'd accumulated since that day at the Civic Center. What was today? Tuesday? Crystal's burial day.

I shook my head quickly trying to clear it, then turned the ignition and waited a count of ten before turning on the air-conditioning. I stuck my head in front of the blast that came out of the dash. For a brief moment, it seemed like a cool, crisp day. On the drive home, something in my head that I choose to call Crystal spoke to me. What she said was "Shit. Don't pretend for me, Sydney. It's all a bunch of shit."

* * *

When the kids and I arrived at the funeral home, I noticed there weren't many cars. I hoped we were early and that more people than the smattering I was looking at would show up. My watch told me we were right on time.

Harry and Bryant is a converted antebellum home with traditional white columns, a slate porch, and a circular drive lined in perfectly pruned boxwood. Its formal first-floor rooms are where they lay out their clients for viewing, an activity Crystal didn't get and wouldn't have wanted. The rooms, however, are exquisite with narrow oak floors, fireplaces, wide moldings, and expansive windows.

The basement is quite different: wall-to-wall carpet covers the cement. Musty floral odor. Artificial light. Services are held here for people who don't belong to a church. Crystal didn't.

The kids and I sat toward the back on the right. Her parents and brother, Curt, sat in the front on the left. If they looked over their shoulders, I wanted them to see someone. I closed my eyes and squeezed the kids' hands. I talked silently to God about Crystal, about her true self, about His wisdom and ability to see through us to the children we still are in His eyes. I felt dishonest, a huckster. It was between God and Crystal. She could take care of herself on this one. Who did I think I was?

I opened my eyes and noticed the small chapel filling with people. Gordon S., Ann H., Susan R., and several people with them whose names I didn't know sat in front of us. I turned to my left and saw other AA people filling the rows behind the Simmonses. With the lack of windows and basement smell, Crystal's funeral could have been an

AA meeting. I smiled in gratitude at my friends and the irony they brought with them.

The minister, I noticed, was an assistant from one of the many Myers Park churches. I'd seen him preside here before for deceased who didn't belong anywhere. As he was about to speak, Fred and Sally entered a side door toward the front of the chapel. Only the kids and I registered shock since no one else in the room knew who they were. The Simmonses slid over as if the entrance was planned. Sally sat beside Curt, and Fred sat on the outside.

The minister nodded at them, first the Simmonses, then at Fred, and began. I hated every minute of Crystal's funeral. The minister didn't know her. I'd be willing to bet he'd never even met her. I resented everything he said about butterflies, ships on horizons, and sleep; about Jesus preparing rooms and the valley of the shadow of death. I wanted to hear him talk about "the presence of mine enemies," for at Crystal's funeral, that was surely the case. Fred, who if not her murderer physically, surely killed her spirit. Sally, who had spent these past six months telling me what a lush and a whore my friend was. The two of them sat there as honorees in grief and remembrance, noble and long-suffering. I even saw Sally squeeze Curt's shoulder as he cried.

By the time the service had ended, I'd built up so much resentment, I needed an AA meeting. Neither Joan, nor George junior, nor I spoke as we walked to the car. "I'm so sorry, Crystal," I said under my breath.

Back at the office later that morning, I learned Sally had not found her mother's diamond ring. In fact, the jewelry box itself was missing. She had enjoyed herself with the

Simmonses, however, and found herself particularly fond of Curt. As if I hadn't noticed at the funeral.

Sally has never married, probably never will, but has been in love with a different man at least every two weeks for the five years I've known her.

"He's a wonderful person," she said. "A New York stockbroker. Not married. Can you believe he doesn't even drink?"

"Unlike his sister in so many ways," I said. In spite of my determination to keep my resentments to myself and work through them privately, the sarcasm came through.

Sally ignored my comment, didn't even look at me. She was into her typing. I stood behind her back and watched her type billboard orders for Miller and Associates.

"How are Crystal's parents today?" I asked.

"Mrs. Simmons has cried pretty much all last night and today. You know what, Sydney? They're withholding their judgment of Freddie. Isn't that bighearted?"

I watched Sally as she typed and realized that her mood always came through in her strokes. Today she was emphatic and it showed in the exclamation point she typed right after Allen Teague.

"Take that exclamation point off the billboard order, Sally," I said pointing to her screen. "You've got to learn to keep your mood from affecting your typing."

Hart sat on the love seat and smirked at the two of us. "Can we have a meeting?" he asked. "I'm beginning to feel there's a lot of work to do that's hiding inside your head, Sydney." He pointed at his own silky thinning hair as he said it.

I'd forgotten momentarily about having two rush jobs to get out this week. If I could get this real estate thing off my mind, I still ought to be able to write all the copy and get it to Hart in plenty of time for art.

"Let me make two quick phone calls," I said. "And Sally, hold those media orders for Miller and Associates until I tell you to release them."

I closed my office door, something I rarely do in front of my staff. It took two or three attempts to get through to Bishop Cates. I thought it more likely they had eliminated lines than they were overwhelmed with business. Barbara's receptionist said she'd called in sick this morning.

"What's wrong with her, do you know? I was with her last night."

"She sounded all stuffed up like she had a cold. Would you like her voice mail?"

"No. I'll call her at home."

The machine picked up at her house. I decided she could be sleeping. "Barbara," I began matter-of-factly, "I'm getting ready to call Detective Thurgood about the problem with Multiple Listing. I wondered if you had any fresh thoughts on it before I do." I waited a few seconds in case she was screening her calls before picking up. When she didn't break in, I added, "I hope you feel better. Get some rest and call me when you want to talk."

The second call was to Thurgood. He wasn't in either.

"It's extremely urgent that I speak with Detective Thurgood," I said to the operator. "Is there any way you can reach him?"

"Who'd you say this is?" she asked.

"Just a friend. But I have to talk to him about police business. It's really very important."

"Who's this?" She sounded irritated.

When I told her, she said, "You've been added to his

list. I can try him on his car phone and have him call you." I felt I'd given the right question on *Jeopardy!*

"What list?" I asked.

A slight hesitation. "His personal list," she said slowly, then laughed. "You're right up there with his mother and his veterinarian. He added you yesterday."

After thanking her, I hung up and sat there flattered for a full minute. When's the last time I'd been on a man's personal list? Maybe never, I decided.

Sally, Hart, and I sat around my conference table, the two of them each with legal pads; I with a hastily thrown-together file on the fire campaign. I couldn't find my notes on the Textile Museum tourism.

I talked about the museum first, the problems I'd encountered with its curator and the need to visually simplify the materials we produce to combat the actuality of clutter inside the museum itself. "If we can come up with one strong visual and copy concept this week, I think we can get away with putting off the actual work until next week." They both nodded and took notes. "Hart, let's you and I work on this separately and simultaneously. The first one to come up with a concept, let the other know. How's that sound?" I was groping for a way to get the work out.

"What about the fire ads?" Hart had eased himself down into his chair and crossed one leg over the other so that his right foot lay sideways on his left knee, thereby serving as a table for his legal pad.

I sat up straight in response. We were a finely tuned balancing act, Hart and I. "That's going to be the problem this week. We're going to have to go ahead and buy the media, then deliver the ads when they're ready."

"God, I hate that," Hart said from his slouched position. "We're stuck with the bills if we can't deliver on time. I hate to go into these buys backwards."

"Can't be helped," I clipped. "You sound like you don't trust our ability to deliver, Hart." I shook my finger. "Shame on you. I'll sleep here if I have to. You ought to know that by now." He studied his fingernails.

It would take Sally the rest of the day to work out the media buys for the fire campaign. Then she'd spend all day tomorrow typing up the orders. I would have hated her job if it had been mine, but she was turned on by deadlines as much as I was.

When we were clear on what each of us needed to do, I poured myself a cup of coffee. Hart still looked worried, but I knew that he liked to fret as much as Sally and I liked the pressure. "Why don't the three of us do a late lunch today?" I asked. "We can give each other progress reports."

Hart sat immobile.

"It's on Allen Teague," I added. "Two o'clock. Snack till then."

He looked at his watch and raised those haughty eyebrows. "That gives us each about two hours to work. We can barely get started." If he didn't watch it, Hart would be in an advanced state of anal retention by the time he was forty.

"Can Freddie come along?" Sally asked sheepishly. "I sort of promised him we'd have lunch today."

"Some business lunch," Hart intoned.

"If he can let us work, he's welcome. You'll have to tell him that, Sally. He'll take it wrong from me."

Hart combined a sigh with a groan and unfolded the

table that was his legs. I was relieved when he'd marched back up the steps to his lair.

Sally reappeared in my office doorway within thirty seconds of having left it. Her perky demeanor in check, she said with a slight stutter: "Detective Thurgood's in the reception room." Panic raced through her eyes, and she put a hand to her stomach. She whispered, "He must have been out there during our meeting."

I whispered back: "Why are you whispering? We don't have anything to hide. None of us. Do we?" I walked over to join her just inside my office door.

She continued in a whisper: "I mentioned Fred. I asked if he could eat with us, remember?"

"So?" I whispered. "We all have to eat, don't we? Get a grip, Sally. Thurgood's human."

He was studying our awards wall, a space found in every agency no matter how large or small. His back was to me, so I cleared my throat. He turned quickly. Not just his head, as I would turn, but his entire six-foot-six-inch frame. Instinctively, I knew he had been trained to react fully like that. His smile was just as quick, the green of his eyes disappearing as his lips turned upward.

"I hope I'm not interrupting. I got a message you called." He walked over to my office door and briefly touched my hand with his.

Sally stood frozen beside me as if in a police lineup. She seemed to be awaiting her turn to be called out.

"You remember Tom Thurgood, don't you, Sally?" I said. "You should see him at the net on the tennis court." This is merely a person, I wanted to scream to her. Finally she spilled her coffee, a very hot cup, on her open-toed sandal, and the pain brought her to action.

I closed my office door for the second time this morning and apologized to Tom for Sally's behavior.

"Don't do that," he said as he pulled a conference chair out from behind the table and sat. "Don't apologize for her. Most people react that way around cops. Even people whose brothers have not been charged with murder."

"You're too good," I said as I pulled a chair out at the end of the rectangular table. "I'd be tempted to arrest people who treat me like that."

He gazed at me with genuine affection, then cocked his head to one side. "No you wouldn't," he said. "You'd get used to it just as I have." He folded his large hands on top of one another. "What can I do for you? I was in the neighborhood when I got the message."

"I think I've learned something very important in connection with the murders of those four women. All their houses were for sale when they were robbed and killed." I took a deep breath and watched him take this in.

"Also," I continued, "at least thirty robberies have occurred at houses for sale in the last three and a half months. All the houses—all the murders—were part of the Multiple Listing Service." His eyes turned from a bright emerald to a deep forest-green as I talked. He did not interrupt but listened patiently. "Tom, I'm afraid something terrible is happening."

He nodded, then pierced me with his dark eyes. "You have a lot of information," he said softly. "We've been going back over every robbery labeled unforced entry and coming up with a whole rash of them this summer. If the house was for sale, it would be hidden somewhere in the report narrative . . ." He threaded one set of fingers into the other, like the beginning of that childhood rhyme about churches and steeples.

I told him about what I'd learned from Barbara. Again I called her office while Thurgood paced beside me. When the receptionist told me Barbara had still not come in, I asked to speak to Oscar. As I expected, he was less than pleased when I told him Barbara had showed me the drop-out program last night.

"Look, Sydney," Oscar barked, "that probably happens all the time. Charlotte has about five hundred robberies a month. So what if ten of 'em happen to houses on the market?" He laughed derisively, a blustery self-confidence easing its way into his voice. As he talked I handed the phone to Thurgood, who caught the end of Oscar's lecture.

"Mr. Cates, this is Detective Thurgood with the Charlotte Police Department. I'd like to take a look at this computer program Ms. Teague is talking about." He smiled at me, then raised his eyes to my ceiling while Oscar backpedaled and offered to run a printout down to the Law Enforcement Center. I motioned that I wanted to speak with Oscar again, so he handed the phone back when he was through.

"Oscar, I'm worried about Barbara. Is she okay?"

There was a long silence on his end. Finally, he said, "She'll be okay. Some kind of flu." Then he hung up. No good-bye, no nothing. I stared at the receiver.

Thurgood took it from my hand and hung it up. "Sometimes it helps that people fear me. It evens out in the long run."

Before Thurgood left, he promised to let me know when there was something he could share with me. After he was gone, I thought about what he had actually said. Lots of words. No real promises.

* * *

I wasn't going to obligate little Miller and Associates to $60,000 in media placements until I knew the repercussions of Thurgood's findings on Charlotte's real estate market. If it was coming to a standstill no matter what we did, the ad spending would sink Jean quickly.

I buzzed Sally and told her I did not want any more calls until we broke for lunch. That gave me only about an hour and a half, but it was enough to get me started on ideas for TV fire spots. If we had time to create visuals in the studio, we could take existing pictures of Hugo destruction, including and especially the trees, and set it afire along with a voice-over. If we didn't have time for the visual, we'd just do sound effects with the voice-over. I decided the sound effects alone would be more powerful. Rain, then wind merging to the rush of fire wind, and finally the crackling sound of forest fires. I had written the script and had my list of sound effects by the time Sally opened my door.

"Here," I said, handing my scribbled pages to her. "It's the fire campaign TV and radio scripts. Use the same words; just change the format for the different media."

She said, "Wow! I'm impressed. You sure can squeeze it out when you need to."

"Is Fred here yet?" I asked.

"I sent him upstairs to get Hart," she said. "Please be sweet to him, Sydney. This whole thing's really hard on him."

Were my feelings that transparent with regard to him? I guess they were. I've been told they come through no matter what I say or don't say. "I'll try, Sally." I looked at her pleading blue eyes. "I really will," I added, and her expression loosened. "Remember though that this is a business lunch. We've got work to get out, and he'll have to bear with us on that."

She was smiling now. "He knows. I told him. He just said he wants to feel like a normal human being going to lunch with other normal human beings."

I grinned. "Are you sure he's going with the right people?"

"I'm going to find some photos of Hugo damage anyway," Hart said as he chewed a slice of hard-boiled egg off his spinach salad. "I'll need them for billboards so I may as well see if they'll work better on TV. Right?" He dabbed at his chin with the wide paper napkin. His attitude had improved now that he believed we might actually be able to meet our deadline.

"I forgot about billboards for a minute," I said as I chuckled and looked to Sally and Hart for reassurance. "That's why there are three brains at this table, right?"

"Sorry, Fred," I said when I saw him flinch. "Three advertising brains. Be proud yours hasn't sunk so low."

He grinned, the pomposity coming through again as if I'd truly given him some kind of compliment. We were finishing our lunch at a nice little cafe called Mykonos on East Boulevard. We were the only people who'd chosen to eat outside here today, so our sometimes loud artistic differences hadn't bothered anyone but Fred.

Again the temperature was in the mid-eighties with humidity at least that high. I noticed that Hart's hair was thinning so much, I could see the perspiration beading between his wispy strands. I had been wrong about the sky being pale gray by now. It was milky white, as if the color had been fried completely out of it.

Mykonos is, as you would guess, a Greek-owned restaurant. The Zrakas family has this one as well as a sports bar on the north end of town near UNC-C. There are two small ethnic communities in Charlotte, Greek and the newer Vietnamese. In and around East Boulevard is the center of the Greek population, since a large Orthodox church consumes an entire block of it. Until recently the Greeks even owned Italian restaurants here. I just wish Jim Zrakas would put more Greek foods on the menu. The Greek salad I had eaten for lunch was too common to count. I told him so when he stopped by the table.

"Don't tell him how to conduct his business, Sydney," Fred said with a smirk. "You ought to stick to advertising and leave everything else alone."

A little over twenty-four hours out of jail, it seemed Fred's ego was bouncing back nicely. In my opinion he was not acting like the human being Sally said he would like to be, so I decided to stop the consideration I'd been affording him and get some answers to my questions.

"Fred," I began, "why did you lie to Detective Thurgood about when you arrived at Crystal's house Thursday morning?"

He didn't have much of an upper lip to start with, but it dissolved completely into a straight line. "I didn't think it would look good," he spit out while meeting my eyes.

"No, I don't think it did, did it? What were you doing? Taking an inventory of all your missing precious things?" Sally put her hand on my forearm, but I raised my hand and pushed my mildewed hair off my face.

He didn't answer, just continued to stare at me.

I said, "What about the night before? Why didn't you tell Thurgood you were at the house then? Huh?"

He dropped his eyes to the table and searched frantically for something to look at. Finally, he picked up the salt shaker and began shining its glass contours with his thumb. "That's none of your business," he said.

"You fought with her." I could hear my voice rising, and Sally's hand was back on my arm. "You called her a slut." I watched him as what I had said sank in.

Hart looked uncomfortable.

Sally said, "Sydney, Freddie would never talk like that."

Fred smirked at her.

"You came to the house and forced Mickey Sutton to leave."

He dropped the salt shaker, then dabbed the fallen white crystals with his forefinger.

"Why are you doing this, Sydney?" Sally asked, on the verge of tears. "Fred's cooperating with the—"

"She was a slut," Fred blurted. "Ask Sutton about that night. He came and went more than I did." He gritted his teeth, wiped the salt off the table onto his sister's lap. "She was a goddamn drunken slut, but I didn't kill her."

Nobody spoke to me as we walked back to the office. I suppose I was being punished. I had, after all, ruined everybody's lunch. I was uncomfortable enough, physically and mentally, to not care. But I did care about Crystal. Just because something's the truth doesn't mean it has to be told. Fred Ball could go to hell for all I cared.

Cottage with personality.
Perfect for couple or singles. ML

Guess how many discoveries are accidents. I mean like mistakes. A whole bunch by my calculations. The kind of situation where a guy is doing one thing, something goes wrong and he has to improvise to get the job done. We got the ice-cream cone that way. Guy runs out of cups so he grabs a waffle and the next thing you know we have the ice-cream cone.

The first death was that way. Pure accident. Pulled my mask off. Thought I'd stop, I guess, since she saw me. My hands acted on their own, went for her throat. Squeezed until her eyes stopped staring at me. I felt so relaxed when it was over, so certain that I had helped make it all better. Not perfect, nothing ever is. But I had done my part.

From then on I knew I would kill them. I knew I could go without the mask, that I could enter with a certain honesty I hadn't had before. Yes, honesty. The honesty to be who I am.

I can't remember a time when I have felt useful like this. It's like I've found my calling, my purpose. Like a secret code has finally been discovered making all the pieces fit for the first time.

14

THE ONLY ADVANTAGE TO HAVING THE PEOPLE you work with mad at you is that you get a lot accomplished in the isolation and silence. That afternoon I wrote the fire billboard copy and the general distribution brochures, which were basically Smokey the Bear rewrites.

I had only three interruptions all afternoon, two of which I instigated myself. One was a call from Gus Georges wanting to unload a storage bin full of textile ad products that had not been imprinted. I could have however many items I wanted below cost. Some York County mill, just over the South Carolina line, had gone out of business, and Gus had bought the residue. As many T-shirts, sweatshirts, and hats as I had to buy every year, it was worth my while to at least take a look. I agreed to drive down to the storage facility with him later in the week.

The second call I made. Jean Miller could not understand, at first, my advice to withhold her ad placements.

The conversation was difficult for both of us since I didn't feel free to tell her what Thurgood was looking into.

"You're going to have to trust me on this, Jean," I told her.

"You know I trust you," Jean said. "I just wish you'd give me a reason for not placing all those ads now. People don't know I exist."

And they won't care that you exist, I thought, if Multiple Listing is shut down and potential customers find out why. "Like I told you, I'll be able to get all the information I need by tomorrow or Thursday at the latest. We'll talk then."

She was silent, weighing either the wisdom or the truth of what I had been telling her. Finally she sighed and said: "Okay. Call me as soon as you find out whatever it is you need to find out."

Then I called Barbara Cates at home again. As it had earlier, the answering machine picked up. I almost did not leave a second message but decided to go ahead since I wanted her to know I really was worried about her. Two messages show more concern than one, I reasoned.

"Barbara," I began, "it's Sydney again. I know you're at home. I've talked with Oscar, and he's taking your drop-out program down to the Law Enforcement Center. If you're there—"

"I'm here, Sydney." She sounded as if she were in some kind of tunnel. "Not in one piece, but here."

"Are you sick? Oscar said you had the flu."

"No. Not any kind of flu," she sniffled. "I've been on one of my crying jags." She cleared her throat. "I've been to my therapist this morning. He changed my medication." She laughed halfheartedly. "Let's hope it works . . . for everybody around me as well as myself."

I didn't know what to say. I never do when someone brings her therapy into conversations as if discussing menstrual cramps. My mental health reference is AA, so I said what I usually say in these circumstances. "First things first, Barbara. You've got to take care of yourself."

"I'm trying," she said weakly.

"Have you talked with Oscar?" I asked, afraid that I might upset her if the question was more pointed.

"He left a message while we were at the doctor."

"So you know the information is getting to the police?"

She took a deep breath. "Yes, I know."

"Is someone with you?"

"Buddy stayed out of school today to take me to the doctor."

"Good for him," I said, not knowing if I meant it or not. My opinion is that kids should be in school.

"Maybe it'll all be over now," she said.

I thought it was probably just beginning, but I didn't tell her that. Instead I told her to rest and we'd talk again later.

George junior's team was playing a soccer match at five, so I wanted to be sure I could get out of the office by four-thirty. I didn't have to drive him, thank God. The game was on a Dilworth field, one belonging to a Catholic school, but used by independent soccer leagues. George junior could ride his bike with another Kingston Avenue boy who was on the same team.

Hart came downstairs at four-fifteen to see how I'd progressed. When I smugly told him I'd finished both the billboards and brochures, he congratulated me. He'd been in a creative zone himself, locating all the photos he needed as well as sound effects. We were going to be able to do this after all.

"What about general press releases and a feature story?" he asked casually.

Damn. I'd forgotten the need for that kind of ancillary material. We didn't have to create them as part of this campaign, but it always helped. "I'm coming back tonight to do them," I said, and resigned myself to the need.

"Good," he said. "I've booked the studio for tomorrow; then we'll be done. Had any ideas on the Textile Museum campaign? I haven't."

"Me neither," I said. Hart was cleaning his fingernails with his X-Acto, so I couldn't look into his eyes. The little noises he was making with his tongue and the roof of his mouth were enough to convey his feelings, however. "I like those sound effects, Hart. Maybe we can talk someone into building a campaign around them, something like 'DON'T JUST DO IT!' "

He put down his X-Acto and finally looked at me. "I know you think I'm negative." He smiled. "I prefer to call myself realistic. One of these days we're going to miss a deadline, and then what are you going to do? Quit? You have too much vested in these deadlines. You're like a mountain climber; you keep looking to set new records, climb new peaks. Why can't you ever say you'll just do the best you can?"

Usually the deadline talk around Allen Teague is light-hearted, but every once in a while Hart turns serious on me like this. To be honest, it made me uncomfortable, which personal history tells me means it probably hit some truth.

I exhaled and more air came out my mouth than I thought possible. Had I been holding my breath? I pulled out the chair beside him at my conference table, sat down, and spread both hands on the table as if I were about to make a mold of them. "Because the question they always ask me is not if I can do my best, but if I can do it by a specific date. Specific questions require specific answers. My only options are yes or no."

He bit the side of his lip, then rolled his tongue against the spot, not a sensual movement at all but rather the kind of tongue movement that indicates deep thought.

"Hart, I don't mean to put you under a strain. Believe it or not, I try to absorb most of the pressure myself." He was looking at me now. "Some things I don't even tell you about."

"I'm not worried about myself," he said. "It's you who worries me."

"Don't you think I'd complain if any of it bothered me?" I raised my eyebrows in search of some kind of understanding from Hart.

He smiled; only it was the kind of smile one makes at a small child who has done something foolish. We would never see eye to eye on this subject.

"What was the point about Mickey Sutton at lunch today?" The question seemed to come out of nowhere, but I guess it had been on his mind for hours.

"I think maybe he's a suspect too."

"Would help things out a bit if he did it, wouldn't it?" Hart had a skewed view of the world, and I agreed with him most of the time.

It really is true. We measure the quality of our efforts by the outcomes they produce.

George junior's team had lost, but he played well. I

was pleased for him but showed what I hoped was the appropriate disappointment at the loss. I hate to admit it, but his playing well made me almost as happy as I would have felt if the team had won. George junior, on the other hand, assumed he'd played poorly since they had ended on the short stick. Sometimes luck makes us look good; sometimes it's the inferiority of our opponents. Today, George junior had made some brilliant saves, but none of that mattered to anyone. Except to his mom and his big sister.

I insisted we eat out. In celebration, I said, of how well he had played. What I did not tell either of the kids was that I had failed to grocery-shop at lunch today, and all that I could have fixed us would have been potato salad, scalloped potatoes, and a baked potato on the side.

George junior chose the Outback Steak House on East Boulevard. I've always loved the Australian atmosphere; it reminds me of a fifties western with class.

Even on positive topics, like how well George junior had played today, my kids tend to bicker. This one had started with Joan complimenting George junior. She did not need to add, however, that she thought his coach was awful.

"Shut up, Joan," he snarled. "You don't know anything about soccer."

She grunted, then looked toward me. "Tell him, Mom, that he doesn't know how to take a compliment. Why's he taking his bad mood out on me?" She humphed a little when she had finished, feigning a hurt too deep for words.

"It wasn't a pure compliment, Joan," I said. "You should have stopped with the first remark and not added the second. You can beef about your own volleyball coach, if you want, but not about George's soccer coach."

"How come?" She sounded somewhere between indignant and enlightened. "Whose rule is that?"

"It's mine," I said brightly. "You can criticize your own anything, but not someone else's." She was listening closely now, as was George junior. "For instance, you can criticize your own mother but not George junior's."

George junior and Joan looked at each other, then at me. Simultaneously, they broke into giggles and refrains of "Oh Mom." They were allies again, siblings with the mutual fact of a strange mother.

As we were finishing our Goolagong pies, I told them that I had to return to the office tonight to get a little work done. I would be home before bedtime.

In the car, Joan said, "We've got a volleyball match tomorrow, Mom. Can you come?"

"Home or away?" I asked.

"Away. At East."

I told her I didn't think I could since we were so busy at the office. Away games usually took an additional hour to attend when I counted the driving time.

"It's just as well. We're going to get our butts kicked. Cindi's out sick. Some mysterious illness."

"You don't know what's wrong with her?" I asked.

"No one knows. How could I know? Her mom won't even let the coach talk to her. You know she won't let me."

The thunderstorms were popping up with such frequency that I couldn't tell by the smell whether one had just ended or one was about to begin. The likelihood was both. This time of year the humidity builds to a point of saturation so that the smell is that of a dirty wet sponge. At its worst, breathing is more like swimming in a blocked-up kitchen sink. After the thunder and the lightning, with the inevitable downpour, the unmistakable scent of sulfur fills the air, cleansing everything. These storms were different. Nothing ever got clean. The smell was wet matchsticks.

One of these storms was building as I walked from my house to the Allen Teague office. Kingston used to be a through street, paralleling East Boulevard all the way to its intersection with South Boulevard. In the seventies, when Charlotte drug dealing was in its infancy, neighborhood leaders petitioned to block off Kingston at Euclid before it reached South Boulevard. The reasoning, of course, was that dealers would move down Kingston from seedy South Boulevard, and, if that route were shut off, the neighborhood would be spared. At the time the dead end was created, the neighborhood association bought two vacant lots at the blockade point and fashioned an overly landscaped park complete with benches and even a goldfish pool. Twenty years later the landscape had overgrown so much that city police cited the park as a haven for drug dealers. The best-laid plans, right?

I did see one hypodermic on the way, just on the edge by Euclid. Taking out every other bush in the park might help the neighborhood, but it wouldn't curb the drug trade. I had grown to believe that it was here to stay in one form or another. Nothing we could do would make it go away. Some forces are just too powerful. Like the weather. Like drugs. I wrapped a Kleenex around the hypodermic and put it carefully in my pocketbook, a habit from when the kids were smaller and in this park daily.

Hell, my neighbors' kids still were. I turned left toward the artificial lights and street noise of East Boulevard.

Allen Teague's driveway enters from East Boulevard but widens to a large parking area in the back where we can put up to eight cars. Since our old house is the second one from Euclid, I sometimes cut through the backyard next door rather than walk the rest of the way to East Boulevard. That's what I did tonight.

I think I saw the van even before I stepped into the yard next door. A pale fuzzy rectangle against the black asphalt. No stars, no moon. A dirty sponge of a sky. An unmistakable shape behind Allen Teague. A small light shone through an upstairs back window, but I saw no others from where I stood in the neighbor's yard.

The likelihood was that whoever was inside my office could not hear me since the central air was on, and all windows were shut, but I took my shoes off anyway so that I could hear myself think rather than the snapping of twigs. I put my short heels into my pocketbook with the hypodermic and, still in the neighbor's yard, tiptoed up to the front. A small pinprick of light darted past Hart's side window, then was gone. Thirty seconds later, it reappeared at his front window.

I circled the building slowly. All my ground-floor windows were closed and seemed untampered with. When I reached the front porch, the door there appeared secure as well. As I turned to go around to the back, the sky turned white with lightning. Down in the sweet autumn clematis, something shiny danced on the edge of my perspective. Like an empty casket, the supralock lay open.

I needed Tom Thurgood. If I went back home to call, whoever this was would be gone before the police could respond. If only I'd bought that pocket cellular instead of the one mounted inside the car.

As long as the intruder was in Hart's room at the front of the house, I could enter through the back door without being heard. A bolt of lightning cracked the sky wide open, streaming a second or two of warped daylight on the van. The color flashed white, then silver as the fireworks lost their power and faded to mist again.

The rain began before I could find my key. In frustration, I tried the door gently just in case he had entered from this side. It moved, and fear punched me so hard that I stepped back. Again I considered going home. The fear was paralyzing me.

I lifted my face to what was now a downpour and hoped it could beat the fear out of me. I sloshed slowly into the tiny hallway, knowing that a water-logged tiptoe is not silent. Except for random flashes of lightning, the first floor was dark. But I didn't need the light. This was my office after all. Dammit. My office.

The pantyhose on my thighs reached out for each other like two hydrogen molecules seeking oxygen. They rubbed while I crept through the downstairs toward a phone. When another sheet of light spread out across my desk, I saw my work stacks in disarray.

I whispered to the emergency operator that a robbery was in progress. I gave her the address, but when she wanted me to spell my name a second time, I hung up. My life was more important than her paperwork.

I heard my old stairs squeak the way they did when someone was on them. A flashlight beamed against the walls of my office, bumping up and down with the rhythm of someone descending the stairs. No matter how hard I tried, I couldn't will myself to stop shaking. I backed off from the side of my desk into a corner. If lightning flashed again, I didn't want to be lit up.

He stood in the doorway to my office and gave the room a cursory glance. Obviously he did not see me. He walked quickly to my desk, restacked the piles of work.

I pulled one shoe and the hypodermic from my pocketbook, then let the pocketbook slide to the floor. Bad idea. The shoe inside sounded like a tap shoe as it struck the hardwood. His head turned.

"You're a goddamn worm, Mickey," I said.

The body turned as well. An arrogant smirk streaked across his face accompanied by a nasal sound indicating his irritation. "Insidious Sydney. You have a nice little setup here."

"What are you looking for?" Amazingly, the fear that had almost kept me out of my own offices had completely dissolved.

"Textiles," he said as if we were at a Chamber meeting. "Anything to do with textiles. I can't get European accounts without a textile."

Now I knew where my Textile Museum file had gone. Mickey had been here before tonight.

"Have you done this before? Have you broken into my offices before?" I couldn't believe this conversation.

"Now, don't go jumping to the wrong conclusions, Sydney babe. I didn't break in here, did I? Nobody'll find any evidence of that. Nobody'll even know I was here." He took a step or two toward me.

I tried to back up, but the wall would not budge.

"Is this what Crystal was trying to warn me about, Mickey? That you were using your wife's supralock combination to break into my office?"

He smiled and stopped. "Good old Crystal. You know,

I don't think I ever saw her sober? Why are you so loyal to such a drunk, Sydney?"

"You haven't answered my question, Mickey. Did you use Gloria's combination to get in here? Did you brag about it to Crystal?"

"You think that's worth killing her for?" He took a step closer.

"Did you have your van with you that night?"

He even laughed. "I drive a Mercedes, babe. You ought to know that."

"That's not a Mercedes in my driveway, Mickey. There was a van like yours at Crystal's that night."

He played with his belt buckle. "Look, babe. I only take the van on business."

"Like tonight?"

The smile widened, and he stepped closer.

The last place I needed to be was in this corner. I moved a couple of steps along the wall toward the door.

A siren blared. Then another.

He shook his head back and forth, then his forefinger in the same motion. "Now, why'd you want to go and call the police, Sydney? I'm going to have to leave you now. Nobody's going to believe you." He walked quickly toward the back of the house, headed for his van, I assumed.

I was a couple of steps behind him when I called out: "What about the supralock? It's wide open. The police can find out through Multiple Listing that Gloria's combination opened it."

He stopped and stared at me.

I continued. "There's a roll of paper in there telling them as if it were your signature that Gloria Sutton's code was used to get into this office."

He hesitated, then turned and ran to the front door.

The sirens were on our block now.

As he leaned over to insert the key back into the supra-lock housing in an effort to undo his imprint, I stuck him in the rear with the hypodermic. He screamed, then straightened up, hands on his butt. That's when I screamed, "Take this, babe," and knocked him in the head with my low heel.

I was on an adrenaline high, invigorated by the fight and gaining momentum to strike again. His face turned toward me in agony; then the agony turned to rage as he raised the flashlight to the sky. Before I lost consciousness, I saw an ever-widening plate of pure light swim toward my eyes.

15

SOMETHING SCREECHING AND SCREAMING broke into my unconsciousness, dragging me upward and out of it. The unmistakable wail of an ambulance, bumping and racing the few short blocks to Carolina Medical Center. I opened my eyes for a brief second to a blurry film that was surely blood, then sank again into my deep black space where everything was smooth and nothing encroached on my serenity.

The light that woke me the second time was just as garish and intrusive as the screaming of the sirens. Had Mickey stabbed me in the head? Why was this pain so sharp, so unrelentingly pointed above my right eye? Then pricks, why the pricks? Like briars from a blackberry bush, not rounded or fully formed like the thorns of a rose. Why was Mickey wrapping my head in blackberry branches? My crown of thorns. What had he done to me? Where had he taken me? A roadside. A briar patch. No one would ever find me.

The voices. Whose were these casual voices talking to

each other as if I were not down here in this blackberry thicket? Out of nowhere, strange insects came, bringing a tingling numbness, crawling and spreading out from my eyelids into my scalp. I tried to stop their approach. I wiggled my eyebrows.

A hand rested on my cheek, and a soothing female voice said: "Try to keep your eyebrows still, Ms. Teague. The doctor is sewing your head."

The last time anyone had sewn my head together was in junior high. Girls' softball. I was the catcher; Barbie Bishop at bat. She said I'd stood up just as she swung. Why would I do that? I couldn't remember.

I lay in a long hallway on a gurney, one gurney among six or seven others in various stages of pain and wakefulness. We were pushed to the sides so that doctors and nurses could stroll unobstructed through their livelihood. I was not a satisfied customer, but no one seemed to notice in spite of my frequently squawked statement: "I'd like to leave, please."

I watched a towering figure come down our hallway. He paused at each stretcher and stooped to peer at the victim. We recognized each other at the same moment.

I said to Thurgood: "Are you looking for me? I sure hope so."

"There you are. How do you feel?"

I winced and sat up holding my head with both hands.

"Did you get Mickey Sutton?" I asked with all my strength.

"Don't worry about Sutton. He's downtown now."

The room began to turn, and I groaned involuntarily.

"I can imagine," he said as he steadied me with his large hands. "Twelve stitches and a concussion. Not a bad one, according to the doctor, but they'd like to keep you overnight for observation. They're getting you a room now."

I waited for the nausea to subside before I answered him. "I can't stay here. I told the kids I'd be home before bedtime."

"What time is bedtime?" he asked.

"Eleven." I slowly swallowed the bile that had inched its way up my throat.

He looked at his watch, then carefully at me. "What if I spend the night at your house? It's ten-thirty now. You can call Joan and George and tell them you've had an accident."

I was touched. I truly was. No man I knew, not even the kids' father, had ever shown that kind of concern. I didn't know what to say.

He misinterpreted my dumbfoundedness. "I can sleep on the couch."

"No. No," I said as I touched the thick bandage on my forehead. It was still numb. "I'm just so grateful. I can call a friend if you—"

He put his finger to his pursed lips. "You rest. It's done. I'll get us a phone over here so that you can talk to your kids."

I didn't give them any details since they would worry unnecessarily. Tomorrow was soon enough for that. That I'd had an accident at the office and hit my head was frightening enough for two kids with only one functional parent. They knew and liked Thurgood. This would work okay.

"Thank you," I said steadily as he took the phone from my sheeted lap.

"You'd do the same" was his matter-of-fact reply.

A sharp pain began to throb under my bandage, and it must have shown in my eyes. He put his hands on my shoulders and eased me back down.

"Do you need anything else?" he asked. His tone of voice was soft and soothing, as if he were afraid I might shatter at a normal one. I might have.

"A file," I croaked. "On my desk. It says 'fire campaign.' " He squinted his eyes but not in the smile I'd come to know. "I need a legal pad and a pen too," I added.

"Are you insane?"

I thought this was rhetorical, but I answered anyway. Just in case. "No," I said with all the strength I had left. "Advertising. Deadline."

While he made the quick trip to my office, an orderly lost no time pushing me to my room. His gusto was such that we could have at least placed in a race for this sort of event. Part of my stomach had been left on the elevator, but it caught up with us just as he was lifting me to my bed. The Outback cheeseburger, in all its ground glory, hit the floor and splattered his shoes. I felt very groggy.

"I'm so sorry," I mumbled. "We were doing so well, you and I."

He seemed to clean it up in record speed as well. As I continued to mutter to him, he muttered to himself as if I were not present.

When he had been gone for a minute or two, a nurse appeared in my doorway. White-haired and stocky, with horn-rims, she marched to the end of my bed and put her hands on her hips. "I understand we lost some stomach contents."

"We did?" I asked, since I genuinely didn't know what she was talking about.

She seemed to misread my confusion for sarcasm because the tone of her voice shifted from that of Mary Poppins to Nurse Ratched. "Let's not make it hard on each other, Ms. Teague. You have a concussion, and I have to watch you all night." Her voice made my head hurt. She stared at me closely, then softened a bit—from general to corporal perhaps.

"We can't let you sleep for a while so we'll try to make you as comfortable as possible. I can give you something for the pain, but nothing that'll make you sleep."

I needn't tell her about my alcoholism since her prescription is exactly the same as AA's: Easing pain is okay as long as reality is not altered in any way. Mickey's flashlight sure had altered it for a while, I thought. "How about a couple of aspirin?" I finally asked.

Thurgood returned with the fire file, the legal pad, and a choice of three different pens. When Nurse Ratched protested, he showed his badge and said that I was under orders to write a detailed description of the operations of a drug ring. "She's been undercover," he whispered, and peeked into the hall to make sure that no one had overheard him.

Her eyebrows rose above her horn-rim glasses as she gazed on me with a newly found respect. Bless Thurgood. He had saved me on two fronts tonight—home and hospital.

Throughout the night and early Wednesday morning, I fell into an unnatural pattern of writing, resting, sleeping, and being awakened by the nurse only to start the cycle again. The story I wrote was dark and ominous, the menace of forest fires lurking in my doomsday wording. My head hurt so much at times that I couldn't stand to proof what I had written. I decided to leave it for Sally to clean up. Press releases are supposed to be emotionless statements of fact. I prayed that mine had been as devoid of emotion as I felt when I finished the last one at seven.

Nurse Ratched and I had become friends during the ordeal of our night together. She even fluffed my pillows twice. My secretive celebrity status rubbed off on her, and she performed valiantly for the cause. I even got sips of ginger ale from four o'clock on.

By seven-thirty I was under the pillows by choice. My work done, so was I. Twelve solid hours in the netherworld seemed like what I needed most.

"Can our stomach take a little breakfast?" Her voice was cheery in spite of the double shift she was obviously pulling.

"Our stomach would like to sleep now," I said out of the little hole I'd created for breathing.

She stood steadfast. "That will have to wait until we get home," she said, and I thought for a second she would really go with me. "If we can keep this breakfast down. All of it, mind you. If we can keep it all down, we get to go home."

"And what if we can't?" I asked because, for my part, I wasn't sure we could.

"I call the doctor." It was the first time since last night that she had spoken of herself in the first person singular. I thought it was a good enough sign to go ahead and try breakfast.

It stayed down. Barely.

* * *

Thurgood arrived at eight-thirty just as I was wondering if I'd have to put on my blood-caked khaki shirt. He'd even thought of that, except the dress he'd brought was a black one I reserved for dinner parties and an odd corporate client or two. But how could he know and who was I to complain? I had no plans to stay dressed any longer than it took to drop my work at the office and go home.

In the car, Thurgood began to chuckle. "You got that Mickey Sutton good last night."

My memory was vague at best. "I did?"

"They tell me he's yelling that he'll sue you for shooting him with that needle. When he posted his bail, he said he was going straight to his doctor for an AIDS test."

"God, I hadn't thought about that. I found it on the ground when I was walking to the office."

"Why in hell did you pick it up?"

"It was where the kids play. There's not a mother in Charlotte who wouldn't have picked it up."

"I didn't think it was yours. Mickey told us he'd heard you were on heroin. He would have told us he was in your office to get you off the stuff if he thought it could have saved his ass." Then he chuckled. "Too late to save that, I guess."

"He's right to be concerned about the needle," I said. "Anybody could have used it. It was the first thing my hands touched when I went looking for a weapon. Dammit, I'm sorry about that."

He looked over at me when we stopped for a light. "Don't tell me you're sorry you stuck him? The little prick deserved a lot worse than that. Look what he did to you."

"He'll say he was defending himself, and, you know, he really was. All he was doing was snooping." I laughed. "I was the one who got aggressive." My head hurt when I talked this much. "Maybe I should drop the charges." I looked to Thurgood for reaction, got none. "He was at Crystal's that night."

"We know" was all he said. Thurgood would not comment on Mickey anymore.

He took my work in to Sally while I rested my head against the car window. I had closed my eyes by the time he returned, Sally and Hart both trailing him like faithful retrievers.

"We called the hospital when we got here, but you had been discharged," Sally said. Instead of asking me, she turned to Thurgood, whom I was pleased to see she was treating as a person, and said, "Is she going to be okay?"

"I like it," quipped Hart, pointing to his forehead. "Patches are always mysterious. Even if they don't cover an eye." The art director's view of battery, I thought.

"Thank you," I said, smiling at him. And then to Sally, "Of course I'm going to be okay. I just need some sleep. How did you two know what happened?"

"It made the morning paper. Local section; B4. Across from the paid obituaries where they usually put business news of note."

"I guess it was in a way," I said reflectively. "Business news, that is."

"Competition foiled," said Hart.

"No TV?" I asked.

"Not that we know," they chimed together.

I was thankful for that since neither of my kids nor

their friends read newspapers unless they have an assignment. TV was a different matter. This way I could tell them both about it when they got home from school.

Thurgood insisted on going inside the house with me. In spite of my protests to the contrary, I was less than steady on my feet and grateful for his support, both physical and emotional.

"Get in bed," he said in a voice resembling that of the nurse I'd just left. "I'll bring you some ice water before I leave."

The black dress got slung on my bathroom door with my bra on top of it. I wore my half-slip and underpants into the bed and pulled the sheets up to my chin.

He knocked lightly.

"Come in," I said, feeling, all of a sudden, like a Norwegian virgin on her wedding night.

I sipped the ice water and returned it to my old mahogany bedside table. "You've been wonderful, Tom. I couldn't have asked for a better friend through this."

He was sitting on the edge of my bed. His shoulders sagged. "Is that all?" he asked softly. "You don't think there's more?" He was perfectly at ease with the question he had asked and seemed ready to accept whatever I might say. Except for his shoulders, I would have thought he didn't care.

I was not ready for this question. After all, we had not really even decided on playing tennis together regularly. I sidestepped as best I could. "I can't have this conversation right now. I'm not up to it." I looked from the crumpled spread at the bottom of my bed to his perceptive eyes. "Okay? We'll talk. Just not now."

His eyes disappeared into his smile as he bent forward and kissed me lightly on the lips. When he stood up, he reached into his pants pocket and pulled out my dead bolt key.

"Thought you might be needing this. We lifted it off Mickey Sutton." He put it on the bedside table next to the water.

"That goes in the supralock at the office. Realtors can't get in without it," I said.

He left it on the table and walked toward the bedroom door. "I don't think they'll be using your supralock for a while."

This was what I'd been afraid would happen, why I had urged Jean to delay her advertising. "You obviously studied Barbara's drop-out causes. What do you think is going on?"

"Something very strange" was all he'd say as he closed my bedroom door. I barely heard his car start before I was asleep.

All I remembered of my six-hour nap were fitful awakenings to stabs of pain. So, when I awoke, I stared at a blank spot on the wall for fear of moving an eyeball. Then I carefully pushed my pillows against the headboard and slid myself up to a half-sitting position, where I waited for my forehead's reaction. A dull throb was all that was left, it seemed. I exhaled in gratitude and lit a Vantage in celebration.

The cool hum of my air conditioner in concert with the restorative powers of the cigarette lulled me to a minor trance. The rhythmical pull and push of the act of smoking had been my mantra for years, a medicine much more than a social tool even when it was that, too, twenty years ago. Like the other few who are left, I gradually withdrew the habit from public display until it became a private thing, a personal thing. The same sequence as the Scotch, I thought, for not the first time. I wondered how one reached a bottom on nicotine without its killing them first. I had been convinced I would die from alcohol. Why couldn't I believe it, gut level, with these little things? Part of the answer, I knew, was that I did not feel dead already, the way I had toward the end of the Scotch.

The shower rejuvenated me further in spite of the old shower cap I had pulled down over my forehead to protect my stitches. I washed my hair in the kitchen sink, avoiding my gauzed patch entirely.

Thurgood had left a note on the kitchen counter. "Used some potatoes," it read. "Kids said best hash browns ever had!" All of a sudden, I knew the problem. He was too good for me. How could I involve a man as good as he with a woman like me? My God, he couldn't even recognize a bad marriage when he saw one. I could have written a book on that sordid subject. A kind man with an angel of a dead wife. He had wonderful memories, and they were intact and unspoiled. I could probably destroy those as well.

Five blinks meant five messages on my machine. Since I'd turned off the ringer on my bedroom phone, I never heard a single call while I slept. I stared at the box on my kitchen counter and debated whether or not I wanted to be involved in this day at all.

I never did punch Play but got in the car instead and drove across town to watch Joan play volleyball. George

junior would be home soon, I reasoned. He could re-
trieve the messages for us, and by the time I got any for
me, surely they would have lost their urgency.

Joan had been right. They were getting their rear ends
kicked. Cindi was our setter, the one who sets up everyone else for what is delicately known in volleyball circles
as the kill. The young girl who had replaced her could
not get the ball high enough for the tall girls on the front
row. More often than not, her sets went into the net.

Out of nowhere, Buddy Cates and his mangy-looking
friend, Jake, appeared at the end of the game. As he had
at the game last week, Jake stood off to the side, nervously taking in the crowd and the noise. Buddy worked
the girls again, hugging tightly whomever he could grab
long enough. Joan saw me before he had reached her and
came over to the bleachers.

"What happened to you, Mom?"

I wondered how much truth a teenager really wants, finally deciding that a watered-down truth is preferable to
a full-strength lie.

"Yuk," she commented when I had told her the pertinent parts. She lightly touched my bandages, then said,
"Ouch. Are you okay? Does it hurt?"

"Just a little now. I don't think I can resume jogging
just yet."

We both laughed since she knew as well as I that the last
time I had jogged intentionally was in pursuit of the Hubba
Bubba ice-cream truck attempting to leave the neighborhood without coming to our end.

"I do want to get home, though. We need to stop by
the grocery store on the way."

She grabbed her duffel bag and her book bag as we headed for the gym parking lot. The lot was dusty, the way they get when the gravel is starting to thin out over the red clay. Obviously no thunderstorms had hit this part of town last night.

I would later chalk it up to my concussed head, but why I did not notice the van beside us until I was pulling out, I will never really know. Maybe I hadn't wanted to see it, self-preservation finally kicking in after last night. Mint green I'd call the color, with a metallic sheen common back in the early eighties. The Kirbys were right about it being an Econoline. The blue Ford logo was encased in metal below the gas cap above the right rear tire. Someone had just washed the van. It was shiny except for the little bit of red dust it had picked up in this parking lot. At gut level, I knew this was the van.

I probably wouldn't have noticed it even then if Joan hadn't rolled down her window and waved to Buddy, who was climbing into the passenger side.

"Don't talk to them," I barked, and swatted at her shoulder with a hand so frantic, I could not control it.

She recoiled instinctively, staring at me in disbelief. "What's wrong with you, Mom?" She rubbed her shoulder where I had hit her.

I put my right hand on her thigh and my left on my bandaged forehead where I'd learned a certain pressure could quell a throb. "I'm sorry. My head just hurts."

She removed my hand from her thigh as if it were an unwanted piece of lint. I held it in my other hand and rubbed it until it felt part of me again.

"Whose van is that?" I asked as calmly as I could.

"It belongs to the company, I think. Buddy's mom's

company. Good Lord, Mom, they didn't steal it." Her furrowed brow let me know the extent of her irritation. In her mind, the problem was with me, not Buddy Cates and his friend. "Let's just go to the grocery store," she said. "Do you want me to drive?"

> **Location, location, location**
> **Grand Dilworth home has seen four**
> **generations raised.**
> **Now it's your turn.**
> **Widow moving to Florida. ML**

The water is running so she doesn't hear me. She's at the sink. Her back to me. Thick-waisted, slim-hipped. Apron tied like a gift-wrapping. Her gray hair curled tight like from an old-fashioned beauty salon. I am out already.

My timing is perfect now: one hand to the mouth, one spread across her pelvic bones lifting her buttocks up to me. She drops a coffee cup into the suds. She stiffens as I carry her down the hall in search of a bedroom. I think I can even smell her fear. I swell.

Her eyes are the size of baseballs, bulging in their sockets. They are the color and consistency of an egg not quite done. Tiny red veins spread out from her lower lids. She will not scream. She is beyond it.

Her terror fills in around me and grips me like concrete-laced quicksand. Down I go, deeper. I seek a depth she doesn't have. The sandpaper grit of her dryness taunts me to thrust once again . . . and again.

She whimpers. From pain, I think. I push the goose-down pillow over her face and press my palms to either side of her head. Like a man with no legs, I lock my elbows and leverage my torso at her cunt with the velocity of an air hammer. I break through her tunnel wall just as she goes limp. The quivering reflex that follows kisses the very root of me. I am filled with awe at this power.

I sit up and listen in the silence. It's time to go now. At the bedroom door I take one last look. She still has the apron on.

16

By thursday morning, I had decided that the light green van didn't necessarily mean anything. How many Econolines that color were on the streets in Charlotte anyway? Hundreds at least. What was I going to do, run to Thurgood and tell him I saw a green van? Besides, why should I believe Mickey Sutton? Simply because he said he drove his Mercedes that night didn't make it true. In fact, with Sutton's track record, saying one thing most certainly meant its opposite.

Before going to work, I finally listened to Wednesday's messages. George junior had obviously punched Save when he heard the ones from Jean Miller.

Sydney? Sydney, where are you? I hear you were beaten and robbed (rumors must have built throughout the day). *I haven't tried the hospital yet.* (pause) *I guess I should. I heard it was pretty bad.* (sigh) *I'll try there next. But, Sydney, listen. You've got to help me.* (mumbles to someone in background) *I'm at the Law Enforcement Center along with thirty other realtors. They've separated three of us from the rest. You're not going to believe why.* (screech)

Hers was the next message as well. She said that the three who had been taken into a separate room owned the personal combinations that were used to enter the most recent houses where women had died, including Crystal's. No one was being held, but the three realtors had been questioned for two hours. *Thank God none of us are men,* her voice said. *No matter what they may want to believe, we women can't rape each other.* (pause) *Can we? They call that a technicality.* (nervous laugh) *Call me.*

The three other messages were a Nature Conservancy solicitation, a dental reminder, and Cynthia Hyatt, in that order. Cynthia's message had included the phrase "no big deal" and had asked about lunch "whenever you've got the time." Since I didn't have the time, I decided I could return her call whenever I felt like it. No guilt there at all.

The call I did need to return was Jean's. In spite of her attempts at humor, she was bound to have been frightened—at the least, intimidated—by her experience at the police station. God, I had been intimidated myself last week when I went down there merely to talk with Sally and Fred. What must it feel like to be connected materially to something as heinous as these murders?

It was not quite nine yet, so I tried her at home on the hope that she was moving slowly after yesterday. No such luck. Not even a machine at Jean's house. She answered her own phone at the office.

"I thought you had one of the 'associates' answering your phone," I said cheerfully.

The nervous agitation showed with her first words. "Oh God, Sydney. I don't even know why I'm answering

it at all. The only calls I'm getting are my few little listings wanting out of their contracts."

"I got your messages."

"It would have been nice to talk with you yesterday,"
she said with no attempt to hide the sarcasm.

"I didn't do yesterday at all. I took it off."

There was a slight hesitation before she answered,
some of the focus taken out of her arrows. "Yeah. I heard
you had a bad night."

She was silent, as if she expected me to tell her about
it. I really didn't want to get into the whole Mickey Sutton thing, so I sat silent with her, waiting her out.

She sighed finally. "Sydney?"

"Yes?"

"I'm ruined. We're all ruined."

"No you're not," I said with conviction. "As long as
the media don't make a big deal out of this, it'll all blow
over as soon as the police catch whoever's broken your
codes."

Her laugh was hearty enough, although driven by sheer
nerves. When she finally stopped, she said, "Have you
looked at your paper or watched TV today? The police
even had a press conference last night." She choked on
something at that point. The gagging and gasping seemed
to go on forever. "Lord, that went down some pipe that's
never been used before." She coughed again. "Gotta get
some water, but we've gotta talk. Lunch?"

"Today?"

Cough. "Well, if not today, it'll be one more day of
business lost. You've got to help me keep what little business I've got."

"It's not going to be that bad, Jean."

"It already is."

"Where do you want to go?" I asked.

"I'll come there. We can decide. One o'clock."

I had missed the morning news. It was nine now, and all major networks would be into Oprah, Sally Jessy, or Kathy Lee and Regis. The paper was hidden in a deep liriope patch behind my nandina bushes. It was three-fourths dry from either rain or dew, but the slug tracks still blurred the headlines: POLICE SHUT DOWN MULTIPLE LISTING.

Good Lord, why'd they have to publicize the whole thing? Wasn't it enough to dismantle the service quietly and efficiently while they look for the person who is robbing and killing homeowners?

Part of the answer became apparent in the early paragraphs of the story. Eight thousand houses were currently on the market through the Greater Charlotte–Mecklenburg Multiple Listing Service. The police wanted to remove each supralock themselves. In fact, they had issued a warning to homeowners and realtors alike that if they tried to disengage their own supralocks, they would risk prosecution. So the police themselves needed to publicize their problem in order to gain cooperation.

Eight thousand supralocks to remove. My God. How long would it take them? The police spokeswoman was vague at best in answering that question.

I was tempted to call Thurgood, just to let him know how hard I knew this case must be on him. Also, to thank him for yesterday. Frankly, I wanted to hear his smooth voice more than anything, but, in the end, I decided against calling him. Surely he would be heading up at least a portion of the whole mess. And I thought I was having a busy week.

On the drive to the office, I forced myself to think about the revolution of the intimate blend and the problem of how to get people to care. I had not heard from the Textile Museum curator since Monday, but he would expect a progress report by tomorrow. Maybe Hart had come up with something.

I detected a note of pride when he told me he had not. He was in one of those see-I-told-you-so moods, which meant that I had gotten us into this mess and I would have to be the one to get us out. Oh well, I couldn't expect the rest of the world to thrive on the same stuff I did. It would be nice, however, if my own employees humored me a bit. The honesty of democracy sometimes impedes progress.

Before I could settle in, I got a call from Mickey Sutton's lawyer. First, he apologized for what he called the misunderstanding between his client and me. Next, he cleared his throat even though I heard nothing there to clear. Then he said that Mickey was willing not to press charges against me for attacking him with a deadly instrument if I would drop the battery and unlawful entry charges.

"What are you calling a deadly instrument?" I asked.

"We have precedents," he said. "Used hypodermic needles are more lethal than small flashlights, Ms. Teague."

I saw deep pink, as close to red as one can get without exploding. Lawyers can make me angrier than any other profession in the world. They say something insane like this and end up being right. Part of their strategy is getting you to react in anger, so I breathed deeply and lit a cigarette before answering him.

"What about the unlawful entry?" I asked politely.

"The poor guy had left a sentimental pen his wife had given him when he was in your office last week. He was in there for a showing, wasn't he?" I could hear papers being rattled on his end. "Yes, here it is. A Barbara Cates took him through your building last week as a potential buyer, is that not right?"

"So?"

This time he dislodged something when he cleared his throat. "So he just thought of it and didn't want to bother you. He used his wife's combination. All a big misunderstanding, I'm afraid, between the two of you."

One phrase kept running through my mind: the little shit.

That phone call set the tone for the rest of my morning, the most irritating part of which was Sally's jubilant celebration. A raping serial killer on the loose in Charlotte was preferable to the doubts she had had about her brother.

The strangest part of her mood, however, was my reaction to it. Last week I'd been convinced that Fred had nothing to do with Crystal's death. I had held this belief in the face of evidence against him. Now that Thurgood and his team were obviously connecting the Ball murder to these other four, I was beginning to doubt Fred. I couldn't figure out why. Hart would say I simply liked to take the opposite side from popular opinion. Some truth to that, granted. But I knew that I knew something that had made me change my mind. I just didn't know what it was.

"Have they dropped the charges against him yet?" I asked Sally.

She was sitting in the blue client chair across from my desk chewing gum with the ferocity of someone on a diet. "Not yet, but Mr. Diehl—ooo, he's so cute, Sydney— says they will."

"Have you met Craig Diehl?" Craig Diehl was a hard-drinking, churchgoing, father-of-five womanizer with the nicest wife in the world.

She giggled. The hint of a small bubble appeared and then was gone, the kind of bubble a baby makes when it coos. "I had dinner with him last night."

The anger that I felt for Mickey Sutton, his lawyer, my brother Bill, Hart, and even Crystal erupted all over Sally. "What in the hell do you think you're doing? The man's married."

She slumped in the chair, dropping her gum onto her bosom. As she picked it off and put it daintily back into her mouth, she whined, "Sydney, stop. We didn't do any-thing. We just talked about Freddie." She looked as if she might cry.

"What happened to Curt Simmons?"

She winced. "He's still in town. He wanted to spend some time with his parents."

I don't know why I was taking all of my frustration out on her. "Oh, that's right. I had forgotten that's why he came to town. Something about a dead sister, wasn't it? Sally, you turn every man you meet into your own pri-vate fantasy."

She removed the gum from her mouth entirely, signi-fying that I had ruined her day. "Do you mind?" she asked as she popped a Kleenex from the dispenser on my desk, deposited the gum into it, and, with great finality, stashed it away in my wastebasket.

"Sydney," she said with more determination than I had heard from her since we'd won our first Addy Award. "Sydney, you'd be much better off if you'd notice men at all. At least one in your life might do something for your disposition." She exited the room the way Loretta Young would have if she had ever gone in that direction.

I couldn't concentrate after Sally's prescription. I fiddled a bit with the Textile Museum and thought about calling the curator, finally deciding against it since I'd had no revelations of my own. Everyone took for granted the existence of poly/cotton clothing. Dammit, the intimate blend *had* been a revolution, but who gave a damn? Hart was at Rogers Sound Studio making the fire spots. He'd probably be there through tomorrow. He was right: I really was stuck alone with creating a concept for the museum. I had a problem.

Jean Miller's arrival was a welcome respite from my work. For all her anxiety over what might happen to her business, she looked like an ad for the success one gleans from an American Express card or some other upwardly mobile device. The lines of her burgundy suit seemed to stretch her five-foot-three-inch frame to model height. Her complexion, usually pasty at best, was almost ruddy, as if all her blood vessels were at attention. Some of her good looks were bound to be attributable to high blood pressure.

We decided to eat across East Boulevard at the White

Horse, a restaurant known for its pasta and heavy sauces. "I need something substantial," she had said. I decided long ago that the Alfredo sauce here could be a suitable glue substitute in the assembly of elementary science projects. I went along with her choice anyway, not wanting to add any unnecessary color to her cheeks. I ordered the chicken salad, but even it seemed heavy on the part that wasn't chicken.

"I feel so much better when I eat," she said as she wiped a white glob of clam sauce off her flushed cheek.

I was busy searching for the chicken in my chicken salad. When I came up short, I pushed the mound to the side of the plate and attacked the iceberg.

"Uh huh," I replied. I wasn't going to be the one to initiate the conversation we were bound to have.

"Of course, I won't be able to eat out anymore if we're shut down more than a few days."

I didn't want this lunch to turn into a poor-Jean-whose-business-is-dying session, so I said something that may have been a bit cruel on my part: "The women who are dead won't be able to eat at all." It did the trick. She straightened up. I added, "The lunch is on Allen Teague. You are a valued client." I smiled as brightly I knew how.

She smiled weakly in return. "What now, maestro?"

"Do you really want to talk about the what-ifs right now? Why don't we go back to the office and not ruin the lunch?"

Her hand flew immediately to her throat. "My God, Sydney. Is it going to be that bad, so bad you can't tell me in a public place?"

I laughed and put my hand on my chest. "Cross my heart. That's not what I meant at all. It's a company policy is all. If I'm paying for lunch, I make damn sure it's pleasant. It's about the only return on investment I can control."

We spent the rest of the lunch chitchatting about light and easy topics—family, friends we had in common. Jean kept asking me if I'd seen certain movies and TV shows, but I'd been so busy lately, I didn't have much to contribute.

As soon as we stepped outside the restaurant, our relaxed mood was spoiled when we saw the police car parked in Allen Teague's driveway. Jean stiffened and backed into the restaurant door, only to be pushed onto the sidewalk by a couple who were leaving behind us. She then grabbed my elbow, pulled herself close to me, and stared at my right shoulder. I wondered if these were the beginnings of a strange new dance.

When I saw Tom Thurgood hop out of the passenger side, I said, "Don't worry, Jean. They haven't come to get you. He's a friend."

Since we had the light, I began to walk across the street. Jean had backed off me somewhat at this point but still was holding on to my elbow. The last person I had crossed a street with in this manner had been my eight-five-year-old grandmother. She mumbled as she hobbled: "Whose friend? Who could have a friend like that?"

When we finally reached the other side, I took her hand off my arm. "Mine," I said strongly, and took note of the pride in my own voice. "It's Tom Thurgood, and he's a very good friend of mine."

Tom didn't see Jean and me. I watched him go into my office. We were walking up the three short steps that separate our yard from the sidewalk when he was coming back out the front door. That contagious smile washed over his face.

"Hi there," he said as he pointed back at the office door. "I was looking for you."

Jean mumbled under her breath. "I bet he means me."

Ignoring her, I returned his smile. "You've found me. We've been to lunch. Tom, you've met Jean Miller, haven't you?"

Thurgood extended his hand, and his arm looked longer than Jean is tall. "Hi. Tom Thurgood." Recognition hit his eyes, although the smile did not fade. "Yeah. We met yesterday. You're a realtor."

"And you're a policeman. Detective, right?"

Tom continued smiling, either not hearing or choosing to ignore the bite in Jean's voice. "In my other life," he said. He moved his gaze to me and cocked his head slightly.

I said to Jean: "Why don't you go on in. I'll be there in just a second."

He wanted to know how I was feeling, bless him. No one else had asked me since yesterday, as if twelve stitches and a concussion vanish overnight. I had begun to feel hypochondriacal about the occasional jabs of pain and dull headache.

"Not a hundred percent but definitely better," I said, touching my head. "Thanks for asking."

He shifted his weight awkwardly the way I'd seen some teenage boys do with Joan. A shock of his rich auburn hair fell onto his forehead from the abrupt movement. His jaw dropped, then his mouth opened—all of this seeming to take a very long time. When the process reached his own personal crescendo, he raised his green eyes toward mine and said, "How about dinner tonight?"

"Do you have time?" I asked. Dammit, Sydney, I thought. Why couldn't I try a little sensitivity with the man? It had taken everything he had to ask, and I hadn't let him reap one bit of victory.

"You mean the Multiple Listing problem?"

"Uh huh." What other "problems" could he have to compare?

"Nothing much I can do until we've collated all the combinations with the realtors they belong to. That's for the houses still on the market. Not much we can do about the ones off the market already. Those women at Multiple Listing move those locks fast."

"Can you tell who's been inside the houses you're taking the locks from?"

He nodded. "Uh huh. That's not a problem. Just a lot of 'em. It'll probably be Sunday before we can determine who's been in every one of those houses."

"But Jean said you isolated three whose combinations had been used at the murder scenes."

"The last two murders. No other rolls of paper still exist." He glanced toward the spot where Jean had stood earlier. "I'm sure your friend told you. They all deny having been in those houses at the times we have them recorded."

She hadn't told me. I hadn't asked. "Then what are you looking for?"

"There've been even more robberies than we thought. We're thinking a pattern will emerge. We can't push it any faster than it takes to get all these locks back in." He watched me think for a few seconds, then said, "So I decided to grab at life while I still had a chance." He raised an eyebrow. "So can you have dinner with me?"

I had been staring at the light on the corner as it

turned from green to yellow. I looked back at him. "Of course. I'd love to have dinner."

"And just what did he want?" Jean's hands were now on her hips, preferable to my elbow any day of the week.

"None of your business," I said playfully, and looked to Sally for collusion in my game. Still injured from Tuesday's lunch, she continued her filing as if I had not walked into the room.

"Come on into my office," I said. Just to swipe back slightly, I added, "We don't want to bother Sally."

"Humph" she said from the bottom file drawer.

"What did he want?" Jean insisted again. We continued to stand just outside my door.

"Dinner. He wants me to have dinner with him tonight."

"You're not going to, are you?" Jean asked combatively. She was clearly shocked. Sally was still posing as a Pendaflex file, so I could not see her expression.

I got the distinct impression Jean thought the purpose of dinner would be to discuss her. This kind of self-centeredness, I'd learned over the years, was a by-product of encroaching paranoia. Understandable, I supposed, under the circumstances.

"Why shouldn't I?" I asked Jean.

"He's a cop," she said, and I liked her less for that—no matter what she may have meant.

Sally surfaced but did not turn to face us. "Sydney is too old," she said sarcastically, "to eliminate men by profession."

I was sick and tired of them both. First I peered at Jean, who was looking more to me like a small rodent than a client. "I'll tell you what I've already told her." I pointed my fully extended arm toward Sally. "He's a goddamn human being, okay?"

Jean shrank to under five feet.

Then I turned toward Sally. "And you. You Miss Take-'Em-Where-You-Can-Find-'Em. You—" I was shaking so badly that I retracted my wobbly arm.

"What?" Sally challenged.

"You're too young to 'humph.' "

I turned to Jean. "Let's go," I barked as I walked into my office and sat in my desk chair.

Over my personal fuming, I could barely hear Sally's parting shot: "It's a beginning; she has a date."

17

MY BLUE LEATHER CLIENT CHAIR ENGULFED poor Jean. She had come to me for solace and become victim of my wrath instead. I had to get hold of myself. Could a concussion, even a slight one like mine, alter one's personality?

"How about some coffee?" I asked.

She went to shake her head, and it jerked instead. No sound came out of her mouth in spite of the fact that she had opened it. I had scared this poor woman beyond words.

I walked around to the back of her chair and pulled her head lightly against my waist in a gesture of peace. "I'm sorry, Jean. You need my help. I'm doing the opposite. Let me get some coffee, and we'll settle down." Before I released her, I felt her body deflating, letting go some of the awful buildup.

We usually keep just one coffeepot going in the reception area. I keep a warmer in my office, however, where I put my Melitta drip pot when I make my own. I rambled around in the little kitchen near our back door while I waited for my water to boil. Believing with all my heart the old adage that a watched pot never boils, I forced my eyes to the speckled linoleum floor that seems always in need of a Clorox rinse. The strange-looking little key was just sitting there, its edges almost hidden by the partially popped-out panel that covers the bottom of the stove. I picked it up and looked at it for a moment, knowing instantly it wasn't mine. The ridges were quite distinct. Maybe it belonged to Sally or Hart. I put it in the pocket of my navy blazer, glanced at the bubbling pot on the stove, and marveled once more at the truth of old sayings.

I poured us both a glass of water after I'd set the fresh pot of French roast on the warmer. With two beverages on the desk in front of me, I was beginning to regain my security and composure. For good measure and my lingering headache, I popped two aspirin.

"How's your head? I sure have been self-centered during this mess."

I could have agreed with her, but in the interest of peace and progress, I merely said, "It's better."

She stared at me, her complexion less ruddy and features softened. "He is a good-looking guy, that detective. I didn't mean anything by my comment. It's just that I'm so scared I'll go under. God, Sydney, I've barely opened my doors."

I sipped the still-hot coffee and swallowed it slowly. "I don't guess it helps," I said, "that you're not alone in your predicament. How many other realtors were called down to the police station?"

"About thirty of us. I knew every one of them. It was awful. You would have thought we were all murderers."

She gulped some of her water, spilling a few drops on the lapel of her burgundy suit.

"Someone is," I said, and immediately regretted it.

"Guess whose combination was the last one to open the Ball house?" she said with an odd combination of pride and guilt. "Mine. Jean Miller's. Eleven-o-four p.m., September seventeenth. Can you imagine them thinking that I'd show a house close to midnight?"

"I doubt if they actually thought you'd been the one to enter it, Jean. Who else has access to your combination?"

She straightened in the big chair. Professional indignation replaced the self-pity in her eyes. "No one. It's like a pin code. You know the secret kind you have with the bank to access your money? Only the Multiple Listing Service and I know my code. I don't even know my associates' codes. God, I signed a contract with the Service practically forfeiting my life if I ever let anybody learn my combination."

"Who exactly is the Multiple Listing Service?" I asked.

Her demeanor slid toward exasperation now. "Two little old ladies in a house on Morehead Street. Oh, they work under the auspices of the Board of Realtors, but they're independent otherwise. The service has offices all over the country."

"Could they have given your code to anybody?"

She shook her head vehemently.

"I didn't say 'would they.' My question is 'could they.' "

"No, Sydney."

"What if somebody who didn't have a combination wanted to show a listing? Couldn't they have gotten it from the women at Multiple Listing?"

"Not on your life." She shifted in the client chair. "Why don't you go ahead and smoke, Sydney. Your mind works better when you do." She motioned at me with her hand upside down, her short thin fingers walking on air.

I held the Vantage before lighting it. I said, "You know, I've given my pin to a friend before to get money from one of those bank machines. Why couldn't that have happened?"

"Smoke it," she said authoritatively. "You wouldn't if it risked your whole career."

I had to admit she was right about us. Everybody wasn't like Jean and me, however. "Is there a cleanup crew or a night watchman who could have gotten into the Multiple Listing offices and accessed everybody's combinations?"

She chewed on her lip for the ten seconds it took me to light my cigarette. She was shaking her head back and forth, but said, "Maybe. But why?"

I didn't know. This was Thurgood's area anyway, not mine. The marketing angle of a standstill industry was bad enough. I said, "Want to talk strategies?"

She slumped in the chair and let out a long sigh. "What am I going to do, Sydney?"

"It depends," I said. "If it blows over by Monday, I don't think anyone will be hurt. We'll just place your ads next week and make certain that the paper does a series of articles on how safe the system is."

She stared at me. "And if it doesn't blow over? What if this mess goes unsolved the way most of the crime does in this city?"

I placed the stub of cigarette that was still burning into the little snuffer I'd bought to sit in my ashtray. "Everyone will be hurt the same," I said. "If the public is scared to list their homes with one realtor, they'll be afraid to list them with all the rest. Nobody doesn't get hurt."

Her laugh was closer to a deep, ragged sigh. "Some

consolation, Sydney. Those of us who are new can't wait it out. The only firms that'll survive this are the old ones like Bishop Cates."

"They may be going under anyway, remember? Either way," I said, "it's best not to spend your money. The ones who are advertising right now will go under before you do. I'll wait to bill you for our work when your business picks up."

"Thank you, Sydney." She reached across my desk to touch my hand and tipped over my coffee cup. The clear brown liquid spread out over my desk blotter and was making headway toward one of my work piles.

I instinctively reached into my blazer pocket for Kleenex and pulled out the key I had found in the kitchen instead. It fell into the liquid in the process. The other pocket held the Kleenex, which I threw at the coffee with the same confidence one might throw a dish towel at a barn fire.

"Let me help," she said, getting up.

"No, no. I've got it." And I did, with half a roll of paper towels I retrieved from the kitchen. The two of us worked together in sopping up the mess, both of us grateful, I think, to have busywork.

Jean said, "Where did you get the supralock key?" She pointed at the odd-shaped key on my desk.

I picked it up. "Is that what this is? Do you think it fits my supralock?"

"All the keys are the same, Sydney. It's only our combinations that are different." She took the key from me. "Where'd you get one of these?"

"Off my kitchen floor." A flash of recognition hit me at that moment. "I'll bet Mickey Sutton left it." I looked back at Jean, who had put the key on my newly mopped desk. "See, Jean? He got into my house by using some-one else's combination. Why can't these others have been done the same way?"

She looked at the floor and shook her head vehe-mently. Still not buying.

I walked her to our back lot where she had parked her car. The asphalt sank with our steps the way soft acrylic tile does. God, this heat. I noticed a yellow oak leaf or two on her fender. Casualties of the extended heat, not the natural death of autumn. I wanted to say something positive to her, to give her hope that the anxiety would soon end.

"Did you really know all the other realtors at the Law Enforcement Center?" I asked, praying that the you-are-not-alone-in-this approach would help.

She laughed. "Every single one of them."

"Do you know why they were all called in?" I asked.

"The tip of the iceberg from what I could see," she said sarcastically. "The three of us, of course, who'd mur-dered those women. The twenty-seven others were from recently robbed houses." She raised her eyebrows and threw her arms out in front of herself like an agitated Vanna White. "Get this," she almost shouted. "These were only the houses that are still on the market. They hadn't even gotten to the ones that had canceled con-tracts because of robberies."

"Oh my God," I said, partly under my breath.

"Yeah." She laughed when she saw my stunned expres-sion. "That's when they decided they had to shut the whole thing down." She got into her car, turned on the engine, and rolled down her window. "It was like old home week down there. Every single one of us had worked for Bishop Cates."

"Was Barbara Cates there?" I asked. I was afraid to hear her answer. Barbara's mind couldn't survive such an experience.

"Nope, I bet Madame had her own private session. She wouldn't want to be seen with us commoners."

Gus Georges was on the phone by the time I'd reached the reception room. Sally seemed cheerful enough. I couldn't predict our relationship minute to minute anymore. We needed one of two things: to keep our personal lives out of the office or simply accept who each other was. Both options looked impossible right now.

"Hello there, Gus," I said, pumping myself up for the kind of animated conversation one always has with Gus Georges. "What can I do for you?"

"Are you ready to go on a little road trip?"

I hadn't the slightest idea what he was talking about.

"The storage bin, Sydney. Remember? It's about as close to the end of the week as we're going to get without it actually being Friday."

Wow. How did that slip completely out of my mind? "Oh yeah. Can't do it this afternoon. How 'bout the morning?"

We settled on ten o'clock. He'd pick me up here at the office.

"Can't wait for ya to see the new headgear, Sydney gal. You're a tennis player, aren't ya?"

"Uh huh."

"Well, I've got a deal for you. A whole truckload of terry cloth tennis hats, the kind that go all the way 'round your head so you don't get any skin cancers on your ears.

Be thinking 'bout which of your great clients might need some of those beauties."

After we hung up, I felt totally drained. Five minutes on the phone with Gus and two hours with Jean had done me in. If I was going to enjoy myself at all tonight, I needed a bath and a nap. Nothing to feel guilty about, I told myself as I said "Good afternoon" to Sally in my most civilized voice.

I slid out of my navy blazer as soon as I got outside. A slight breeze fluttered against my white cotton blouse. I lifted my arms to catch it, to cool off. The first breeze I'd felt in several months. Funny about these thunder-storms we kept having: not even a hint they were coming until, like a runaway train, they were on you. At most, a gust or two of wind. No breeze though. I pulled the blouse from my chest. Maybe this breeze meant things would change soon.

Both kids were home. Joan had an American lit test to-morrow and George junior, Spanish. They were diligently studying in their bedrooms. The refrigerator yielded a cornucopia of the five food groups, or was it four? Had someone combined fruits and vegetables in recent years? I pulled out pork chops, bread, broccoli, and milk, and then some grapes just in case there were five. My kids would go balanced into academia tomorrow. And I would go guiltless into this good night.

It was five o'clock. Thurgood would be here at seven. I started my bath and was just about to undress when the front doorbell rang. Joan screamed she would get it, but I screamed louder that she wouldn't. One interruption, I knew from observation, could throw a kid like her off for the rest of her life.

Buddy Cates stood taller than I'd remembered him only last week. At least six feet, probably six two. His square jaw, grayish blue eyes, and crew cut reminded me of a thirties German youth. He looked so serious I was tempted to salute, but, sensing no humor in this boy, I said, "Hey, Buddy. Joan can't see you right now. She's got a big test tomorrow."

His gaze didn't falter the way most boys' would when they're talking with a girl's mother. He must have held that gaze for a full thirty seconds. I couldn't tell if he was about to challenge me or if he was waiting for me to say something else. I finally said, "Okay?"

Only then did he move at all, a smooth one-hundred-eighty-degree turn during which a shoulder never even dipped. The boy had not said a word. As he walked away, I called out to him. "Is your mom feeling better?" A legitimate question, I decided, since Buddy had been the one to take her to her therapist.

He hesitated for a brief second, then said, "She will. Oscar's left."

I followed him out into my front yard. "What do you mean by 'Oscar's left'?"

"Left Mom, left Charlotte, left the face of the earth for all I care." His voice had a coolness to it I hadn't heard before. His blank expression didn't change.

I touched his arm, and he recoiled. "Oh no, Buddy. How's your mom taking it? As if she didn't have enough troubles."

He seemed to stare right through me, the gray of his eyes blotting out the blue. He clenched his jaw. "She'll be fine," he said. "Now that he's gone, everything ought to be fine."

I gripped his arm again, this time tight enough that he didn't pull away. "Buddy, I care about your mom. I'm not some enemy."

He relaxed. Only then did I see the boy I used to know.

"Mrs. Teague, my mom needs someone to take care of her." He studied me, as if sizing up my friendship, then spoke again. "Oscar made her worse. I can take care of her." He took my hand off his arm, turned, and walked down my sidewalk.

I stood mesmerized watching him walk away. His gait had a military quality to it; his arms pumped back and forth like an oil rig on a strike. Waiting at the street was that light green van. From where it was parked, I couldn't see who was driving, but I was willing to bet it was that Jake. The van door slammed. The vehicle cut a wheel leaving the curb of quiet little Kingston Avenue.

Joan yelled, "Who was that, Mom?"

"Nobody," I answered and didn't know why I lied.

Sometimes a thirty-minute nap can do the trick. Today I'd needed more but didn't get it. I couldn't stop worrying about Barbara. I had never liked Oscar, and his leaving only proved to me I was right to dislike him so. Now was a hell of a time for a husband to leave a wife no matter what the problems between them. Maybe he'd always been just a hanger-on, true only for the good times and poised to leave when the easy money and prestige dried up. One thing was certain: Buddy was angry about something, something to do with Oscar and his mother probably, something more than the simple dislike he'd shown last week. Maybe it was a godsend that Buddy had come home. His devotion to Barbara was just what she needed. Not too healthy for a nineteen-year-old, though. I decided to give the boy a chance, to try a little harder. No boy should have the burden of his mother's happiness.

18

If HE RECOGNIZED THE BLACK DRESS AS THE one he had brought me at the hospital, Thurgood hid it well. He concentrated, instead, on the prime rib in front of him. His was the kind of appetite I'd only read about before tonight. I even gave him my baked potato, which came prestuffed with several cheeses, bacon, and scallions.

After several attempts at table chatter, to which he'd politely smile and continue eating, I finally said, "You don't like to talk while you're eating, do you?"

He finished chewing a piece of French bread, wiped his lips with the bedspread-size red napkin, and smiled, first with his eyes and then his whole face. "Do you want to talk? I thought we could eat now and talk afterwards."

I returned his honest, wide-open smile and admitted to myself that his was a reasonable suggestion. "Go ahead," I said. "Enjoy your food."

He had started to order wine when we first arrived.

When I reminded him that I no longer drank, he returned the list. "Please, have your wine," I said. "Don't change anything you'd normally do because I don't drink. The only time I'm uncomfortable is when people make concessions for—"

He grabbed my hand and squeezed it as if trying to shut my mouth by depressing some distant lever. His other hand he had put to his lips and said, "Shh. Don't want any. I drink to be sociable only. It doesn't make sense to do it alone." He let go of my hand and laughed. "Besides, I don't need it to stoke my appetite."

He'd been right about the appetite. I'd thoroughly enjoyed my sea bass, but it had long been gone by the time Tom Thurgood had finished his time at the trough. In the interim I'd taken in the views of the outstretched, twinkling city. To the west rose the newest and tallest of the banking monsters who own this town, the sixty-story NationsBank Corporate Center. All men I know see a warhead when viewing it, at the least a gigantic bullet. All women see a massive, erect penis—complete with lights at night and a bulging red tip. From where I sat, with floor-to-ceiling glass, I could see to the southeast, into neighboring South Carolina. Along the way, neighborhoods sprawled and the busy corridor of Independence Boulevard looked like a poorly strung Christmas tree. Crystal had been killed within my view. Who was dying out there tonight? Heart attacks, traffic accidents, bathtub falls. I hoped no murders. What else?

"Are they out there right now?" I asked.

"Who?" he mumbled as he stabbed at the heart of an unsuspecting lettuce.

"Your men. Are they out there tonight removing supralocks?"

He wiped his mouth again, looked at his watch, and shook his head back and forth. "Women too." He winked in a contradictory show of liberation. "Not after dark. People are too scared. They'll use the night to assemble the imprints left by combinations."

"How's that going to help? I mean those imprints can't tell you much of anything if the houses haven't been robbed. Can they?"

"Depends. We're looking for trends. For anything linking all these houses in the Multiple Listing Service." At that he returned to the slaughter of his salad, which he ate last rather than first. A strange culinary ritual from my point of view.

The order of his courses, it turned out, was only the first of many contradictions I found interesting about Tom Thurgood. He wore French cuffs when dining out like tonight, but he held them together with paper clips, one having popped out while returning the check to our waiter. The tailoring of his suit was impeccable on his oversize body, but when a breeze flapped his jacket I saw that red dog hairs were covering his rear.

"I'd like to meet your dog," I said as he opened the car door for me.

"I didn't think I'd mentioned them," he said, tipping his head as if trying to shake something loose. "I don't remember that."

"Don't worry; you didn't. I just guessed. Them?"

"Two goldens, husband and wife. Red and Rosie, a great study in matrimony and parenthood."

"Do you have puppies?" I asked.

"Not right now, thank God. I couldn't be entering this

city tennis tournament if I had a litter at home." He closed my door and returned to the driver's side. When he had started the engine, he asked, "Did you mean tonight?" He hesitated only slightly. "Did you mean you'd like to go to my place?"

"Is it far?"

"Twenty minutes on the interstate. On the river. Do you have time?"

"Think of me as an early-variety pumpkin," I said. "On school nights, eleven's my latest. I believe Cinderella had till twelve."

In a deadpan serious tone, Thurgood said, "But, you know, I doubt the prince would throw a big party like that on a school night so it's really not fair to compare."

He had me laughing, something I had not done much of recently. "I've never liked the comparison anyway," I said. "I'd die before I'd put on a glass slipper. Prince or no prince."

"No comfort, right?"

"Right," I agreed.

"Well, there you go. We have some things in common after all. I believe in comfort first."

That belief was evident in his home, which was really a boathouse with more square footage in the water than flooring. As we approached it through a massive entanglement of tall pines, dogwood, kudzu, and honeysuckle, I thought it was simply a small cabin, one of hundreds dotting the banks of the Catawba River. Because of the overgrown rhododendron bushes flanking both sides of the house, I had no idea that the bank dropped off into the river ten feet behind those bushes. He lived on the one floor with several canoes and a bass boat occupying the lower level. The dogs came and went through one of those doggie doors downstairs on the small portion of the house that was actually on the land. After his wife had died, he explained, the two dogs had slept with him. Now they preferred the bass boat. I watched him bed them down in the boat for the night, and the thought occurred to me that the process was similar to my nightly ritual with Joan and George junior. I told him so.

"I enjoyed being with your kids," he said warmly. "They're good people."

He fixed me a ginger ale, and I insisted he have a beer. His living room extended to a wide screened porch that jutted into the river, which in turn surrounded us on three sides as we sat. The furniture was an old, basic, heavy rattan with thick cushions covered in green canvas.

Cicadas fought for the night with ancient bullfrogs whose instruments were deeper and more resonant. The former were like bass guitars in need of tuning, the latter like runaway tubas and oboes. The resulting cacophony was somehow comforting. Nature's harmony; not man's. It was as sticky and steamy on the river as it was in the city, maybe more. He lit a citronella candle to keep the mosquitoes at bay.

Neither of us spoke for a very long time. There was no need. The longer we sat, the more relaxed I became until finally I eased myself into that wonderful hollow between his open arm and his hip. I laid my head on his chest as he let his arm slide down my shoulder to my elbow. Through his shirt, I could feel tiny mattings of hair against my cheek as my head slid toward his center. His aftershave had long ago faded. The humidity opened his pores. I was engulfed in the smell of his maleness.

"What was your wife's name?" I asked.

"Carol. Carol Delany."

"Different last names?"

I felt the chuckle, like a low rumble, within his chest. "Yeah," Thurgood said. "My doing, not hers. Carol didn't care; I insisted."

"Why?"

He squeezed my hand, then let it go. "She had a reputation. Been practicing five years when we were married. It made sense to me that she keep her name. Hell, if anybody was going to change, it should have been me."

"She was that good?" I asked.

"Yeah. That good."

I kicked my shoes off, leaving them to perch like odd-shaped blackbirds on his catchall coffee table. "What kind of law did she practice?" I asked.

"Carol was a public defender."

I leaned forward and looked back into his face. "A public defender? You two were on opposite sides."

He chuckled. "It worked out okay. She was great at what she did. Sometimes, when it wasn't even my case, I'd slip into court to watch her work."

A houseboat, ablaze with strung-up lights and pulsating with reggae music, appeared from inside a cove on our right and made its way for the wide waters in front of us. I kept time to their music with my bare feet and eventually found myself tapping a toe on Thurgood's calf.

"Why don't you take your shoes off?" I asked.

He bent his left knee, then dug into the heel of one wing-tip and kicked it across the room. He let the other slide off to the floor beside the sofa. He put his foot back on the table and looked at his watch.

"What time?" I asked.

"Ten-thirty. Time's about up, Cinderella." He didn't stand up; he pressed my head to his chest and kissed my hair lightly.

My hand fell to his thigh; I felt my way along it as if it were a road to some exotic land. He tensed in response to my touch, and his muscles grouped themselves into patterns that threw off my journey.

He turned my face toward his, and I slid into his lap, his thighs propping me up. His lips were honest, welcoming and full. I could feel their slight upturn even in a kiss. His tongue darted, probing me, not assaulting me. As if asking a question rather than making a statement. I answered by meeting it with my own, softly, playfully. Like flirting or dancing. His probe went gradually deeper, his tongue bolder, his lips hard-pressed against my teeth. From deep inside him a quiet, yet painful, moan arose. He gently led my hand to the heart of his lap where the bulge was so great that my light touch made him shiver.

"Oh God," he groaned. "Timing." He guided me by the shoulders back to a sitting position and covered his face with his hands for a few seconds. "God, what timing. I'm sorry, Sydney." He looked at me. "I shouldn't have let myself go like that."

I took his face in my hands and said, "Don't you apologize for that. You're human." Then I kissed him very lightly on the lips and repeated, "Very human. And I like it."

We both took the time to throw some water on our faces before the drive back to the city.

* * *

My tub ritual gained a new and profound dimension that night. I used a lavender oil in combination with a raspberry bubble; the result was close to transformational. All my muscles came alive, their usual plea for relief yielding to a celebration of their existence. I thought about Thurgood and the paradox that he was. So cool and tough, so much a man's man in a man's world. So willing to deal with the baser side of who we are, yet so honestly open to the vulnerable as well. So what if he was still in love with his wife. I liked him more for that. Who wouldn't respect that kind of commitment? I even wished I'd known her. I wondered why I couldn't willingly lay myself open the way he did. I found it so hard. Too much damage; too many years. Thurgood was living his life at the core of its extremes, hard where life is hard and soft where it should be so. I muddled somewhere in the middle on everything.

19

────────────────────────

SOMETIMES CREATIVITY IS BORN OF FAR-FLUNG
associations. I awoke brimming with ideas for
the Textile Museum campaign. Why hadn't I thought of
it before? Of course! The natural metaphor for the intimate blend revolution was sex. After all, polyester and
cotton had formed an intimate, exquisite union to create
a brand-new kind of product: the poly/cotton fabric. I
saw animation depicting a female puff of cotton and a
hard-nosed piece of male polyester approaching each other
longingly. They inject each other, they entwine, they inter-
weave themselves. They give birth to a beautiful baby
poly/cotton shirt. I could call it "The Birth of an American Shirt" and give all three, Mama Cotton, Daddy Polyester, and Baby Shirt personalities to attract brochure
readers and TV viewers. Maybe a comic book as educational tool for the kids to learn how textiles are manufac-
tured. I could practically copy the copy of sex manuals.

All this creativity came out of the blue while I was

driving through my little neighborhood figuratively patting myself on the back. At the intersection of Euclid and Dowd, police cars, yellow tape barricades, and an ambulance blocked my normal route to East Boulevard. A traffic cop was rerouting all commuters away from this part of Euclid. I drove up to him, ignoring his powerful arm movements, and rolled my window down. He looked perturbed since everyone else had followed his directorial show without questioning.

"What's going on, Officer?" I asked from the secure height of my Trooper. Just beyond the yellow tape that surrounded a small Tudor house, I saw a Prudential sign. I didn't need his answer to know that Charlotte had another real estate murder on its hands.

He wasn't going to tell me anyway. All he said was "Move on, ma'am."

I backed up in someone's driveway and took a left onto Dowd like everyone else. Only I pulled over to the curve while the rest of the cars gunned it up to South Boulevard in the hope that they wouldn't be late to work. If this was another Multiple Listing murder, as I thought it must be, Thurgood would be inside.

I got out of the Trooper and walked casually up Dowd toward Euclid. The cordoned house was the third one from the intersection, about as much distance as I could handle in casual mode. I studied a perfectly healthy helleri planted between the drives of houses two and three until the policeman out front was overly busy with clogged cars. My march to the front door was swift and purposeful. Knowing Thurgood was inside gave me enough confidence to stride through the front door as if I lived there.

The gurney was in the entrance hall. A police photographer was putting away his equipment in the living room.

Two men in white jackets held a black body bag, were unfolding it, smoothing its creases. She could have been my mother. Her gray hair looked like my mother's, tightly curled with a rinse to add sparkle. She seemed asleep. Peaceful. When I saw she was wearing an apron, I thought for a second I'd been wrong. This woman couldn't have been killed by the monster who'd killed Crystal. Then I saw Thurgood, and I knew that she had been.

He was coming from the kitchen, a styrofoam cup of coffee in his hand. He was talking to another man. He stopped the moment he saw me and stared, his naturally curved mouth straight for the first time since I'd known him. The other man, probably a detective too, first looked at him, then followed his line of sight to me. I felt uneasy immediately. Why had I come here? Why did I think I would be welcome?

The photographer and I spoke simultaneously, he saying "Detective Thurgood, this woman barged in here" and I saying "Tom, do we have another murder?"

Thurgood answered the rookie, but the anger in his voice came through clearly for me. "Well, get her out of here."

I put my hand up toward him. "But, Tom, I—"

"Now! If she doesn't cooperate, arrest her." He never even looked at me once he'd seen who I was, a nuisance to be swept away like nonevidentiary trash at a crime scene.

Tom turned to his peer, and the two of them went back toward the kitchen area to avoid the unpleasant distraction that was me. I apologized to the men handling the poor woman on the gurney.

Outside in the yard, I felt like a fool. But I was angry too. I'd been involved in what was happening to these women. I had not asked to know all the stuff I'd learned.

Chances were I knew every bit as much as Thurgood. He had not even had the decency to acknowledge he knew me. Damn him. Macho to the core, after all. Like every other guy I'd ever known. When it really came down to it, he had to look tough in front of the guys. I stared at the front door with thoughts of going back inside. Just to show him. Just to let his peers know who I was. Hey guys! I dated the self-serving snob last night. Take that! I wasn't, after all, some nosy, busybody woman who felt a God-given right to boss the whole world around. Why did I feel like one, then?

I was shrinking into the sidewalk when the traffic director spotted me again and shoved me off like a stray dog at an outdoor wedding. If I had had a tail, it would have been between my legs. Damn Thurgood.

By the time I got to the office, I wanted to go home for the day. I did not want any part of the adult world with its protocol, its unspoken rules and mixed messages. Fortunately, Sally and Hart do not play by those rules. Not allowed at Allen Teague. Advertising has no protocol. A certain amount of immaturity is desirable. At least, I thought so today.

The two of them were again sitting on the love seats leisurely taking their morning coffee. A sharp jab of irritation pierced through my rapidly fading dull headache when I saw them so comfortable with each other. I said, "Good morning," perfunctorily, hoping that I sounded normal enough not to elicit any questions about my mood.

"There's been another murder, Sydney." Sally said it quietly as if the evenness of her tone might render the content less heavy somehow. They both stared at me, waiting, I felt, for something I could not give them.

"I saw" was all I could say.

"I thought it would stop after they closed down Multiple Listing, Sydney. How could it have happened again?" The softness in her voice belied a fear that had reduced these gruesome crimes to the universal word for the unspeakable: it.

I did not answer her. I poured a cup of coffee for myself and sat beside Hart, who had been staring at me since my less than enthusiastic entrance.

Hart looked from me to Sally. "At least some of the locks are still out there," he said. "The police said there were eight thousand. God, it could take forever."

"Monday," I said. "They should finish by Monday."

The softness now gone from her voice, Sally said, "They got ours this morning. A nice woman police officer was taking it off when I got here. She used some kind of saw." She scrunched her face as if to say she considered the method distasteful.

Hart looked back at me. "You okay?"

I could not bring myself to say "yes," so I nodded and said, "Tired is all. Tired of the whole mess."

An unusual silence among the three of us followed. Finally Sally said, "How was your date with the detective?" To her credit, there was not a drop of sarcasm in her voice. Like she really wanted to know.

"Okay," I said with sufficient noncommitment. I turned to Hart. "By the way, I came up with the Textile Museum solution. Intercourse."

He looked befuddled. "Like talk?"

I shook my head. "No. The sexual kind. Polyester screws cotton. Cotton puffs up until she births a poly/cotton shirt or something." I got up to go into my office for a much-needed cigarette.

Sally began to giggle, but Hart showed visible signs of

anxiety, sex of any kind not being a big draw for him. "Hold it," he said. "Sex is specific. A penis has to enter a vagina. You two may think it's funny, but I have to illustrate it. Polyester has no penis." He fell quickly into deep thought, then added, "I suppose cotton is soft enough to take penetration."

"Show her like one of those clouds in those old toilet paper ads, Hart," Sally said through her laughter.

Hart thought some more, then looked at me. "Okay, okay, but what about polyester? It's nothing but long filaments."

I opened my door. "Right. Long, skinny, coiling. Like a tightly coiled snake. Perfect, don't you think? It all seemed so wonderfully romantic when I awoke this morning. You can make it work, Hart. Use your imagination." I started to close the door behind me but said as I did, "You've got the easy part this time. I have to sell the curator."

I had smoked hardly half my Vantage when Sally poked her head in to tell me that Gus Georges was waiting in reception. I'd completely forgotten our plans to drive to South Carolina.

"Tell him he'll have to wait a few minutes," I said. "Give him some coffee out of one of those mugs he sold us. Maybe he'll notice the discoloration." I made no attempt to exhale away from her direction. "I've got to call the textile curator. I promised him an idea by today."

The curator was not in. I was relieved. I told his assistant, a woman of indeterminate age who dresses in early pre-poly/cotton textiles, that we'd solved the campaign problem. "Tell him polyester and cotton got married."

She was writing this down. "Married?"

"Yes, married. You know, like a union. The intimate blend, right?"

"Oh, yes. How lovely," she said dubiously. "I will tell him."

"And tell him not to worry. We're doing it with cartoons so nobody will think his fibers would actually have sex."

Silence on her end.

"Very tasteful," I added. "Tell him we'll send him some illustrations next week. The little shirt will be adorable."

"The little shirt?"

"Their offspring."

She repeated back to me slowly, "Off spring. One word or two?" She was really writing every bit of this down.

"One. Because of the union, you know."

"Yes, of course," she said like someone answering a four-year-old. "I'm not certain I got this down correctly, Miss Teague. I'll have the curator call you if he can't understand your message."

"Well, tell him not to think about it too hard. It's one of those campaigns he has to see. It doesn't work as well in the abstract. We'll call him next week to show some visuals."

20

YORK COUNTY, SOUTH CAROLINA, IS JUST OVER the state line, south of Charlotte, a geographical extension of our city the way Newark, New Jersey, extends New York. Not that Charlotte and New York have anything else in common. I'd bet there are probably more storage bins per capita in York County than anyplace in the country, most of their contents belonging to businesses and residents of its neighboring county.

Gus drove, and I was grateful. Except for the marathon sleep imposed by my concussion, I felt as if I'd been dragging the world around on my shoulders. I knew I'd been carrying Allen Teague, but that was par for the course. I always had in spite of the fact that every now and then the salesman would actually snare us a new client or Hart would appear out of his lair for a client meeting. For all public purposes, I was Allen Teague. I usually liked it that way, but recently I'd been envious of society's drop-outs.

It took Gus thirty minutes to get us out of Charlotte

and fifteen after that to get us into South Carolina and the storage facility. The sky was bleached white again and it was not even eleven o'clock in the morning.

I wondered if the trend spotters have noticed the big growth in the storage bin business. Row upon row of cheap aluminum containers keep us Americans feeling as footloose as our cowboy heritage while holding what we might need someday if ever we settle down. The grandmother's attic that no longer exists. I'm not criticizing. I've got stuff stored myself. My bin is on the west end of Charlotte toward Gastonia. It holds manual typewriters in case a pandemic of computer viruses should send us back to the 1950s. Old client records and campaigns are there. So, too, my personal tax returns back to 1970 and several bicycles of the same vintage. If I bought these T-shirts and hats from Gus, I'd store them there too.

"Here we are, Sydney girl." Gus pulled off the sprawling six-lane interstate, drove through the service lanes of a McDonald's, veered sharply down a hill to our left, and parked us in front of a gated aluminum city. Four rows, each hundreds of feet long, lay against the asphalt like hastily built barracks in a metropolitan war. Or it could have been carefully assembled spinal columns from prehistoric creatures. Some future humans, ten centuries hence, may think that these things ruled us.

We pulled up to a window-level lock pad that looked to me like an automated teller machine. As Gus punched in his numbers, he said, "Put . . . It . . . On" and the gate opened at the fingertips' command. Grinning, he pulled through.

"Sixteen, nine, fifteen. Most people use their birthday or some portion of their social security number, but I use the company's initials. I wouldn't want Uncle Sam to think there was anything personal down here." He patted me on the knee. "No ma'am, this bin's business all the way." Suddenly I felt guilty about the bicycles in my storage bin and wondered how I'd justify their presence to the IRS. The strange demands of creativity, sir.

One shiny aluminum building sat off from the four long rows. It was only about ten feet wide and thirty or forty feet long, and one long side of it lay on a grassy patch, the only green on this asphalt island. The grass was immaculate, like a putting green in its tight smoothness and even color. An awning, also aluminum, hung across the grassy side with a slab of concrete under it. My God, this was a home! Four cheap aluminum chairs sat in conversational format on the slab, a man and a woman in two of them.

I put my hand on his arm as he started to open his door. "Wait a minute, Gus! I'm here to see your goods. Only! I don't want to get into anything else. Who are that man and woman?"

"Jewel and Betty. They own this place. Make a damn good living, and—" he waved his arm out toward the long, skinny building—"they don't have any living expenses."

"Uh huh," I mused. "I can see that. They actually live in that thing?"

Before he could answer me, both Jewel and Betty were at the car, opening our doors, beckoning us to join them "on the patio." Just before we were both pulled out of the car, I whispered to Gus: "This had better be quick, Gus. I need to get back to the office." He grinned back with those puffed-up cheeks of his.

Betty and Jewel turned out to be much more pleasant

than I had anticipated. Eccentric but charming. Jewel was sharp, physically as well as mentally. From the beak of his nose to the razor sharpness of his elbows, the man was all angles. Betty was the opposite, her plumpness being the kind that must have originated the adverb "pleasantly." Her hair was thinning angel fuzz, and the deep rouge on her cheeks worked visibly into her scalp above her ears. She collected antiques, filling two-thirds of their aluminum building with her collection. He wrote a Mr. Fixit column for *The Charlotte Observer* and freelance for four or five magazines. Between the two of them, they kept an interesting banter going on topics about which I knew very little. Gus dropped his salesman persona for the first time since I'd known him and fully engaged Jewel in the finer points of furniture restoration and historical pieces.

Inevitably the conversation worked its way around to the present. Betty said, "Gus, tell me about these awful murders up in Charlotte. Who's killing these poor women?" I stiffened automatically as if hearing about it for the first time.

"Wow! Isn't that something?" He turned to me. "You read about that, Sydney?" he asked.

I raised my eyebrows, but neither shook nor nodded my head. I was afraid of what I might say if I opened my mouth.

Gus has an opinion on everything, and the real estate murders were no exception. "Well, I'll tell you, Betty, I think it's some real estate salesman who got into the business for the wrong reasons. Yessiree, I do!" He slapped his own knee for a change.

Betty asked, "But how did he get into all those houses without breaking in?"

"He was an agent so he could," said Gus.

I couldn't stand it. "No one agent could ever have done all this, Gus. Each agent has a personal code to get into a house. You read the paper. Many codes have been used to commit these crimes."

He dismissed my comments with the flick of his hand. "I still think it's one guy," he said.

Jewel looked at me. "I have to agree with Gus. It's hard to believe that a group of people would be raping, murdering, and robbing as a team."

"You bet your life, Jewel buddy. It's just amazing what one really crazy guy can do. Look at that Dahmer freak. He sure did look normal, didn't he?"

Betty shrugged visibly. "His features were quite nice," she said, quaking.

To disentangle myself from this conversation I sought something to do with my eyes. The muddy bank leading to the back of McDonald's was infinitely more interesting than the rows of aluminum, which were my other option. Bridging the two views was the gate itself. While staring at the bank, my eyes sensed an object at the gate. I automatically turned. The back of the Bishop Cates van was stopped no more than twenty-five feet from where we sat. Its driver pushed in his personal code. In less than thirty seconds the gate opened, and Jake pulled out into McDonald's backyard.

I was on my feet screaming at him to stop. He bypassed the drive-through, and as he did, turned his full scraggly mane in my direction. He had heard me. Thank God he didn't stop. I don't know what I would have said to him if he had, or why I screamed in the first place.

Gus grabbed my arm, pulled me back to my seat.

"That's the Bishop Cates van, Gus!" I said, anxiety clipping my words. I forgot for a moment that he couldn't possibly understand, nor could I tell him, what my reaction was all about.

"So what?" Gus said.

Jewel looked at us both. "No, that's Jake Furman," he said. "He's had a bin for a couple of months now."

I sat lightly on my aluminum chair. "The company doesn't have a bin here?"

Jewel rubbed his angular knee with long, thin fingers. "Nope. Nope, that's his bin. If he's renting it for a company, he sure didn't tell Betty and me."

"What's the big deal anyway, Sydney?" Gus asked. "Half the world has storage bins. You do too. Why can't that poor guy?"

Betty spoke up: "For heaven's sake, boys, she was just trying to speak to a friend." She looked over at me and smiled, a female conspiracy. "Weren't you, dear?"

The smile I returned was genuine. "Why, of course. These men can't recognize enthusiasm, can they, Betty?" I hoped that the quiver in my voice sounded like Betty's did naturally. "I do know that young man. He works for a friend of mine so I thought that perhaps she, not he, was renting down here."

"That boy comes down several times a week. A messy one, isn't he?" Jewel said, raising his eyebrows into two carets. "He doesn't cause us any trouble though."

Betty snickered. "Aw now, honey. How's anybody going to cause us any trouble? It's not like people have parties down here. Sydney, people come and people go and in between they load or unload. That's about it."

"What's his bin number?" I asked as casually as I could, still looking at Jewel.

He said, "You'll have to ask Betty. She keeps the books and the keys." He chuckled. "I do the labor."

I looked over at Betty. "Well, let's look inside," she said. She rose and motioned me to follow. "We have over four hundred customers, Sydney. It's hard to keep track of who's where. Why do you want to know?"

I didn't have an answer; my face showed it.

She chuckled, shook her head like a woman who meets all kinds of people. "I don't suppose it'll do any harm to tell you. Not like you can cause any trouble without a key and a code to get inside here."

I had the code. I needed the key.

The "business office" of Jewel and Betty's aluminum home comprised the first ten-by-fifteen segment of their string of personal storage bins. It consisted of a half-wall kitchenette with a small conference table in front, a couple of customer chairs, and a long counter three feet off the back wall, the wall separating this area from their living quarters.

"How did you get used to living like this?" I asked as she pulled a large ledger onto the long counter.

She laughed. "I like it. Our house wasn't anything but a shrine to my antiques anyway. And I was always afraid Jewel or somebody would hurt something."

"But you don't even get to see them here. Don't you miss getting up and looking at them every morning?"

"Oh, I go back in there every day," she said. "Some days I spend all my time in there. I get to see them plenty. I never did like living with them. Made me too nervous." She was bent over the ledger and running her finger across a long horizontal column.

I scanned the room and spotted a large board on the

wall opposite the kitchen. On the board were keys. Must have been hundreds of them. Each was pegged over a number. Duplicates.

"Here we go. Here it is," she said. "One-one-five. Second building. West side. It's one of our larger ones, a fifteen by thirty. He must have a whole house in there."

"I just can't imagine how a boy that age could accumulate so much stuff he'd have to store it," I said. I located one-one-five on the board.

Betty laughed again as she closed the ledger and put it away on an out-of-sight shelf. "You'd be surprised. We have one teenager with a beer bottle collection that takes up a twenty-by-twenty. His mama said 'out' so the boy brought it here. He comes down from Charlotte every Sunday afternoon to look at it." She caught my eye. "I'm not the only crazy one, Sydney. Don't you collect anything?"

I walked over to her counter and rested my elbows on it as I thought. "Well, I collected marbles when I was a kid. I still have the better ones, maybe ten or twelve, in a crystal jar in my living room."

"Marbles? That's usually a boy's hobby."

It was my turn to laugh. "You got me. I was a tomboy, and my marble collection was the envy of every boy I knew. The first boy I ever dated asked if he could come into my house to see it."

Betty held her right index finger to her cheekbone and thumped it a couple of times. "Let's see . . . yes. Yes, you are in luck, Sydney. I happen to have some rare amber marbles." She turned toward a door on the wall behind the counter. "Would you like one?"

"Oh, Betty, I'd be thrilled. I haven't added any marbles in thirty-five years."

A soon as she closed the door, I reached for key one-one-five. To cover my misdeed, I moved the key next to it into its spot and moved one from the bottom row to where it had been. I felt as if I'd rearranged a puzzle someone had worked on for two months. Jewel would have himself a project fixing this mess.

I dropped it into the side pouch of my pocketbook. Betty reappeared behind her counter. The marble was exquisite, the color of translucent maple leaves in fall. The color deepened in its center.

"It's beautiful, Betty. Look at that color. Wow! What's the diameter?"

"Oh, I don't know. About an inch, I guess."

"That's big for a marble. I don't think I ever had any that big." I took it from her, held it up to the light one more time, and dropped it into the pouch inside my pocketbook as well. It clanged as it hit the just-deposited key.

The T-shirts were not one hundred percent cotton. Blends are throwaways. I want people to hold on to whatever has a client's name or slogan on it. I know. I know. I was hawking the wonders of poly/cotton these days, but I wouldn't buy a truckload of T-shirts made out of it.

"Cotton shrinks, Sydney. Then your people will get mad at you." Gus was doing his level best to sell me. His best wasn't good enough.

"Preshrunk. I always buy preshrunk."

Gus scratched his head and wiped the beaded sweat from his forehead in the process. "Okay, okay. Mickey Sutton said he'd take 'em off my hands if I couldn't unload 'em. He just moved his stuff to a bigger bin."

"Mickey? You're saying he has storage down here too? Since when?"

Gus gestured to the metal door to the right of his. "He was in this one here beside me, but moved to one of the larger bins on the end last week. He said he'd have room for the T-shirts."

Damn. Mickey seemed to be popping up everywhere.

"But what about these great hats? Terry cloth. You can't complain about them." He picked up one, made a fist, placed the tennis hat on it as if it were a shrunken head, and twirled. "See that beauty. Can't beat it, Sydney girl."

I'd learned with Gus that, when he starts adding "girl" to my name, he's in some kind of sales zone and will not be denied. The hats did look good, I had to admit. More important, I wanted to get out of there.

"How many you got there, Gus?" I asked. "Looks like enough to outfit the whole audience at the U.S. Open."

"Ten thousand," he said with such pride, you'd have thought he'd birthed them.

"Ten thousand! What am I going to do with ten thousand?"

The only way I was going to get them dirt cheap was to take them all, so, like a fool, I did. In my gut, I knew that I'd be thinking up themes like "Serving You Since . . ." and "Love is . . ." until retirement. Maybe I could snare an Ace Hardware and unload them all. The problem became how to move one hundred not-so-small boxes out of there. Gus told me not to worry about it, that he'd see they got to my office. I suppose it was providence that I'd had to take the building off the market. These boxes would consume all our free space.

"What if I wanted to bring the Trooper down in a couple of days and pick up a few boxes? Could you arrange with Betty and Jewel for me to do that?" I needed to get back into this place as soon as possible.

Gus rolled down the heavy door and locked it. His white shirt was soaked. All this aluminum created its own sauna. "You don't have to do that," he said. "How soon do you need them?"

"I don't need the whole truckful until it's convenient for you. I just might want to drop by and pick up one box sometime next week." This was one time I didn't need such a full-service salesman.

He started to unlock his bin again. Gee, he was making this hard. "Well, I'll just get you a box now. We'll—"

"Forget it, Gus," I said angrily. "Stop being so damned accommodating."

He stopped abruptly and slowly shook his head. "I'm just trying to help you out . . ."

I touched his arm briefly. "I know you are, Gus. Please just humor me on this and arrange for me to come by in the next few days."

Although it was after noon by the time we got back to Charlotte, I begged off lunch with Gus and had him drop me at the office. An unfamiliar car sat in the lot. Because everything out of the ordinary made me suspicious these days, I peered in through its windows to see if I could figure out who it was. No paperwork. No books. Just two fishing rods, taken apart to fit, and a worn basketball. Maybe it was a friend of Hart's. This person obviously did not work.

"Whose car is that?" I yelled out as I entered through the backdoor.

Nobody answered. I continued walking into Sally's reception area. At her desk sat the salesman, whose name, I believe, was Bob.

"Do you know whose car that is in the back lot?"

He looked up from his paperwork, smiled and said, "Do you mean mine?"

"Do you have an old basketball in the backseat?"

He grinned. "Yes, I do, Sydney. Seen a lot of cement in its day."

"That's more than you can say for yourself," I said sharply. "Where's Sally and Hart?"

"At lunch," he said as if I were making polite conversation. "I'm trying to get caught up on some paperwork. I'll be out of your hair in a minute."

"You're not in my hair," I said as I opened my door and closed it behind me.

I sat at my desk and tried to decide what I should be doing. Work was out of the question. The textile campaign was in Hart's court, the fire campaign was with production people and being sent to Raleigh today, Jean Miller was on hold. There was nothing else I really wanted to get into right now. I wanted to leave.

Through my closed door I could hear Hart and Sally returning from lunch. The door opened, spewing forth the laughing twosome. I caught the aftermath of some off-color joke Sally delights in telling Hart to see if she can get him to react. His laughter told me she'd scored. They were both at the edge of my desk before the giggles and sputtering stopped.

"It looks like you two had a fun lunch," I said. "Where'd you go?"

Sally answered me. "Across the street. We both had white sauce at the White Horse." Minor giggles as they beamed at each other.

"Do both of you have enough work to keep you busy this afternoon?" I asked.

Hart merely nodded. Sally giggled some more. "We're doing the sex thing together. I mean Hart wanted my help, my insights as a woman. I'm thinking like cotton, and Hart's trying to imagine what it feels like to be polyester."

I couldn't bring myself to look either of them in the eyes, especially Hart. I knew I'd laugh. The exercise was, after all, worthwhile. I wasn't about to sabotage creativity at Allen Teague. No matter how it came about.

"Okay. Good. I'm beat and hungry. Haven't eaten today." I looked at my watch. It was past one.

Hart said, "It would do you good to get a little rest. That bump on your head is only a few days old. Why don't you go home?"

"I think I will." I shifted to a whisper. "What about the salesman? Is he still out there?"

Sally tiptoed to the door, peered out, and returned as if on a reconnaissance mission. "Gone." She grinned.

"That's more like it," I said.

"Before you go," Sally said, "you might want to call a Cynthia Hyatt. She's called twice this morning. Could be some new business."

"No. That's personal. Anything else?"

"Just Tom Thurgood," she said.

I was pleased a call from him no longer bothered her. She must have assumed Fred was no longer in danger. I hoped, for her sake, she was right. I wasn't so sure.

After they left, I tried Cynthia Hyatt at home. As far as I knew, she didn't work. All we really knew of each other were the volleyball skills of our daughters. She'd wanted to have lunch. Maybe I'd be in luck and find that she hadn't eaten yet either. God, I was starving. Eight rings. No answer. No machine. It was sort of refreshing not to get a machine.

After being so rudely ignored this morning, I wasn't about to call Thurgood. He'd dismiss anything I'd tell him anyway.

21

THE MCDONALD'S LINE AT SOUTH BOULEVARD was backed up to the street, so I decided to try out Bojangle's, where things looked nice and empty. I pulled up to the drive-through and ordered the two-piece chicken Meal Deal with an extra cup of dirty rice. My hunger was so fierce, I couldn't make it home with the food. I parked next to the store Dumpster and tore into my lunch, devouring a drumstick in such a vicious frenzy that I felt at one with other carnivores. Two large end-of-season blackflies fought me for my biscuit, finally settling for a few crumbs I'd dropped on the passenger seat.

I considered my options on Jake's storage bin. I could have called Thurgood, but that didn't seem like a very good idea. After all, he didn't seem to be putting much credence in what I had to offer. I hadn't told him about seeing Jake in the green van earlier in the week. It hadn't seemed so important at the time. I wasn't about to tell him now.

Maybe I should just go on down there myself. Not tell anyone.

But maybe I owed it to Barbara to tell her what I suspected. Even if she couldn't handle it. With Oscar gone and Barbara in the condition she was, I was suddenly grateful Buddy was home. He seemed to be the key to her being okay. Jake was his friend, though, whether by choice or by necessity.

I decided to drive down to South Carolina tonight and see for myself. Since Jake had already been down there once today, I hoped it was a safe bet he wouldn't be down there again tonight. If Crystal and Fred's electronics or Crystal's jewelry were in that storage bin, then Jake killed Crystal and the other women too. I'd hand the whole case solved to Thurgood on a platter. That would show him!

Barbara lived in Foxcroft, an affluent neighborhood near her beloved SouthPark megamall. Getting there took me nearly thirty minutes because I was wedged behind a massive yellow school bus. Every half mile or so the stop sign extended from the bus's side, everything on both sides of the road stopped, and out popped elementary-age children, lunchboxes and book bags in tow.

The lots in Foxcroft are all at least an acre. Most homes do not front directly on the street, or if they do, you can't see them because of winding drives, lots of trees, and high bushes. Barbara's was no different. In fact, the Cateses' lot looked closer to two acres to me. I pulled into the drive with faith it would eventually lead me to the house itself. Funny, I had known Barbara most of my life and had never been to her house.

The front walk seemed as long as the driveway and was flanked on both sides by twenty-year-old boxwood. The house was Georgian, massive and square, the architectural destination of most upwardly mobile Charlotteans.

I rang the front doorbell and waited. After a half minute or so, Barbara's voice jolted me out of my rehearsal for talking to her. The intercom was expertly hidden among the ivy on the brick wall beside the door.

"It's Sydney, Barbara. I hate to bother you, but I really need to talk with you a few minutes."

"Go around to the back by the kitchen if you don't mind. I keep a key on the ledge over the door. I'm upstairs in my nightgown. Just come on up."

She sounded better. I immediately felt guilty, a familiar state for me. I would take whatever modicum of well-being she'd been able to muster. But there wasn't any way I could see around this conversation. Jake was her employee, and her son was hanging around with him. I felt I needed to warn her what I thought was coming. The shock would be worse if she heard it directly from the police.

I went around to the back of her house, no easy feat with a home this size. Overgrown fall camellias were everywhere. Their buds were enormous, but none had flowers. I felt above the rim of the only door I saw and, sure enough, found a dead bolt key. Once in the kitchen, I called her name, softly the first time, but loud and clear the second.

"Up here," she yelled back, and I followed the voice up a winding stairway with a large chandelier hanging between its curl.

The master bedroom, or suite as it turned out, was at the stairway landing. Barbara greeted me at the door.

"Sydney, I hate for you to see me like this. I'm really lying low. Didn't expect any company." She waved the back of her hand across her face as if trying to wipe off her own features.

"But come in," she said. "Come let's sit over here in the sitting room."

She took my hand and led me to an adjoining room with a love seat, two comfortable chairs, and a large floral ottoman. I couldn't remember ever having seen Barbara without any makeup. I caught myself when I fully took in her worn features. The paleness of her skin was rivaled only by the weakness of her eyes. They looked as if they'd seen more than their share of tears recently. God, I hated to contribute more.

"How are you feeling?" I asked as I sat on the ottoman. "Your voice sounds stronger," I added in an attempt to make it so.

She fidgeted with her matted hair before answering. "Oh, I'm better . . . I suppose. Buddy and I will get used to being alone." Her voice broke on the word "alone."

I touched her knee. "You've had a lot of stress lately. Oscar's leaving was probably the straw, you know." I smiled, hoping to hold her eyes and steady her for what I needed to say. "You wait and see. You're going to be better off in the long run."

She cleared her throat. "Would you like something to drink? Nonalcoholic. Coffee, Coke?" She rubbed one of the knuckles of her left hand as if it were arthritic. Maybe it was.

I shook my head. "No thank you, Barbara. I'm only going to stay for a few minutes. You need your rest. There's something I feel I must tell you. I hate to, but I feel I must."

She threw her hand to her neck and blinked. She opened her mouth but closed it without saying anything and shrank back in her chair. A woman retreating from the world.

"It's okay," I said as I squeezed her trembling fingers. "Where's Buddy?"

She dug her nails into her neck. When she removed her hand, deep red pits sprouted where the tips of her fingers had been. "In his room," she rasped. "Why? Where would you expect him to be? He's still helping me. That's why he's not in school."

"I'd rather he not hear what I'm going to say is all," I said, lowering my voice.

"Why? What's going on?" she said as she rubbed her mottled neck.

" 'Cause it's about Jake, and I know they're friends. I don't want to put Buddy in a difficult position. If he doesn't hear this, he won't be. Okay?" I waited for her to ease herself back into her chair before I continued.

"Barbara, I have reason to believe Jake is involved in these murders."

Her hand flew to her mouth this time.

"Let me tell you what I know before you get upset. Do you know that Jake has a storage bin down in York?"

She was slowly shaking her head back and forth, her mouth slightly ajar.

"I saw him down there this morning. In your Bishop Cates green van." I hesitated between each statement, then took a deep breath. "And, Barbara, I think it's the van that's been spotted at least one time at these murders."

Finally she was listening to me. "Who?" she asked. "Who saw the van?"

"A couple across the street from Crystal Ball's house

described a van that sounds like yours. They were watching the robbery as if it were a movie. On top of that, they described someone carrying a TV set out of her house. The police thought it was Fred Ball. The description fits Jake."

"Oh no," she said softly. "I thought the boy was doing okay. I knew he'd had some problems when we hired him, but—" Her voice broke, and she stifled a cry. "But how could he be getting into these homes?"

She answered herself before I could speak. "My office," she said breathlessly. "Oh my God. He took codes from realtors' desks before they left the firm. That must be it. I had wondered how . . ." Her voice trailed off, as if she had left me for another world.

"Well, if I'm right," I said, "that answers another big part of this puzzle. How did he gain access to their desks? Didn't they keep them locked?"

"He must have gotten the master desk key from Oscar." A hardness came over her. "Oscar gave him the run of the place. I warned Oscar. Goddamn him, I warned him."

She stopped and grabbed both my hands. "What do we do now? Are you going to call the police?"

"Not yet," I said. "My theory could be all wrong. I could be dragging the boy into something that I shouldn't. Besides, I have personal reasons for not wanting to report any of this to the police just now."

"You're not going to confront Jake, are you? I'd be afraid for you. . . ."

"Oh no. That's the last thing I'd do," I said. "I have access to the storage bin where I saw him this morning."

She looked as if she were going to ask me how, so I waved her off. "Don't ask me how, but I do. I'll go down there tonight and look inside. If I find anything that appears to be stolen from one of these houses, I'll let you know. Then I'll call the police."

"Sydney, that could be dangerous. Don't you want me to go with you? Let me get Buddy. He could go with you."

"Buddy mustn't know about this, Barbara. Promise me you won't tell him. Jake's his friend, and you'll put him in a bad situation. It'll be hard enough on him if all this is true."

She answered slowly. "Okay, Sydney. I'm scared for you, though. Won't you let me go?"

I patted her on the knee before I rose to go. "Some help you'd be." I smiled, and she hugged me tightly, what felt like desperately. "You'll be okay when this whole mess is settled."

As I was leaving her bedroom, she pulled me close again and whispered as if we were in a crowded room: "You're a great friend, Sydney. You've always been a great friend, haven't you? You've stood by me."

So lonely. I let myself out and put the key back over the kitchen door. So lonely and so desperately needing not to be. Just like she was in junior high. The pressure of her need repelled me. The irony of it all. The opposite of the reaction she wanted.

George junior was arriving home from school when I drove up. He looked as tired as I felt. This lingering heat and humidity was getting to all of us.

"Hey there," I said cheerfully. "Want some ice cream? Maybe put it in some ginger ale and make a float?"

His open smile gave me back some of my energy. I

slipped his book bag off his shoulders and bent over to kiss him. In a few short years he would be taller than I was.

"Boy, your bag is heavy," I said. "Big test Monday?"

He ran his fingers through thick, unruly hair. "Ugh! Yeah. Science. Everything we've studied so far this year. It's almost as bad as math."

"I know, Georgie. I felt the same way. It's funny, though. Now that I'm a grown-up, I like both subjects. You're right, though. As school subjects, they're not very exciting."

While we were slurping our floats at the kitchen table, Joan came in. Her arms were full of books as well.

"It looks like a quiet weekend around this house," I said. "You got a test on Monday too?"

"Term paper." She groaned. "The Salem witch trials. It's actually pretty interesting stuff. I've written most of it already." She fixed herself a float and joined us.

"So, you're staying in tonight?" I asked her.

"Carolyn Bitters is having a surprise spend-the-night for Sissy Warden. It's her birthday." I felt her eyes on my forehead as I studied the foam in my glass. "I thought it'd be okay with you since most of the paper's done."

"Have you told her you'd come?" I asked.

She squinted as she smiled. "I thought you wouldn't mind."

Normally I would. "It's okay," I said.

"I've got to get her a present. Do we have any wrapping paper?"

"In the attic. The box that our computer came in. If we have any, it'll be there." I wiped my mouth with a piece of the paper towel roll I'd put in the middle of the kitchen table.

"So you're invited for dinner?" I asked. I didn't want to sound too excited, but I wanted to reach the storage facility before dark.

"No," she said. "Why?" She squinted her eyes and smiled conspiratorially. "Are you trying to get rid of us? Is that Tom Thurgood coming over?"

"I may never see him again. He's too in-charge for my tastes." I took my glass to the sink to wash and pitched the wadded paper towel into the trash can on the way.

"Seems easygoing to me," Joan commented. "You want to see in-charge, you read about the men in charge of these witch trials. Wow! I bet some men still think that way."

"Do not!" said George junior.

"Do so!" said Joan. She turned to me. "And please don't ask me to take care of the whining baby here. He wouldn't be welcome at a spend-the-night party." She followed me to the sink with her glass and George junior's.

"I've got plans," George junior said defensively, then looked to me pleadingly. "Is that okay, Mom?" He continued talking to his sister as if I'd answered. "I'm sleeping over at Jimmy Hyatt's. Randy Metz is too. So there."

She turned toward him. "Well, don't you little boys go playing with any matches."

"What's that supposed to mean?" he asked her. Then he looked at me. "What's she mean, Mom?"

"Honey, I really don't know. I guess it's a history joke. Are you invited for supper?" My mind was beginning to groove on one track only.

He wiped the foam off his lips with the back of his hand. "I don't think so, but I could ask."

"No, no. That's okay. How about Chinese? I'll call it in and then go pick it up. Let's eat before seven, though. I need to go out while it's still light." I picked up the roll of paper towels and took them to the kitchen sink, where I tore off four sections and ran them under the water, then wrung them out. As I knew he would, George junior was drawing designs with the float residue onto my laminate table top. First I cleaned his fingers, then the laminate.

That little bit of sheen I rose from the kitchen table spurred me on to an afternoon of cleaning. I have no schedule for this type of activity, so when it hits me, I've learned to go with it. The older I get, the less often it hits.

By five-fifteen I felt I'd merely transferred all the grime to my own body. I showered and washed my hair, letting it air-dry while I walked around the yard and looked for spots in which to plug a few more daffodil bulbs. It may have been my imagination, but the air didn't seem so dense. There was the hint of a breeze, but not enough to move the air around much. Swarms of tiny gnats still hung just below the lowest of the oak tree branches.

Yards like mine in Dilworth are mostly long and narrow. I was halfway back in a bed of wilting hosta when he drove into the drive that culminates beside the kitchen door. Thurgood was knocking on the door for the second time when I finally reached the driveway myself. Although I was no longer angry, I chose not to speak. I didn't care whether he came and went without seeing me.

He did see me, though. As he was turning to get back into his car. With no hesitation, he lifted his long arms, opened his palms to the sky, then lowered his arms. Some kind of cinematic framing of the scene, I supposed.

"Hi," I said without much enthusiasm.

"There you are," he said, still flailing his arms around

as he approached me. I watched the movements more closely and realized that Thurgood was trying out various tennis strokes. Very poorly, but at least all this movement had a purpose.

"I went by your office. Sally said you were taking the afternoon off." His hair fell across one of those sparkling green eyes.

"Why didn't you return my call?" he asked.

My shoulders slumped as I continued past him toward the house. "It's okay, Tom. You don't have to apologize."

"Huh?" he muttered.

"This morning. You don't have to say you're sorry. I know you had to act that way in front of your peers."

My hand was on the railing beside the short steps leading to my kitchen. He grabbed it and turned me around to face him. Something close to anger was in his eyes, a hardness like this morning's.

"I want to get something straight with you. I don't act a prescribed way for anybody. I do what's right as I see it and that's that."

His eyes were so piercing that I couldn't keep looking at him. I rubbed my hand.

"Look at me," he said, and waited until I did. "You had no business crossing a crime scene barrier this morning. I would have treated the governor the same way. You just don't do that, Sydney. It's a crime scene, for Pete's sake."

I chewed on the inside of my cheek. "So, you're not here to apologize?"

"Tennis," he said. "I want to play tennis." His eyes softened with the topic shift. "It's too late today, I know, but what about tomorrow afternoon?" The metal was gone from his voice, replaced by boyish enthusiasm.

"We'll see," I said noncommittally. This guy surely

seemed to segregate his life. I didn't think I could move so easily from one arena to another.

"Are you going to be home tonight?" I asked. "I can let you know later." I wanted to be able to reach him. Just in case.

He said he would be and put his home number on the back of his card.

"I might need to call you about something else tonight too."

He didn't probe; he didn't even look curious. How did he pull it off?

As he was getting into his car, I tried to make it sound offhand, more casual than casual, an afterthought at most: "What's the latest on the real estate murders?"

"You saw it. Another one" was all he said, as if that was enough for me.

Chinese restaurants are punctual, but my kids are not. George junior was asked to come to the Hyatts' any time after seven, but it was seven forty-five before he and I pulled out of our driveway. Joan had hitched a ride with one of her girlfriends just before we left.

The Hyatts lived on the other side of Freedom Park in the Myers Park area. I could keep going in the same general direction when I let George junior off and be at the storage facility in thirty minutes at most. I would have a race for the last of the daylight. Their house was an added-on ranch with all kinds of breezeways and odd angles to make it work. It looked to me more like an elementary school than a home. But what did I know? I was beginning to think not much—about anything.

When George junior was bounding from the Trooper,

I pulled on his shirt sleeve and gave him a kiss. "Ask Mrs. Hyatt to come out to the car for a sec, honey. We've been playing telephone tag for a couple of days."

"Okay, Mom," he said. "I'll be home before lunch tomorrow."

I waited and fooled with the radio enough to hear a portion of the life history of some violinist I'd never heard of on PBS. His mother had been Russian, but he'd been raised in Budapest. I couldn't get into it.

George junior came running back to the car. "Mr. Hyatt said to tell you that Mrs. Hyatt and Cindi are out of town. Get this, Mom. They're looking at boarding schools. Wait till Joan hears this. She'll freak out!"

It made no sense, not this late. The school year had already started. I decided they must be looking for next year. A lot of kids went off then to make their records look better for college. Maybe that's what Cynthia Hyatt wanted to talk about. I'd hate to be present when the coach finds out. She'll be the one to what-did-Georgie-call-it? Freak out?

Large family home. Needs repair.
Owner says reduce for quick sale. ML

When I was young, real young like seven or eight, I had an ant farm. Two separate packages came in the mail from some-place in Texas. The first contained ant food, glass panels with snap-on plastic bottom and top, and the sand to go in it. A cou-ple of days later, a box of frozen black ants arrived with a book-let about their civilization and a magnifying glass to watch it.

I set up their world on the table beside my bed, and by the next morning, two tunnels were already begun. I was hooked. I de-voured the booklet, then found a thin hardback at the library too.

In the ant farm, everybody knew what they were supposed to do. There was a leader for each tunnel dug, and they appeared to take turns at this role without prodding. When I'd open the plastic top and drop in their food, the same group would heave it onto their backs and distribute it to the others. Meaning for each came genetically embedded, a code so clear one had no choice but to follow.

Everything important to me I learned from those ants. Sounds stupid, I know, but it's true. Like understanding your role, tak-ing the time to pay attention to who you really are, then accept-ing it—like the ants did. And being responsible. Hey, I don't smoke cigarettes. I've decided it's like infecting our civilization.

I don't have control over much, but when I do, I try to be responsible.

There was even an undertaker in the ant farm. Tunnels collapsed despite the greatest of care in building them. No matter if the undertaker was in another quadrant entirely, he attended his dead posthaste. He would drag bodies one at a time through a tunnel used only by him. To a burial ground only he and the dead ever touched. Sometimes it took him three full days to clear out a landslide. I'd try to stay with him during those times, draping my lamp late at night with a beach towel big enough for my upper body to share the space.

He was the only ant who worked alone. As time passed the burden of his code grew heavier. Ant farms don't last forever, like anything else.

The day came when only four ants were left, the undertaker and three who seemed to have lost their coding. I dropped in food; they ignored it. They ran back and forth, into each other and over each other, the undertaker working so diligently just beyond their flurry. I grew so angry at these three that I did something I'd never done before: I tapped the glass at the point of their frenzy. Instead of collapsing in on them as I'd planned it, the sand heaved, then sifted itself onto the valiant little undertaker, leaving his body crooked and stiff.

So the big question finally came down. Who would bury the ant who buried the rest? The three remaining insects ignored their brother, continued their systemless ramblings. Hey, you creeps, I screamed, help the undertaker! Nothing.

I took the plastic top off their world and poured them onto the smooth wood surface of my desk. The three renegades emerged from a mound still moving. I grabbed a #2 pencil and plunged its eraser onto each of them, ending their meaningless existence.

I sat for hours looking at the salt-and-pepper landscape that had transformed my desk. I swept the three losers into my plas-

tic Redskins trash can so as not to violate the others. *Which corpse the undertaker was I could never tell. The first strobe of daylight pulsated red on the horizon, and I knew what I must do.*

I shivered in the unexpected chill of early autumn as I carried my friends in a simple brown lunch bag to the azalea garden. I dug my heel into the earth's surface to loosen the crusty frost, then scooped an area out with my hands, replacing it with the contents of my bag. I wanted to say a prayer for them, especially the undertaker, but no words powerful enough ever found their way into my thoughts. Instead I stood as the sun came up and turned the frosted azalea pink, I stood there and cried.

A light came on in the kitchen, and I went inside to breakfast.

22

PART OF THE PROBLEM WITH CHARLOTTE'S road system is the distance one has to drive to pick up its beltway. Developers have used their power to create pockets of land that have easy access; the rest of us drive as much as forty-five minutes to get on the roads that are supposed to make living here easier. When I finally hit the southwestern belt, I was two city blocks north of South Carolina.

I watched the hazy sun slap itself against objects as it made a beeline for the horizon. First it hit the top stories of the cheap glass-and-stucco towers that riddle the southern boundaries of the city. Then it flashed itself along the tops of cars. Dazzling and random like a rainless electric storm. As its last hurrah, it poised itself on the edge of the world and, for five long minutes, blinded every driver on Interstate 77 and all roads sprouting westward. A swaggering, obnoxious drunken sun, its sunset was unremarkable. A pink so pale, I wouldn't have even noticed it if I hadn't been praying for it to stay with me until I was through with my task.

What I had in light was this piddling spit of a sunset. About ten minutes till total dark, I figured. Enough, I hoped, to get a cursory feel for what Jake had in his bin and leave. I did plan on calling Thurgood if the kinds of things I thought would be here actually turned out to be. Like televisions, stereos, and VCRs. If I was wrong, if Jake's having this bin was just a coincidence and in it I found ten million baseball cards, so be it. I wouldn't have to worry anymore that there was something I alone knew and should be acting on. That damn feeling had plagued me for days, and I was at a point where I was willing to do whatever it took to put it to rest.

The crowd at McDonald's was typical Friday night, families inside and teenagers cruising the lanes. In trying merely to get through the circling tribe, I offended two surly big shots who laid on their horns, ranted and spat in my direction. Like dodging through a minefield.

Juxtaposed to the mayhem of the McDonald's in front of it, the storage facility seemed a respite from a world gone mad. I pulled up to the gate, which sat high above the sprawling asphalt lot. I looked around. The entire facility was fifty feet below the land around it, as if someone had excavated for a multistoried building, then changed his mind. If I were Betty or Jewel, I would lose my mind in this sterile place. Like living inside a crater.

Two high dusk-to-dawn vapor lights popped on, casting shadows onto the metal roofs of the bins. The air was so thick with moisture and interstate exhaust fumes that I could see it in streams in front of one of the lights. I knew another rain would come tonight, a rain like all the others we'd known for the past month.

I had to count on my fingers to resurrect Gus's entry code. At first I gave "I" a numerical value of seven, two short of reality, then panicked that I might have misunderstood what he'd not only showed me but actually bragged about. When the gate finally opened, its moaning hinges made my skin tingle as if someone were teasing me with very long fingernails. I hugged myself and rubbed my upper arms to stop the sensation. I breathed deeply, then pulled through just before the gate automatically closed after me.

The vapor lights reflected off the metal roofs but didn't illuminate between the bins. At ground level the only real light I could see was coming from Betty and Jewel's detached house. Their light didn't help me since no windows faced in the direction of the bins. Wise architectural planning, considering the view. If I could get inside Jake's bin quickly, I could see well enough to decide whether or not to call Tom Thurgood.

I could hear the Trooper's tires rotating atop the asphalt surface. The same rhythm as the blood rushing between my ears. I needed to calm down. Breathe deeply. When I did, I realized I had been holding my breath while I looked for number one-one-five. It was barely visible in the waning light. Second building, west side. Just like Betty said. About a fourth of the way into the row. I wished it were on the end, where I wouldn't feel so much like a trapped field mouse.

The flashlight I usually carry in the glove compartment had disappeared, and for a brief moment I considered going home. My plan had been to do this in daylight. Quick and easy. The rectangular shadows cast by the Trooper made me feel I was about to unearth a grave. But I backed up the Trooper and turned it to face the bin.

My headlights would shine on enough of the contents for me to determine what was inside.

The lock was another one of those semi-bicycle types, only this one was permanently attached just outside the bin's door frame. The door was the aluminum roll type and spanned most of the bin's fifteen-foot front. When I turned the key, the round lock opened just enough to re-semble a metal Pac-Man releasing its victim. It was heavy as hell, upper-body strength a plus to pull and push its opening with ease.

Two rivers of sweat, one between my breasts, the other between my shoulder blades, erupted as I stood back to look inside. At first I couldn't see anything, then realized I was throwing shadows on the objects by standing in front of the car's headlights. I backed up to the front of the Trooper and propped myself against the grille be-tween the lights. The front portion of the bin lit up like the beginning of act 1 in some makeshift small-town the-ater. Really more like act 3, I thought, as the first of the obviously stolen objects came into view.

The first thing I saw was a twenty-seven-inch JVC television, one of those new stereo models with the big black screen and sleek housing. Near it were at least a dozen more TVs close to the same size. To the left front were stereos and compact disc players along with four or five small cabinets that had probably held some of the music systems. Just behind those items I could see the tops of full-size home computers that must have been sit-ting on workstations or desks of some kind because the computers were waist-high as I was seeing them. My God, he had it all arranged like a retail environment. What was the guy doing? Did he come down here every day and work on his inventory display as if his customers would arrive at any minute?

From where I stood everything could have been carried by one man. Easily. This was no "gang of realtors" or even two people the way I saw it. God, this was going to look bad for Barbara. An employee of her firm robbing and murdering with access coming from the personal codes of realtors at Bishop Cates. If Thurgood could track Oscar down, he should be tarred and feathered for hiring this guy. Barbara did not deserve what Jake's arrest would do to her. For a fleeting second I allowed myself to think about the public relations effort I might put forth to avert such a disaster.

I had decided on the drive down here that I would look for Sally's mother's ring and the jewelry box it had disappeared in. It would be my hands-down confirmation that put Jake at one murder scene at least. The Trooper's high beams didn't reach beyond the larger items in the front part of the bin. I stood at the personal computers and stared into the darkness beyond them.

Something smelled rancid. Like two whole laundry loads of mildew. I looked around for a washing machine but didn't see one. Would have been too big for him anyway. I couldn't pinpoint where the smell was coming from, but it made my eyes water and nose burn.

After thirty seconds my eyes adjusted enough to see that what was back there were boxes. Brown, corrugated boxes. Most of them were large, the size you pack your towels in when you're moving. A few were smaller, book size. If he was packing away jewelry boxes, I figured he'd put them in these smaller boxes. I wound my way around two larger ones to get to a short stack of small ones.

He hadn't bothered to tape up any of them. I took a

box off the top and held it while I bent over to look inside the one under it. Sterling flatware filled the whole box. Next I rummaged through the box in my hands, pushing necklaces aside in search of rings in case he had removed it from the jewelry box. God, the whole box was necklaces. A tremendous amount of time had gone into the organization of this take. Jake was meticulous in his booty if not in his person.

I squatted to go through the bottom box in the stack. Bingo. Rings. But there must have been two or three hundred. How was I going to figure out which ones had been Crystal's engagement and wedding rings without the jewelry box Sally had told me about?

I took a deep breath, rubbed my nose to stop the burning, rubbed between my breasts to sop up some of the wet. Was this enough to take to Thurgood? Surely it was, but I didn't feel as safe with him as I had yesterday. What now?

With the box in my hands, I stood up to ease the pain that had begun in the small of my back. A sharp shadow crossed my face, and I instinctively looked toward the Trooper.

I dropped the box. With his back against the headlights, he loomed massive and black, a silhouetted Neanderthal with grizzled hair straddling a thick neck. I tried to breathe again but couldn't get any air back in after expelling it.

"Jake?"

No answer. His legs spread out as if he planned to stand there awhile.

"Jake, I know it's you." I took a small step toward him, which was also the only way out.

"Stop," he commanded, and I realized I had never

heard his voice before. It was high, not what I'd expected at all. "Back where you were!"

I stumbled against one of the larger boxes, packed so fully that I didn't fall. Maybe I could hide behind it, but what good would it do me? There was still only one way out.

"You saw me," he said. "Today. You were here, weren't you?"

"I was looking at T-shirts, Jake. I wasn't following you." It occurred to me that he knew as little about me as I knew about him. "I don't know anything, Jake. Can't we forget about this?"

He laughed.

I waited.

"You know what this is," he said. His voice was decidedly deeper now, his confidence gaining. He saw me as weak. His instincts were right: I was feeling weaker as each second passed.

"So you robbed some people. Maybe you didn't. Maybe I don't know. There's no proof in here." Why wasn't my voice getting any deeper?

"You're Joan's mom, aren't you?" He shifted his weight ever so slightly. At least he didn't seem poised to strike at this second.

I did not answer.

"What do you think you see?"

What an odd question. "What does that mean? I don't know how to answer that," I said.

"Have you looked in that box you're standing next to? The big one." He motioned toward the box I'd fallen against, and then he chuckled.

I could see his edges well since he was backlit. No

bulges in the sides of his pants. Nothing in his hands either. Then I remembered that his hands *were* his weapon. I noticed I was rubbing my neck.

"Answer me. Have you looked in that box?"

"No."

"Open it. Now! You may as well see the whole movie now you're here." More chuckling.

"I can't open it. You've taped it. You didn't tape the others." I thought, if I could get him back here with me, I might get the chance to squeeze out somehow. Not a very good chance, but the only chance I had.

"Pull the tape," he said evenly.

I tried. My fingernail, being part of my hand, was shaking too much to hook the edges well. So I got a partial hold on one side of the wide packing tape. As I pulled, the tape ripped in two so that the lid opened only slightly. The stench literally knocked me back. I thought I would be sick.

Jake started toward me. Slowly. Deliberately. He was maybe fifteen feet from me at most.

"You need to understand," he said as he came forward. "It's important to me someone understand. I'm going to open that box for you so you will see."

I backed up against the box again as he continued his certain stride. My stomach seemed to catch in my throat. I choked and tasted something putrid. He was no more than six feet from me now, his large frame blocking all light like a sudden eclipse. My knees buckled and I started to go down. I tried to hold myself upright by pressing my shoulders against the box. How was I going to make a run for my car if I couldn't even stand up?

It was a series of three pops. Pop . . . pop . . . pop. Like counting by thousands while waiting for water to boil. At first I thought he was lunging for me, to strangle me as he had strangled so many other women. My own hands shot to my neck in self-defense. My elbows pointed toward him, their bony angles my only hope of a weapon.

He had toppled both me and my stalwart box onto our sides and pinned me to the floor beside it. I struggled and screamed, but he made no effort to restrain me, muffle me, or strangle me. I couldn't push him up, so I pulled my upper body to the side enough to get out from under his chest and breathe.

I saw Barbara's two-inch lizard heels, then the .38 in her hand, and finally her face. She was saying something, but the rushing in my head blocked her out. I looked from her hand to the body beside me, and only then did I realize that she had shot Jake. He was dead.

"Oh God, Barbara," I sputtered. "He was going to kill me. You saved my life."

She was shaking as much as I was.

"I followed him," she rasped. "I knew he was coming after you, Sydney. I just knew—" She broke off with a garbled cry.

With great effort, I tried to free the rest of my body from Jake's crushing weight. Barbara put the gun on the floor and pushed at his hips while I dragged myself out. At the exact moment of my freedom, Jake's body flipped to its side, his arms sprawled up against the half-open box.

I gasped. Hanging out of the top of the box, straining at the wrist against the severed tape, was a hand. A dead hand. Dark gray, like someone had rubbed ashes all over it. Dead awhile.

Both Barbara and I simply stared, our mouths literally unable to close but also unable to make sounds either one of us could understand. Together we bent over the top of the box. Neither of us made a move to open it all the way.

A voice from outside the bin yelled: "You in there! Whoever's in there come out now!"

Gladly. "We're coming," I said.

We held each other around the waist as we walked toward Betty's wonderfully commanding voice. Silhouetted, she looked like a plump witch, a plump witch with a very long broom. When we reached her side, I could see that she held a musket. A genuine two-hundred-year-old musket, the kind that you load from the front of the barrel with gunpowder. Jewel stood behind her with a hammer in one hand and a Civil War sword in the other.

"You've got to help us," I said breathlessly. "Jake tried to kill me, but Barbara—thank God—shot him when he was attacking me."

Barbara and I both said together, "There's a body in a box in there."

I hate to admit to a gender observation at a time like this, but I couldn't help it. Of the four of us, Jewel was the only man. He was also the only one of us who was willing to open the box.

Continuing in his wartime mind-set, he ordered Betty to circle back for a flashlight and return "posthaste." While we waited, I explained more of what this was all about to Jewel; then I slumped beside Barbara, who was sitting like a sack of potatoes on a nearby computer workstation. Neither of us spoke. I remember thinking that Barbara seemed almost in a trance. Emotionless, mindless. A part of me envied her.

The flashlight was what I call a lamp, the kind that takes

lots of D cells or a nine-volt battery. It was the size I could have used earlier. What I personally thought we needed now was one of those little ones that double as key chains. We had to find out who this was, I supposed, but I didn't see the necessity of putting the poor corpse in floodlights. Or my stomach in more peril, for that matter.

Betty and Jewel stood at the head of the box. It was lying on its side like a large tan rectangular robot beside a dead Jake, who looked and was as lifeless as the box. I took Barbara's hand, and we joined them. Jewel pulled out a pocketknife and split the box at the seam from bottom to top while Betty held the lamp.

Barbara screamed before my eyes could focus. When I did finally see, the scene was something I am sure I will never forget. Even though the corrugated board no longer held him in, his knees were pulled up to his navel, his chest was bloated barrel-like, his back arched as if pride somehow figured in. His arms were reaching above his twisted head with elbows bent. Someone had stuffed him into the box in order make him fit. At the time, he must have been flexible enough to contort like this. With full-blown rigor mortis now stapling his ligaments, he looked like an ugly ballerina frozen in a poorly executed pirouette. His only clothing was an undershirt and briefs. To say that sharp features go soft in death would be misleading, for there is nothing soft about death. But Oscar's sharp features were now blurred. As if someone had taken pastels and smudged around his edges. Needless to say, his most remarkable feature—the pink of his skin—had been altered forever. The bullet hole above his left eyebrow had seen to that.

My first instinct was to shield Barbara, but she was on top of him, holding him. Her screams sprayed palpable grief through the thick, putrid air. I tried to pull her off, but she gripped him tightly, began to rock him and wail. The overwhelming smell of decay didn't stop her. I fumbled in my pants pocket for Thurgood's card with his home phone number, gave it to Betty, and told her to get him down here quickly. I then gave in and hugged Barbara's back while she held her husband. I did it as much for myself as for her.

Jewel stood with the open pocketknife at this side, not having moved since opening the box. His angular features had fallen, his chin seeking refuge in his neck. His mouth was slightly open, unmoving. Our eyes met and tears fell from us both. Pain this huge begged to be shared.

23

BARBARA WAS ALMOST CATATONIC. BETTY HAD taken her back to the office, where she was going to try to get her to drink something hot and put a blanket over her. In spite of the hot, humid night, Barbara had been shivering when Betty took her away. The only words she had spoken were "Why? Oh my baby, why?"

Jewel and I continued as sentries over the dead, neither of us speaking or even moving. I heard a horn honk several times and realized only after he appeared in front of the bin that it must have been Thurgood trying to get past the gate.

Tom acknowledged me with a nod of his head, then inspected the bodies. He returned to the box where I sat and asked me if I was okay.

Okay by what standard? I wondered. Okayness in my life is defined by a certain sense of well-being that was decidedly lacking here tonight. Maybe in Thurgood's line of work okayness is defined by being the person present who is not dead. In that case, a little more than half of us were okay.

"I guess so," I said, but I noticed that my lip was quivering when I said it.

He put his large hand on my thigh and squeezed it rhythmically, the way a hungry infant primes its mother's breast. As he soothed me this way, he spoke into a portable phone that he alternately held in his hand or cradled between his jaw and shoulder.

When he was through talking, he turned from me to Jewel. I thought that we might feel better if we went outside. The smell, although not quite as strong as it had been earlier, was still overpowering. Jewel looked like he'd feel a whole lot better if he'd go ahead and throw up. Thurgood took the pocketknife from him, looked closely at it, folded it, and returned it to Jewel. The small action seemed to bring Jewel around a little, involve him with the living once more.

"Can you tell me what happened here?" Tom asked him. Why, in God's name, was he asking a complete stranger when I was standing right beside him?

Jewel hesitated, looked at me, then said to Thurgood: "All that you see, sir, had happened already by the time I got here. My wife and I run this facility. We heard gunshots."

Any other cop in the world, I am convinced, would have turned to me to ask what had happened. Not Thurgood. He pulled a small notepad, the size I keep beside my bed for 3:00 a.m. ad ideas, out of his trouser pocket. He next took a pen from his shirt pocket and wet it against his tongue as if it were an old pencil.

"Name, please," he said to Jewel.

My mind wandered out of this bin, over the state line,

to the Bishop Cates offices in Charlotte. What could have happened between Oscar and Jake for it to come to this? Did Oscar figure out what Jake was doing the day I forced him to take Barbara's computer program to the police? When was that? Tuesday? Had anybody seen Oscar since? Wasn't that the same day Barbara went into seclusion and Buddy told me Oscar had left town? Maybe he'd intended to leave town but decided to confront Jake before he did. What if Oscar had somehow been involved in this mess in a more material way? What if they had come to blows as partners? How would we ever know now that both of them were dead? What did it even matter now that both of them were dead?

With Thurgood's back still to me, I stood and walked outside. I breathed as deeply as I could. The first few drops of our nightly rain hit my face as I turned it to the sky. I wished it would pour tonight and wash away all that I had experienced here.

The Trooper's lights had dimmed. I turned them off, but I knew the battery had weakened. I'd probably need help to get home tonight. Thurgood had left his car in front of the office, so the only light inside the bin was the lamp, which Thurgood had placed on the floor facing upward. The shadows it cast only added to the surreal landscape of this place.

I walked to the end of the row and turned toward the light that was the office. I went around to the window on their patio and looked in. Barbara was sipping something out of a mug and curled up on the lone sofa. She was crying, genuine healthy tears of grief. She would be okay.

I kept walking. I felt selfish. I didn't want to be a part of Barbara's grief right now. I wanted to help myself instead.

* * *

Five minutes later a police car almost hit me while it rounded a row of bins as if taking the inside lane at the Winston 500. Immediately on its heels, three or four more came screeching into the facility at various rates of speed and recklessness. I saw Charlotte cars and at least one York sheriff's car.

I pointed them toward one-one-five and kept walking. I climbed a muddy bank fifty feet to its top where an eight-foot chain link fence beckoned me to rest against it. In my blue jeans I found a crumpled pack of cigarettes and two damp matches in a matchbook that said *Smokers, protect your rights!* I propped myself against the fence and attempted to light a Vantage. The first match tore itself to pieces trying to accommodate me, so I blew on the second one awhile to dry it. If it had not lit, I am not certain I would have been able to pull myself together.

I can honestly say that I have no idea how much time passed up on that hill. Nor do I know what I thought about while I sat there. I do know it had begun to rain steadily by the time I saw Tom climbing up to me.

"Come on." He held his hand out.

"I don't want to," I said, my voice sounding as if it belonged to someone else.

He bent down and lifted me by my upper arms anyway.

"I don't want to go back in there," I repeated.

He took off his jacket and put it around my shoulders. "You don't have to," he said. "You can sit in one of the cars. You'll get sick like this."

I let him lead me down the hill. Once on the asphalt, I looked into his eyes. "I know everything, Tom. Jake did everything. He tried to kill me, and Barbara shot him just before he did. Then we saw Oscar—" My voice broke.

"It's okay, Sydney. You don't have to tell me anything. Jeep Anderson's going to take your statement."

I stopped walking. "Jeep Anderson? Who in the hell is Jeep Anderson?"

"I think it's best if I'm not the one to take your statement."

I spun away from his grip and turned to face him. Ready-made anger rose in me like a full-term new-born after a one-day gestation. Impossible. Where did it come from?

"What in the hell is this all about?" I screamed. "I'm the one this all happened to, not the damn manager of the storage bins. I'm the one who was backed into the bowels of that place with a rotting corpse as my only compan-ion." I held my right thumb and forefinger a half inch from each other and thrust them up to his eyes. "I'm the one who came this close to losing her life. All so you can again decide what looks right in front of your goddamn men."

He remained calm. Like I'd just forecasted the weather. "I don't know anything about how things look, Sydney. I do know that you mean too much to me. I'd be biased lis-tening to you." He scratched the back of his hand. "It's best if someone else takes your statement."

"You make it sound as if I'm the one who's committed a crime here," I continued.

"It's my problem. Not yours. I am the one who can muddy these waters." He clasped both his hands around my still-gesturing fingers. A crease threw angles on the bridge of his nose.

He wasn't being romantic. On the contrary, he was

stating a troublesome feeling. A feeling that hurt his performance. Like the symptom of some dread disease. He shared this with me as one might a trusted friend—as if I were not the problem as well.

I let him lead me to Anderson's patrol car and deposit me in the front seat, where Anderson was waiting with his notepad. I noticed Thurgood heading for the office, notepad in hand. To take Barbara's statement, I assumed.

The rains that came this night were off and on. When it did rain, the downpour was so concentrated that I couldn't see and so hard that it hurt my skin. Sometimes it didn't rain at all. The whole experience felt to me like being in the bottom of a toilet awaiting someone's flush.

Jeep Anderson was a very direct inquisitor. I detected no undertones in his manner nor double meanings in his words. He made me feel so comfortable that I could have been giving project times to Sally for billing to clients. He wasn't interested in my thoughts or my opinion, only short one-sentence reasons why I did what I did.

Still, it was after midnight when I emerged from his patrol car. Thurgood was still in the office with Barbara, and I knew I wouldn't be welcomed there. I congratulated myself for having learned some of the basics.

While I was in Anderson's car, the Trooper had been moved to a parking space beside the office. Had it started or had they pushed it? Two coroner's vans were where the Trooper had been. One-one-five, both inside and out, was illuminated with portable lighting systems like ones I'd seen once on a night photo shoot. Jake would have been proud: with the place lit up, the bin could have passed for an electronics store with a Midnight Madness Sale.

A white Town Car idled at the yellow crime tape spread across the opened entrance gate. I watched the driver gesture frantically and the uniformed officer standing guard let him on through. The car's lights washed across me as I stood purposelessly between the bins and the office.

"Mrs. Teague," Buddy yelled as he pulled the car over and jumped out, grabbing me by the arm. "They told me my mother was here. Have you seen her?" The boy was breathless. His throat made a noise when he pulled his breath in as if his esophagus and pharynx hadn't separated properly. He shook my arms. "Is she . . . is she okay?" The panic boiled over to a single tear that fell from his left eye onto the side of his nose. He let go of my arms to wipe it away.

As he did, I put my arm around his back. So intense was his fear that I would have cuddled him like a toddler.

"Your mom's okay, Buddy. Not even hurt."

His face sagged in relief.

"She saved my life, Buddy." I told him this part not so much to brag about his mother as to ease the transition to the rest of what his mother and Thurgood would tell him.

I knew he would ask it and he did: "Saved your life from what?"

I couldn't tell him. Even if I could, I was the wrong one to be doing it.

Protocol or no protocol, we were going inside.

I walked in front of Buddy as we entered the room. The first words out of Thurgood's mouth were "Where've you been? We thought you'd have come in for some coffee long ago."

Figure that out because I couldn't.

Then he saw Buddy behind me and his demeanor changed from light to grave.

When Barbara saw Buddy, she cried "Oh my baby" and the two of them embraced for a long time. For my money, the mother needed a little babying now far more than the son.

I think Buddy must have sensed what had happened because his expression didn't change much when Thurgood told him about Oscar and Jake.

I gratefully took a hot cup of black coffee from Betty. She looked worn out. Her thin, normally wispy, almost fuzzy hair was flat on her very white scalp and turned toward her forehead in Caesar-like half-curls. Either the rain or the humidity, or the stress, had disassembled her. Probably all three. An unreasonable guilt jabbed at me for having involved both Betty and Jewel in our "world-class-city" crime. I know it was unreasonable, but it was how I felt: so sorry for everything. I had an overwhelming need to apologize to someone for it all.

The antique school clock behind Betty's counter said 2:54 a.m. I had put in the equivalent of an entire workday here tonight and I wanted to go home.

Thurgood saw me look at the clock and said: "You can go, Sydney. We've got your statement. There's nothing else holding you." He raised his eyebrows in the direction of the door as if to say that he would leave himself if he could.

Betty stifled a yawn.

Barbara and Buddy both looked at Thurgood, but Buddy spoke: "May I take my mother home, sir?" So polite. I thought again of the virtues of a military school education. Would George junior ever learn that kind of composure?

Thurgood told us all that we were free to go. There might be more questions for each of us. He knew where we were.

"Will you jump my battery?" I asked.

The deep pink began at his shirt collar and flowed upward and under his auburn hair. It occurred to me that we were perhaps on different topics.

"My car," I added. "My battery might need a charge."

In spite of her weariness, Betty winked at me.

The Trooper did crank without the charge. I found myself thinking that another kind of jump might have been what I needed after all.

We were like animals in a city zoo. The entire facility was cordoned with bright yellow tape. Close to a dozen police cruisers and crime scene wagons sat in awkward angles around the lot, their blue lights flashing in a rhythm reminding me oddly of seventies disco.

Beyond the tape, circling our crater in the earth, loomed high-powered media lights and zoom cameras. I could count eight television vans, each with its satellite dish cocked precariously toward unseen distant stars. The static of their radios fought the static of police radios. The new Cold War.

I murmured in gratitude to the deluge that hit as I drove slowly toward the gate. If the media saw me, stopping me would be difficult. Harder for vultures to attack in such rain.

24

THE ONLY GOOD THING ABOUT CONTINUOUS, steady rain is the white noise of its wake. The intermittent downpour in the early morning hours had tapered to a soothing static that kept my brain from bugging me.

I was still in bed although I had no idea what "still" meant since no sun plotted shadows across my bedroom wall. My alarm clock was facedown on my Berber rug, a sign that sleep had not been restful.

For a brief second I considered thinking or perhaps even living. Then rejected them both. Not today. Not in this world. Blessed, merciful static zapped me again. I succumbed to the fog of the netherworld.

From somewhere inside all this I heard a phone ring. Knowing the machine in the kitchen would pick up on the fourth ring, I pulled the pillow over my head to counter the intrusion. It stopped after two rings, which meant someone else was in the house. I forced myself to listen. Joan's voice, muffled and distant, broke through the rain's airwaves.

I tiptoed into the bathroom. Inside the door is a full-length mirror that I rarely use. This morning I pulled my nightshirt over my head to inspect for signs of last night. Amazing. Not even a bruise. Not even on my upper arms where two or three people had grabbed me tightly.

When I heard the soft rap on my bedroom door, I had shifted my focus to the creases on my chest. They couldn't be wrinkles. I refused to believe these persistent tracks were anything other than some athletic anomaly. Maybe the way I was sleeping. I'd try to sleep on my back.

I quickly rubbed my chest with night cream, threw my old white cotton robe around my naked body, and pulled open the door.

"Good morning, honey," I said to my daughter.

"Morning, Mom?" She stuck her watch-clad wrist in my face. "It's after one o'clock."

"I had a really late night."

She stared at me. "Mom, it's on TV. You've had a zillion phone calls. I was so worried I came in here to make sure you were still breathing. It sounds like it must have been horrible." Bless her, she didn't ask for details.

I patted her cheek and wrapped my robe more securely. "It was, honey, and thanks for letting me sleep. Where's your brother? Is he home?"

"In and out," she said as we walked downstairs to the kitchen. "Somebody gave him a ride home, then he took off on his bike to play soccer at the park."

I poured water for my coffee, put it on a burner to boil, and discovered that I was out of #6 filters.

"How was the spend-the-night party?" I was folding a paper towel into a makeshift funnel.

She cocked her head slightly and pouted her lips. "Oh, okay." She covered what looked to me like a fake yawn. "I think I'm getting too old for those things."

The orange juice was empty, but the Five Alive provided a little more than three ounces of vitamin C. "Don't get too old for fun things, honey. Life's going to get real serious on its own without your help." I sat at the kitchen table and waited for my coffee to drip through.

Joan picked up the morning paper, putting it and a piece of yellow legal paper in front of me. The entire page was scribbled with notes from calls.

"It wasn't fun," she said. "Believe me, Mom, I wish it had been. I'll be in my room." With that, she was gone. If she hadn't left so quickly, I would have talked to her more about it. Her voice had been laced with sadness, not boredom, and I wondered how a group of teenage girls at a birthday party could have colored my daughter's mood so darkly.

The yellow sheet lay on top of the *Observer*. Barbara had called. Joan had scribbled details of last night all around Barbara's name. None of the gruesome stuff. Just that Oscar and Jake had died and that I had been put in a "scary predicament." Barbara's choice of word were euphemistic to my way of thinking. The creases on my chest were a "scary predicament." Last night was something else. I assumed I was supposed to call her, and I would. First I needed some distance.

I poured my coffee and lit my first cigarette of the day. I waited for the guaranteed, surefire connection that the first cigarette always gives me. It's like when I'm fishing and get a backlash. That's how I awake most mornings, a line in backlash. Helplessly tangled in myself. But that first deep drag, sometimes the second or third, straightens me out and hoists me mentally into the sea for a productive day of floating the waters. I'm sure there's a scientific explanation for how the whole thing works. Endorphins, neurotransmitters, and stuff. But I like to fish, and it works for me.

Only today it didn't. Not only were my lines hopelessly crossed, I knew I didn't want to be cast back into the world.

The phone rang, and I answered tentatively.

"Sydney, are you okay?" It was Jean.

"Yes, I'm okay. Considering."

"Well, you certainly did go beyond the call of duty for your client." Jean's tone was playful, but I wondered if there was some self-preservative at work in her statement.

I couldn't laugh at her attempts to lighten my mood. All I could say was "Uh huh."

"You sound tired," she said.

"Last night was tiring. I'm wiped out, okay?" Maybe she would hang up out of consideration.

My complaint didn't faze her. "I knew there was something fishy going on at Bishop Cates. Oscar was always a weird one. Never sold anything, but had to have his finger in everybody's business."

"Jean, we don't know that Oscar did anything wrong other than make his fix-it boy mad."

"Fix it? What fix-it boy are you talking about?"

"Jake," I said impatiently. "Who else would I be talking about?"

"Jake never fixed a damn thing. Not while I was there. He just drove around on trumped-up errands." She made a guttural "ugh," then "He gave me the creeps."

I sighed. "We'll never know what really happened,

Jean. All I know is Barbara didn't deserve this. She's going to need a lot of support to get over it all."

A harsh laugh. "Don't expect anybody who ever worked for her to give her any sympathy. She was still rotten to all of us. The feeling's universal on that score." She hesitated. "The television hasn't mentioned Mickey. He was down there, wasn't he?"

"Mickey?" I said in disbelief. "What makes you think Mickey would have been involved?"

"Well, he's been involved the whole time, hasn't he? You yourself told me he was at Crystal's house the night she was killed. Hell, he broke into your office and put you in the hospital. That's pretty damn involved, if you ask me!"

I paused for a moment. Mickey did have a storage bin down there too. Could it be just a coincidence? I sighed. "I don't want to talk about it anymore, Jean."

"Okay, okay," she said, "but I can picture him raping women before I can picture Jake. Jake was a sloppy bum of a guy who never looked at any of us. Like he didn't even notice that some of us were—well, we are—attractive women."

I couldn't believe this. "Rape is violence, Jean. It's about power. Not attraction."

She cleared her throat. "Well, he never seemed very powerful either."

"My point exactly," I said. "I've really got to go."

I decided to spend the rest of the day in bed. I felt I deserved it. Neither kid had a ball game, and Joan could do the grocery shopping.

I poured the rest of the pot of coffee into a thermal carafe, stuffed the Vantage pack into my bathrobe pocket, grabbed my legal sheet and newspaper, and trod back to the bedroom, where I intended to alternately piddle and sleep until tomorrow with a little bit of reading and television punctuating the experience.

The article was a small two-inch block at the bottom of page one. PROMINENT EXECUTIVE SLAIN. The basics only: two men dead at a York County storage facility, no photos, Oscar Cates and Jake Furman, both associated with Bishop Cates. No other names, no connections to the other deaths. Given newspaper deadlines, it was a hasty piece of journalism to get it in at all. I felt certain tomorrow's paper would flesh out the rest of the story.

The murders still commanded the headlines. Law enforcement had finally committed to saying that all Multiple Listing locks would be removed by the end of the weekend. The big news on the subject was yesterday's new murder. God, was that only yesterday? The *Observer*, usually not a paper to preach, even went so far as to suggest no woman with a lock still on her door should sleep alone tonight.

Would tomorrow's paper tell us that the killings had ended with Jake's death? Would it tell us all that a sick young man had gone on a psychotic tear through Charlotte and symbolic womanhood? That he had been raised by poor sick parents who beat him regularly, especially the mother who humiliated him into submission? That he had been waiting his whole sick life for an opportunity to get back at that mother? That this entire affair was the result of a personality and life so depraved and deprived that none of us would ever have to consider the possibility that such a string of horror could happen in our world-class city again? I bet myself it would.

I saw Sally's name on my legal sheet of calls to return. Where had Fred been Thursday night? I wondered. Why did I still believe that there was more to Fred's involvement in these deaths than coincidence? The nagging in the back of my head was still there. Something wasn't completely answered.

Sally answered on the first ring.

"Sydney," she said, "they're talking about you all over the television."

"What are they saying?"

She told me the news said I had accidentally come upon Jake Furman's robbery holdings, that Oscar Cates was already dead at the same location, that Barbara Cates had suspected Jake Furman, followed him to the location, and shot him when he was attempting to kill me. That the fear gripping the city could now be banished, that Furman was obviously the man who had been murdering women in their homes. Police would not confirm.

Just what I thought they would say, except for the part about the police. I would have thought they'd be holding congratulatory press conferences by now.

"How's Fred?" I asked her.

"He's fine, I guess. In fact, I'm sure he's more relieved than anybody that this is all over."

"You haven't talked with him?"

A bit defensively she said: "No. Should I have? We're not very close, you know."

Good old Sally. Whatever suits the moment.

"Listen . . . you're not hurt, are you?"

Not the kind you can see, I thought.

"No," I said instead. "No, I'm not. Why?"

"The TV people didn't say, and Hart called all worried. Said he didn't want to bother you, but to find out if you needed anything."

So much like Hart. So much like Sally.

I took a deep breath. "Tell Hart I'm fine. I've decided to lie low for the rest of the weekend, but I really am okay. But tell Hart when you talk to him that come Monday morning I'll expect a full demonstration on the sex life of fibers."

She giggled. "Okay, Sydney. By the way, the curator called you after you left yesterday. He sounded odd."

"That's how he is, Sally. He's odd."

"Well, he was different odd, not his normal odd."

"We're going to have to sell him on this sex thing. I'm sure that's why he sounded odd."

I had barely put the phone back on its hook when it rang. The six o'clock news anchor wanting to lead off with a live interview tonight.

No thank you. No comment.

I screamed for Joan to get the phone if it rang. To tell all reporters I was not available for comment now and I would not comment at any time in the future either.

"So there!" she screamed back.

Saturday afternoon on public television is fanciful. Garden and cooking shows alternate, titillating my dulled-out senses and bolstering my faith in the human animal's essential creativity. I was thoroughly engrossed in a sensuous tour of some French wine cellars when the phone rang again as it had all afternoon.

"Mom, it's Tom Thurgood. You want him, don't you?" Joan yelled.

"I've got it, Joan," I said, with just enough edge in my voice to let her know that I had gotten her joke as well.

"How are you doing today?" He asked it like he really wanted to know.

"I'm taking the day off," I said. "Second one this week. You ought to think about doing the same thing."

"I'm at the Center. Nobody's got this weekend off. Not until this real estate thing is all over."

"I thought you guys could relax a little now. What's going on?"

He hesitated as if debating with himself what to say. "We're going ahead with the lock removals. We were over half through anyway. Need to take a real good look at this Multiple Listing thing before we give the system a clean bill of health."

I thought about Jean again and the fragile state of her new company. "How long do you think it will be shut down?"

"Don't know. Can't say for sure. It's not entirely up to me."

Something about his talkativeness was bothering me.

"Tom, you do think the murders have been solved, don't you? I mean last night. . . . Didn't last night settle everything?"

He tried to laugh but didn't do it very well. "You just never know about these things, Sydney."

There was silence between us as I tried to divine what he meant.

Finally he said, "It's still raining so I guess we can't play tennis. How about tomorrow if I get finished here?"

"I don't think so," I said. "I don't want anything physical or mental this weekend. Thanks just the same."

He hesitated again, although less so than before. "We've got to start practicing if we're going to stand a chance in the city tournament—"

"Hold it," I interrupted. "I've never said I'd be your partner, Thurgood. You're presuming a lot."

"Aw, stop playing so damn hard to get." Genuine exasperation. I liked it.

The rest of the afternoon was spent, truly spent. I have always felt I'd have made a marvelous lady of leisure since doing nothing, literally nothing, has never bothered me. No guilt, no anxiety: feelings my friends tell me accompany the normal person's periods of sloth.

This afternoon I watched an old Charlie Chan, read a Margaret Maron short story, slept some more, and lost an hour entirely just staring at the wall while blowing smoke rings.

George junior came home, Joan never left, and the three of us shared a quiet dinner of hot dogs on the Jenn-Air. Our conversation revolved around frog anatomy, the possibility of real witches, the unfairness of teachers who overloaded kids with work on the weekends, and whether or not to get a puppy to replace poor Butterfly, our twelve-year-old Lhasa Apso who had died last spring of a skin infection gone systemic.

I was beginning to feel human again.

My weekly Saturday night meeting was a speaker, a once-a-month break from our usual discussion groups. I was grateful for the speaker. In spite of the fact that we stick to the subject of alcoholism and its effects on our lives, someone would surely have said in a voice as sincere as all get-out, "Sydney, you must be feeling pretty low. Want to talk about it?"

Our speaker was Harold V., a sixty-year-old black man celebrating his first anniversary sober. The guy had been ahead of his time. All his life. He'd been young and eager before doors had opened for young, eager black men. He'd been a gifted athlete relegated to Negro leagues. A CPA when no blacks had money, or need of his expertise. And no white had the inclination. A bitter man, a combative man, who ended his talk by saying how grateful he was that the door to AA was open when he needed it. I identified with his feelings, if not his life. I always do. It's why it works.

The fat Sunday paper bulged inside its plastic bag. Although spotty residue of rain sparkled in the bright morning sunlight, I could tell that it had not rained in several hours.

I was beginning to think it was just wishful thinking, but the air felt lighter. Like maybe God felt we were clean enough at last. He could move on down to Atlanta with His dirty sponge.

I removed the plastic and shook the water off it into my scrubby nandina. A burgundy Taurus was parked in front of the house next door. A man sat in the driver's seat reading the paper. I didn't recognize the man or the car. Maybe he was waiting for my neighbor, whom I wouldn't have recognized either. I acknowledged that many people went to church on Sundays. My neighbor and his friend were probably two of them.

The *Observer* this morning had done just what I expected. Dug into Jake's background and fashioned a monster so gruesome that none of us would have to associate him or his actions with any part of the world as we knew it. We could fictionalize him. Our reality was secure. I read the first paragraph, then put it down. I flipped to the Sunday crossword instead and spent a good two hours on my living room sofa.

I even took the time to organize my grocery list for the week. After lunch, George junior and I cruised the Bi-Lo together. He took cereal, drinks, and snacks while I secured the vegetables, fruit, and meat. We met back on aisle four and marched directly to the checkout lane in front of us like two foot soldiers on a well-planned mission. When we arrived back home, I noticed a blue Accord where the Taurus had been.

That afternoon I did something that I hadn't done since the kids were elementary age: I made two vegetable casseroles and froze them and homemade chocolate chips and a lemon pound cake.

I marinated squash, peppers, and mushrooms in a rosemary-laced oil. We ate them off the Jenn-Air and peeled boiled shrimp for dinner.

I felt almost myself again.

After dinner George junior resequestered himself for the big science test, but Joan had finished her paper so we planned to watch the Sunday Night Movie together.

While washing the dishes, I remembered I hadn't called Barbara. The machine picked up. I was relieved in a way. I had begun to leave my message when she came on the line.

"I'm here. I'm here, Sydney. The calls have been awful. I bet they have for you too."

"Not so much today," I said, "but yesterday was pretty bad. Sorry it took me this long to call you back."

I didn't know what to say to her, how to support someone who'd found her husband murdered, whose company had been violated and manipulated as an instrument of that murder and so many before it. This woman had saved my life.

"Barbara, you know I'm here for you," I said. "What can I do? How about the funeral home? Can I deal with them for you?"

"No, no," she told me. "Oscar's sister will be here tomorrow. She said she'd handle everything. Buddy and I will make it through this somehow." Her voice was so much stronger.

"How is Buddy? He was shaken by this too. I know he thought of Jake as a friend."

Barbara coughed. Something caught in her throat.

"We'll both be okay, Sydney," she managed to get out.

Except for my reconnaissance mission to the grocery store and my ritual meeting, I had not left my home all weekend. Curled up on the den sofa with Joan likewise on the oversize chair next to me, I felt secure and whole. Almost as if nothing had ever happened.

I am a *60 Minutes* junkie. Part of beginning each week on a productive note is watching the program every Sunday night. As Mike Wallace explained to me some of the more esoteric aspects of our crumbling economy. I realized that *60 Minutes* is probably my Sunday church. Fortification for the week ahead. The ritual more than the content.

After two segments, the network took a break. Joan stretched her arms.

"How about some ice cream, Mom?"

I smiled and nodded.

"I'll get it," she said as she hopped out of the chair and headed for the kitchen.

Something clicked, some kind of déjà vu feeling that didn't flutter by but stuck inside my mind instead. That couple across the street from Crystal's. They were eating ice cream. What did they say that had been bothering me all this time? Something about a commercial. They'd left their view of the Ball house just long enough to get their ice cream. The time it took for a TV commercial. I looked at the television set. Three bullfrogs were attempting to synchronize their notes as they peered at a Budweiser sign from their lily pads. Leslie Stahl's smiling face replaced the frogs just as Joan was back with two big bowls of van-choc-straw. In no time at all. The length of a TV commercial.

If Jake had been carrying a TV to the van when the neighbors got back to their window, where was Crystal at the time? He was in the van when they left to get ice cream. He was carrying a TV when they returned. No time even to tie Crystal up, much less rape and strangle her. Nobody watches someone strip her house without putting up some kind of fight. The BMW had disappeared. Did that mean Fred was gone or had he only moved it? Had Mickey come back when he saw Fred leaving? Dammit! Somebody was in that house with Crystal while Jake was moving things out.

"Ice cream, Mom. Take it, my hands are cold."

We resumed our relative positions of ease while the blood rushed through my arteries like streams at flood stage. Ever quickening, darting, overflowing, seeking some-place larger to deposit their burdensome cargo. Andy Rooney babbled on about the difficulties he'd encountered opening medicine bottles; Joan was laughing. I managed to scrape all three flavors onto my spoon and put the largest scoop of ice cream I have ever had into my mouth. I let it gradually slide down my throat until a lump sat in my chest so huge and so cold that I thought this must be what it's like to be dead.

The Sunday Night Movie was a Farrah Fawcett don't-take-my-baby-away-from-me thriller/tearjerker. Halfway through, when it appeared poor Farrah would have to kill her abusive ex-husband or be killed herself, Joan began to sob. At first I chalked it up to the stellar perform-ances, but by the big network break at the hour, she was out of control. I reached over, touched her foot, and tried to soothe her to a stop.

"Oh, Mom," she gasped, "I need to tell you something, but I can't." Tears were pouring down her face. I reached into my bathrobe pocket and gave her a handful of Kleenex.

"Why can't you, honey? I'm your mother. You can tell me anything." I was stroking her foot now.

"I promised Cindi," she wailed.

"Cindi Hyatt?"

She could only nod her head as she held a wad of Kleenex to her nose.

"I meant to tell you," I said. "Cindi's looking at board-ing schools. Did you know?"

"That's not going to help," she gulped, beginning to

cry in earnest again. "She can't just pretend it never happened. Her mother—" Joan choked and blew her nose. "Her mother thinks sending her off will erase it. It won't. It won't, Mom." She sat beside me on the sofa and threw herself into my lap. The last time I remember comforting my daughter like this was when her first love broke her heart in the eighth grade. The emotions that gripped her tonight dug deeper than the hurt of adolescent anxiety.

"What never happened?" I stroked her long hair and patted her back gently.

She pulled herself up from my lap, blew her nose again, and gazed at me tentatively. "Mom, don't judge Cindi."

"Honey, in spite of what you seem to believe, I don't judge harshly. I try to live and let live."

She lowered her eyes, then raised them again. "Okay, 'cause none of it's Cindi's fault."

I waited.

"You know how Buddy's been hanging around Cindi?"

I didn't, but I said nothing.

"Last week they were in the Hyatts' playroom alone." She swallowed hard, then continued. "Mrs. Hyatt was upstairs in their kitchen, so it's not like Cindi knew what was coming."

My skin had begun to tingle with some kind of foreknowledge, like nerve endings poised for flight.

"He . . . he . . ." She had to stop. The rest of it came out in artillery bursts of words and sobs. "He forced her to have sex, Mom. Really forced. He took his belt off and held it across her neck while he did it. Like an animal. She screamed when it was over. He threw a lamp at her. He told her he'd kill her if she didn't shut up."

I never thought I would hear anything like this from my daughter. The only thing worse would be if it had happened to her. Keeping my anxiety at bay was close to impossible.

"God. Poor, poor Cindi . . ."

"Kill her, Mom. He said he'd kill her."

"What about Mrs. Hyatt? Was she in the kitchen the whole time?"

"She was until Cindi screamed. Buddy ran out their patio door and kept running. When her mother got down there, Cindi was bleeding all over. Her head was cut, and she was bleeding where he—" Her breath caught, although the sobs had stopped. She pulled herself up to eye level with me on the sofa. No childhood was left in her eyes. "—he raped her. He raped her, Mom."

I hugged my daughter tighter than I ever remembered doing. "Oh my God," I kept saying as I rocked her.

Moving Up? Check out this gem. Owner financing to qualified buyer. ML

I am lying on my bed. I have been here since four o'clock watching the shapes and shadows of my clothes and furniture. I have discovered something. When you concentrate on an object long enough, with undivided attention, you give it life. It doesn't talk or get up and move across the room, not that kind of life. Crude life, I mean. Basic life, breathing like an ocean swell, glistening like sweat on a horse's flank. Likewise, I reason, if I ignore something, I take away its life. I try hard to make the shoe in the corner die, then laugh at the silliness of the effort. You're forgetting the whole point, you fool. Forget the shoe, and it dies. Think about the shoe, even its death, and you bring it to life. Paradox.

I hold the gun at my crotch, direct its nozzle toward the pulsating bathrobe on the back of the door. It seems to me that my cock should hold the gun, could hold it, did hold it, will hold it. Grow fingers, extend itself. Safety off . . . cocked.

I have done my best by her. Women are not to be trusted. I learned that well. I have done all that I could to even the score, bring her some peace, make it okay.

Shit. I'm tired. I'm tired, but I'm not confused. The one real beauty of acceptance is clarity. I am encoded, genetically embedded. We all are. One foot in front of the other, cradle to grave.

Under glass.

Like ants, no more, no less.

25

THESE WERE THE FIRST STARS I'D SEEN IN OVER a month. Like strange, bright birds, they perched on invisible branches in the southern sky high above SouthPark Mall. I drove in their direction.

Still no flashlight, but the three-quarter moon and my flock of stars lit up the Cateses' backyard. The small yellow bug-light was on above the kitchen door. The light was on in Barbara's room above it.

How do you tell a mother that her only child is a rapist and a murderer? When I called her, she'd wanted to talk tomorrow. I insisted on tonight. My only concern was the whereabouts of Buddy. Asleep, she had said. Exhausted from the ordeal.

I knew I had come to her house tonight for myself as well. For Joanie. For Cindi Hyatt and her mother. For my part in friendships, past and present. And for Crystal. Buddy's acts seemed to spring from all of us, from friends who somehow let each other down. From mothers who couldn't own their children's pain.

I guess I could have called Tom Thurgood. I was going to—after I talked to her. He wasn't, after all, a mother. Nor was he her friend. Barbara deserved a friend right now. I needed to break this horrible news myself. I make it sound as if I thought about it more than I did. The truth is, I did not really think at all. I left my daughter in the den with Farrah Fawcett crying on the tube and got in the car.

The key was where it had been before, above the door. I let myself in.

I didn't call her name this time. Instead, I walked quietly and deliberately up the circular stairs and stood at her bedroom door. Barbara was sitting on the love seat in her adjoining room. She had one leg pulled up as if polishing her toe nails, the other extended on the coffee table. She was giving full attention to someone whom I couldn't see but whose voice seemed vaguely familiar. Then the person cried in agony, and I recognized Farrah's voice.

I stepped into the bedroom and stopped.

"Barbara," I said quietly.

Startled, she thrust her hands to her mouth as she turned toward me.

"It's a bad movie," I said.

"I've seen it before," she said. "She deserves whatever she gets, but, for the life of me, I can't remember what happens."

She relaxed visibly, leaned over and patted a chair for me to sit in. "How did you get in?"

"The key over the door, remember?"

She nodded; her eyes still held questions.

Dread was building in me. I wasn't at all sure Barbara could survive this information.

She looked nervous, nerves of anticipation. Like maybe she knew something already, even what I was going to say. Her eyes darted, their questions gone. She sat up straight with knees together while her hands held each other as if weaving a lone thread that might hold her body together.

I pulled the chair closer to her sofa so that I could touch those fragile hands and comfort her as I broke the news.

"Where's Buddy?" I had to ask again.

"Like I said, asleep. Why?"

Her tone was challenging me.

Then I knew. Barbara knew about Buddy already. I took a deep breath and sat back in the chair.

"You know, Barbara. Don't you?"

She kept her eyes level with mine, her chin up although quivering visibly. She was going to make me say it.

"We both know about Buddy," I said. "We know what he's done, don't we?"

I paused.

She withheld.

"Buddy needs to turn himself in, Barbara. You need to help him do that."

The delicate balance of her face began to give way. Her teetering chin slipped like the crumbling foundation of a tall building during a quake. Her mouth flew open, but no sound came out. Only a quickly bursting bubble where her lips had pursed.

I put my left hand over her two. "Barbara, he needs help. You're his mother. You—"

"Help?" she sobbed loudly. "Nobody's ever helped him.

Nobody. No matter what I've done." She choked briefly. Deep wrinkles appeared on her cheeks as if instantly etched by pain.

"I sent him to that school." She stood abruptly, the delicate thread holding her together was replaced by a wire. She walked the length of the short room and turned with her hand shaking at me, her fingers pointing.

"Discipline!" She seemed to spit the words at me. "They said he'd get discipline. I didn't know they'd admitted girls. It was a goddamn military school. Why'd they go letting girls in, Sydney?"

"Did all this start there?" I asked. I needed to calm her, but how?

Her head jerked toward me again. Sarcasm spread across her face. "You mean the 'violation'? They called it 'violation.' Couldn't even deal with it honestly. The girl lied."

"He raped a girl at VMA?" I was dismayed. Barbara's defense of Buddy was beyond reason. So was a mother's love.

"The school just wanted him out." Abruptly the air seemed to rush out of her, leaving her limp and shaking. She stumbled and sat on the ottoman in front of me.

"Why?" The ends of her mouth fell as if she was about to cry. "I told them I didn't want him around girls. Girls have always been a problem, Sydney."

She was trying to build herself up again. Her roller-coaster emotions were exhausting me.

"Barbara—"

"You don't know," she said. "Your little Georgie isn't old enough." Her eyes were desperate to hold mine now, to force me into understanding. She tried to laugh, but the sound was one of pain.

I squeezed her hands. "Shhh, Barbara . . . shhh. I know what you're feeling. You love him. He's your baby. That's what you were saying last night, wasn't it?"

"What do you mean?"

"You kept saying 'my baby' when we found Oscar. I thought you meant Oscar. Then, when Buddy arrived to get you, you called him 'my baby.' He killed Oscar, too, didn't he?"

Barbara was leaning toward me, swooning almost. I wanted to cradle her, to take some of this from her. She seemed to have slipped across some invisible line, the line that's there for all of us when our particular reality is too much. Some people call it insanity, but right now I could see how logical the process really was.

"I should have killed him a long time ago. I just didn't know how easy it was to kill someone." His voice was calm compared to his mother's. I didn't turn toward Buddy, but I could tell he was less than six feet from us.

I sought Barbara's eyes, those colorless slits that had always shifted hues with her clothes, her makeup, her friends. I looked into them and thought I saw straight through to her soul. I had never seen so much pain.

"What did you tell her, Mother?" His tone was stern and confident, as if he were the parent and she the child.

Barbara didn't answer. At this point I wasn't sure she could.

I turned to face Buddy.

"Jake never killed anybody. Did he, Buddy?" Call it hormones, call it God. I think it was nerves. Whatever it was kicked in for me, and I felt so calm I could have been questioning a friend of George junior's who'd just lifted a two-liter from my fridge.

"No," he said to me. "Poor Jake was just doing his job. Guess who gave him that job." He looked at his mother. "Did you tell your old school chum about Jake's job, Mother?"

He walked slowly to her. She was pushing down on the ottoman with both hands like a survivor at sea, the ottoman her life raft. The sway of her back seemed more like a hump. He jabbed at her shoulder with his fingers, and I knew he had hurt her.

"Tell her, Mother. Tell her what you did." He punctuated each word with another jab.

Barbara's head jerked up, but her eyes were vacant. Something dribbled from the side of her mouth.

"Buddy," I said, "she can't tell me anything. Can't you see? You tell me. You tell me what you want me to hear." Deep stores of anger colored Buddy's eyes. He kept pushing her. She held on to the ottoman.

"Mother dear set the whole thing up." Like bitter poison touching his tongue, he spit the words at me.

He pushed at her again. I caught her as she almost toppled over.

"Just stop pushing her," I pleaded.

His outstretched fingers flew at my face, snapping my head back against the chair. He whirled around, grabbed the back of the love seat as if seeking protection from his own destructiveness.

"*She* hired Jake, not wiseass Oscar. Surprise, huh? Not professional Barbara Bishop Cates. You know why she hired him?" His laugh was laden with irony. "She gave him the codes and told him to steal things. 'Enter as many houses as you can, Jake,' she said. 'Take as much as you want, Jake. They'll shut down Multiple Listing,' she said. 'When they see the pattern, they'll shut it down.' No harm done, right?"

What was he saying? Barbara had set all this death in motion? I didn't want to believe him.

"Barbara? Is this true?"

She stared through me.

"Why, Barbara?"

"Only she didn't count on me coming home and riding with Jake. Doing my thing." Buddy mocked me. "Why, Barbara? Why, why, why, Barbara?" He laughed. He grabbed his mother's hair, raised her a half foot, and let go.

Barbara's hand shot to her scalp, a reflex from the pain. She looked at me from somewhere deep inside her world.

"Barbara?" I said. "Talk to me."

"They left me," she said in a lilting voice. "Every single one of those girls just picked up and left me. Like I didn't mean anything to them. Like junior high, Sydney." Her pupils were dilated as if she were drugged. The ends of her sentences rose like everything was a question. She groped for me, grabbing at my hand. "But you're my friend, Sydney. You haven't left me. Look, Buddy, Sydney's here."

She leaned back to look at her son. "This is my friend, Sydney Allen. Don't be mean to her."

Buddy's wooden demeanor softened as he realized the magnitude of his mother's break from us. I thought he would hold her. He looked as if he wanted to, needed to.

"Buddy," I said, "let me get help for both of you."

He tried to smile. "There isn't any. Not for either of us."

He reached into his pocket and pulled out a .38 similar to the one his mother had taken to the storage facility. The utter calm with which I'd faced this whole ordeal vanished at the sight. I realized he'd kill me now, his mother too. I should have been prepared. For Buddy, it was probably the only solution.

He stood behind his mother and held her back against his groin with his left arm. With his right arm, he held the gun up, his elbow cocked. Barbara's expression was blank.

The faint wail of a siren picked at the outer layers of my awareness. Like an auditory mirage, it came, and it went, and I would not believe I was hearing it until it grew constant and fuller and screeching and I was finally awash in the race between it and us.

There was nothing I could do. My mind raced uselessly. I envied Barbara's insanity. I tried to shut myself off, brain and all, like one might the water supply to the house when a pipe is broken.

I remember watching Buddy. I remember thinking he'd shoot his mother first, then me. He held her loosely, as if steadying a wobbly doll for a child's tea party. The way he'd positioned his arm with the gun, he could have shot her then.

Instead, he looked at me. This boy I'd thought so composed, so aloof; this demon, who'd raped countless women and murdered at least three, probably more; who'd killed the man who raised him; this monster, who could take my life in a nanosecond. He was trembling. His face was wet, as if tears had oozed from his pores. His eyes were bloodshot, but they were dry.

"Ms. Teague," he said so calmly that the contrast to his

body astounded me. "Some things just are. You can't fix them. You can't change them. I've tried to fix a lot of things. I've tried to fix her." He looked down at her with an expression I'd never seen before. Sadness, regret, hatred, and love all mingled in his eyes and pulled at his mouth to create a face both determined and somehow dead. "She tried to fix me too."

"We'll get you the help you need, Buddy. I promise you that."

"There is no help for people like me. It is clear. I am who I am. So is she. Why can't you see that?"

Still holding Barbara with his left hand, he shot himself in the temple with his right. He slumped onto her, the two of them hitting the ottoman, then the floor.

The only emotion I felt when I came out of my protective shell was an overwhelming sadness. Somehow I pulled him off Barbara, who gradually became aware of her dead son at her side. Although her plaintive sobs were so intense that the presence of her pain engulfed me, I could not bring myself to comfort her.

I was still sitting in the chair when Thurgood and two other men arrived.

Nobody talked to me at first. I watched them check Buddy's pulse. I watched them help Barbara off the floor. I murmured thanks to Thurgood when he brought me some water. A fog seemed to engulf us all.

Eventually Buddy's body was gone, Barbara had been led away by a policewoman, and Thurgood helped me to stand. A sharp pain stabbed at my shoulders and the back of my neck where Buddy had pushed me down.

I winced.

"How did you know to come?" I finally asked.

"You've got a smart daughter," he said to me. Insinuation that her mother was not. "We've also been watching your house."

The cars at my neighbor's. I nodded.

"Why?"

"We knew somebody else was in on it. We thought it might have been Buddy, but we weren't positive. In the meantime, whoever else had been involved was probably pretty concerned Jake may have told you something before he died."

"He tried," I whispered. "Just before Barbara shot him, he was trying."

I tried to breathe deeply, to diffuse the lump in my chest that had been there all night. It still felt cold and hard. Malignant. It wouldn't budge.

When I was safely behind the steering wheel of the Trooper and Thurgood was leaning his elbows on my open window, I told him what had been gnawing at me. I'd known Barbara for thirty years. She'd shown me her vindictive side time and time again. She'd do anything to get back at those who'd rejected her. Especially women. Every woman who'd ever known her knew she was dangerous. Except me.

"I knew it, dammit, Tom. Why didn't I act on what I knew about her?" My hair had fallen over my eyes. I pushed it back behind my ears.

His index finger followed the line of my hair where I'd just pushed it. "Because you couldn't, you wouldn't believe it. You believe in people. It's not a fault." He stood back and squinted his eyes as if formally assessing me. "I bet you defended her in junior high, didn't you? I bet you've been giving her second chances all these thirty years."

"I'm a fool."

26

For those who believe their lives are linear, Crystal Ball's death was next to last in an illogical progression of a sick killer. An accident of place and time.

I see it differently. We're more like concentric circles. We pass where we've been and where we're going with each revolution. Today is altered by tomorrow; yesterday is never gone. Crystal died when the circles lined up. I was a point in her circle just as Buddy was. Who she was and who we were converged at the moment of her death.

Oscar's sister took his body home to Minnesota. A few Charlotteans flew up for his funeral. I wasn't one of them. Buddy was buried with his grandfather in Charlotte's finest cemetery. Jake's body was never claimed.

Almost a month has passed since that night in Barbara's house. She's been in Dorothea Dix Hospital in Raleigh all this time, not able to attend her son's funeral, nor her husband's. Officially, they're calling her condition paranoia.

I talk to Crystal every day. When your life is a circle,

people don't die. I'm a better friend to her now than I was in her life. She is to me as well. She gives me the humor I need at work, the peace I need to sleep, the courage to speak up when the time is right. I take her to AA meetings too. I laugh when I think about it; I think she'd understand. She keeps me "fuzzy."

Above me the sky is the color of robin's eggs. We call it Carolina Blue. We are not blessed with it as often as we used to be, but you can bet, when we are, the air will be crisp as well. And it is. A nice fifty-five degrees with scant humidity and a slight southerly breeze. Textbook mid-October weather in world-class Charlotte, North Carolina.

In front of me Tom Thurgood's compact butt is poised at the net for my serve. We are in the third and final set of the city tournament, and, if his hyperactive gyrations in the front court are to mean anything, Tom Thurgood thinks I will ace it.

We are playing at Renaissance Park, and the stands are almost full. Unusual for an amateur event like this tournament, but both Thurgood and I are a bit better known than most of the other entries. In front of us a sea of white tennis hats, each with ALLEN TEAGUE emblazoned across it. Even our opponents are wearing them. A thousand down. Nine thousand to go.

I see Sally with some men I've never seen before. She's not really watching us play. Hart is standing beside the bleachers rather than on them. His arms are crossed as if he's studying our situation. As usual, he is alone. Neither Mickey Sutton nor Gloria are here that I can tell. I wouldn't expect them to be. Mickey is reinterpreting my involvement in the murders to anyone who will listen, and he's been calling on my clients with regularity. I need to watch out for my textile accounts. I see Jean Miller sitting on the other side of Sally. Fred's not here, and I haven't seen him since we argued that day at lunch. I hear my children, but I can't see them from where I stand at the service line. Joanie is shushing George junior. It's time to be quiet.

The Textile Museum curator languishes at the fence, his fingers splayed through the linked chain. He has called me four times for a date since hearing our campaign ideas. I've obviously oversold him. His ardor has made no sense to me, has scared me, in fact.

That's the way I am these days. My antennae are frayed. People and things that would have amused me last summer make me skittish now. I don't trust my own instincts. In fact, feel I should run from what attracts me, laugh at what saddens me, go left when told to go right.

For that reason I choose to serve into the net, barely missing the proud man who wants so badly to win today. If we are going to win, I don't want it to be on my serve. I don't want anything to depend on me. Take that for a warped point of view.

I hear George junior's voice screaming above the crowd: "Come on, Mom. You can do it!"

Yeah, sweet boy, but I don't want to right now.

Maybe next year.